ICE RIVALS

EAST COAST
BOOK 4

KRISTEN GRANATA

ICE RIVALS

KRISTEN GRANATA

A NOTE FROM THE AUTHOR

This book contains scenes in the past with a homophobic, abusive father.

It also touches upon grief over the loss of a loved one that happened off the page in the past.

As always, your mental health is important to me. Feel free to DM me on social media if you need spoilers before reading.

This is the fourth and final book in my East Coast hockey series. They're all standalones, so you don't need to read the others before reading this story (but I recommend it!)

They can try to take away our rights.
They can try to take away our voices.
But they'll never be able to take away the love in our hearts.
Don't let them extinguish it.
Keep fighting.

"Would you put your dick away?"

I smirk as I whip my team captain in the ass with my towel. "What's the matter, Big Man? You jealous that your dick isn't as big as mine?"

Alexander points his index finger at me. "First of all, my wife is the only one who gets to call me *Big Man*. Secondly, my dick is bigger."

Jason, our defenseman, arches a brow as he laces up his sneakers on the bench. "Bigger than *that*? How is Aarya walking around right now?"

Alex grins. "With a limp."

I toss my head back and laugh. I love seeing my best friend so happy. It's been a long time coming, and Alex's new wife is to thank for that. Even though the only reason they're married is to secure his family villa in Italy, they're so gone for each other, it's obvious to everyone but them. So, I'll let him think whatever he wants as long as it keeps that smile on his face. He's been through a lot, and he deserves to be happy.

But for the record, my dick is bigger.

"Where are we going tonight?" I bend forward and pull on my sweatpants. "We have another win to celebrate."

Alex is the first one to shake his head. "I'm going home so I can tuck Giuls in before bed."

"I'm heading home too." Trenton, our goalie, grins. "Cassidy is working on a new scene for her next book, and she's going to need someone to act it out with. You know, for research purposes."

I groan. "Come on. We haven't been out together in a while."

"I'll come out for a drink or two." Jason rubs the back of his neck. "But I'm not up for one of your wild and crazy nights, if that's what you're looking for."

"This is bullshit," I grumble.

All of my best friends are wifed-up, and don't want to go out anymore. Not that I can blame them. If I had someone waiting for me—or *two* someone's, like Jason—I'd be running home to them too.

Sometimes it feels like that day will never come for me.

Jason is the perfect person to be around tonight. He found not one but two women to fall in love with, who also love each other just as much. The three of them have been best friends since high school, and last year they finally admitted their feelings for one another and decided to make it official.

If his wives can fall in love with a man *and* a woman, then there has to be hope for me too, right?

After we clear out of the locker room, Jason and I head to the pub, a chill local spot near the arena. None of the tourists know about this little hole in the wall, so we never get bothered for autographs or pictures.

But all my chill goes out the window when I spot some of the Philly players from tonight's game sitting in a booth across the room when we walk in.

"Fuck," Jason mutters. "Want to go somewhere else?"

I shake my head, making a beeline to the bar. "Nope. This is our town. They can leave if they feel uncomfortable."

And they should. We handed them their asses tonight.

"You gonna behave?" Jason asks.

I grunt, locking eyes with Chance Kellerman, their team's winger. "Maybe."

Kellerman's jaw tics right before he averts that dark and stormy gaze of his.

That's right, you coward. Look away.

It's no secret that Kellerman and I have history. My teammates know about our college rivalry—dorming together while playing on the same team, constantly trying to outshine the other to get noticed by the scouts; they know about his shit attitude when all I did was try to be his friend; and they know about us vying for the same girl's attention sophomore year.

What they don't know is how much deeper our relationship went during that time.

It's not that I'm ashamed to tell my friends about that part of the story. I'm open with my sexual orientation, and they know I've been with men in addition to women.

It's Kellerman's secret that I'm keeping.

He came from a broken home with an alcoholic homophobe for a father, so he's kept his sexuality under wraps his whole life. It was beyond frustrating to watch him conceal his true self. I've always been out in the open with who I am, so I can't understand that kind of mentality.

Be who you are, and fuck anyone who doesn't accept that.

A lot happened between us over the course of those four college years, leading to a blowout fight after graduation. Landing spots on rival NHL teams only drove the wedge further between us. Now, the only time we speak is with our fists on the ice.

"We'll have one beer, and then we'll leave." Jason slides onto the stool beside me. "I'm not getting into a bar fight tonight."

I scoff. "Who said anything about fighting?"

Jason shoots me a dubious look. "There's always fighting when the two of you are involved."

Jeff, the owner of the pub, places a bottle of Corona down in front of each of us. "You boys want me to throw them out?"

"Nah, let's send them a round of drinks instead." I wink at him. "Something fruity."

Jason stifles a groan beside me. "Here we fucking go."

Jeff grins. "Four strawberry daiquiris coming right up."

"Oh! With little umbrellas in them," I add, making Jeff chuckle.

Jason gulps down his beer like he's in a rush. "Why do you have to instigate?"

I grin. "Because it's fun."

"There's four of them, and two of us."

"I thought you said you're not getting into a bar fight?"

He rolls his eyes. "I can't just leave you in here to fend for yourself. I would, if I thought it'd teach you a lesson."

I shrug. "I'm just unteachable."

Jason shakes his head. "How have you been doing? You don't seem like yourself since you ended things with Erika."

Erika and I flirted for a while, being the only single ones in our friend group, but she pumped the brakes when I wanted to take things further.

She'd just recovered from vaginoplasty, transitioning from a man to a woman, and she wasn't ready to get into a serious relationship.

"We want two different things, and that's okay. She's been through a lot and she needs to find out who she is."

Jason nods. "I can't imagine going from being a man my whole life to transitioning to a woman. It must feel like she's starting a new life."

"Erika felt like she was a woman the whole time she was a man, so I don't think it's as new or scary as it might seem to us. But when it comes to dating and her new body, she has a lot to experience."

I'd never take that away from her. She deserves to experience life the way we all have—those of us who've been lucky enough to feel comfortable in our own bodies. Besides, we weren't going to be an epic love story. Now, she's one of my closest friends, and I wouldn't change a thing.

"So, if you're cool with Erika, then what is it?" Jason presses.

"It's hard being the only single friend in our group. I never had a problem with it before, but recently..." I stare down at my beer. "I think Cassidy's romance books are messing with my head or something. Or maybe it's the fact that I'm surrounded by married people. Maybe monogamy and commitment are contagious, and they've rubbed off on me."

Jason smiles. "I don't think it's the books. You're getting older, and you want different things than you used to. The meaningless partying gets old after a while, even for you."

My friends know me as the clown; the one who fools around and has fun, but never settles down. Sure, I can be a bit wild, and okay *fine*, I've woken up in an empty apartment without my clothes or any recollection of how I got there, and had to cover my dick with a McDonald's paper bag while I walk-of-shamed home. But seeing my friends find unconditional love makes me wonder if that's in the cards for someone like me. I play it off with lighthearted jesting, but I think about it more often than I care to admit.

I felt true love once, and I don't think I'll ever get that feeling back.
Not for anyone else.

Jason clinks his bottle against mine. "The right one will come to you when he or she is meant to."

I glance over my shoulder as Jeff walks the strawberry drinks over to Kellerman's booth. When four sets of eyes glare at me from across the bar, I blow them a kiss for good measure.

Two of them flip us off, while a third shakes his head, clearly not as amused as I am.

I expect Kellerman to fly out of his seat and mouth off to me, or come knock me off my stool. I'm itching for it. He gets under my skin—always has since the moment we met—and I'm ready for a fight.

But he simply raises the glass with the yellow umbrella sticking out of it in cheers, and takes a big gulp.

Jason chuckles under his breath. "Feel better now that you fucked with him?"

Not quite.

"Come on. Let's get out of here and call it a night." Jason throws down cash on the bar. "I promise, we'll convince the guys to come out with us next time."

I shake my head. "You go. I'm gonna stay for another beer."

Jason steals another glance over his shoulder. "You sure that's a good idea?"

"I'll be fine." I clap him on the shoulder. "Go enjoy your hot threesome sex."

He flashes me a grin. "You know I will."

After Jason leaves, I chat with Jeff until I drain my third beer. I pay for a round of drinks for everyone in the bar along with my tab, and then I head out the back door.

I don't make it more than two feet before I'm shoved from behind.

I stagger forward and then whirl around. "What the—"

A fist connects with my jaw before I can get my hands up. When I regain my footing, my eyes lock with the man who sucker-punched me.

Dark eyes flash with malice. "Just wanted to say thanks for the drink, asshole."

I lift my hand and wipe the blood dripping from the corner of my mouth as I grin. "I knew you wouldn't be able to sit there and take it like a man, Kellerman. Which is surprising, because I remember you *taking it* so well."

His fists clench at his sides. "Fuck you."

"Right here in the alley?" I hike a shoulder. "I'm down."

He throws another punch, but I dodge it this time.

I spin him around, yanking him by his hoodie, and press him against the brick building to hold him in place. "Why do you bother with this every time we cross paths, hmm? You punch me, and I punch you, but it only leaves us frustrated and wanting more."

He shoves me back a few steps. "The only thing I *want* is to wipe that smug look off your face."

I laugh before spitting blood onto the street. "We both know that's not the only thing you want. You used to beg for it. Do you remember that? I bet you do. I bet you think about the things we did all the time."

Kellerman swings and I let him punch me.

"The way you'd moan around my dick in your mouth—"

Another punch.

"The way you'd whimper my name right before you came."

This time when he swings, I dodge it and give him a right hook to the jaw. He lunges at me, and takes me to the ground. We scuffle on the pavement, each of us trying to gain control.

I roll him onto his back and mount him, pinning his arms down on either side of his head while he struggles underneath me. I roll my hips against him, and sure enough, he's hard as a fucking rock.

Just like me.

"You can act like you hate me all you want, Kellerman." I lean down, so close to his face that our noses touch. "But I know the truth. You can't fake it with me. I know your dirty little secret."

"Trust me, it's not an act." He spits his words like venom, lifting his head to speak his words against my mouth. "I fucking hate you."

I roll my hips again, rubbing our erections against each other. "Doesn't feel that way."

His eyes drop to my mouth, and time slows down around us. In this moment, it's just the two of us, back in our dorm room, without the eyes of the world on us; without the pressure of society weighing down on our shoulders.

"You don't have to live like this anymore," I whisper, brushing my lips against his. "Aren't you tired of hiding? Isn't the pretending exhausting?"

He sucks in ragged breaths as his inner turmoil swirls in his dark irises. He tilts his head a fraction of an inch like he's going to close the gap and kiss me.

I'm dying for it.

Yearning.

Practically begging.

I haven't felt this alive since college, and I hate that my heart still beats for someone who's too ashamed to admit that he loves me back.

Jeff's voice echoes in the alley. "Everything okay out here, Mac?"

Kellerman crawls out from under me, and we both brush ourselves off as we push to our feet.

I lift my hand and wave at Jeff. "All good. Just working out our shit."

Jeff chuckles and shakes his head as he tosses the garbage bag in his hand into the dumpster.

I wait for Jeff to disappear back inside the bar before swinging my gaze to Kellerman. "Still don't have answers for my questions, do you?"

He glares at me before he turns around and walks away like he always does. "Not the answers you want to hear."

I'M SITTING IN BED WITH AN ICE PACK ON MY FACE WHEN A notification pings on my phone.

ScoringChance217 wants to chat.

My best friend's wife, Kourtney, created an innovative porn-infused dating app called *FreeMe*. People can match with those who have the same sexual preferences as them, and are also looking for long-term love. It's ingenious. It saves you the disappointment of connecting with someone you aren't sexually compatible with, or someone who isn't looking for the same things you are.

Plus, the videos people post are *really* hot.

I don't post my face, for obvious reasons. I want people to get to know me before finding out I'm a professional hockey player with a shit ton of money. I haven't figured out what I'll say when I get past the talking stage, and try to meet someone in real life, but I'll cross that bridge when I get there.

Because I haven't gotten past the talking stage yet. I haven't clicked with anyone, haven't felt that spark of excitement.

I click on *ScoringChance*'s profile, but there isn't much to see. No pictures, and an empty bio, which isn't uncommon for an app like this. Many people are here to watch, afraid to make that first step toward their true desires. It's crazy how many people suppress the things they truly want in life. But Kourtney's website allows people to unlock that side of themselves and explore.

I accept the message request, and a private chat opens on my screen.

ScoringChance217: Hi. Looks like we're a match.
Me: Hi there. Looks that way.
Me: Not much to see on your profile though.
ScoringChance217: Yeah, I'm new here. Just feeling it out.
Me: I get it. Tell me a little about yourself.
Me: Whatever you're comfortable sharing.
ScoringChance217: You first.
Me: Well, I'm a man, for starters. I'm 26. I love sports, specifically hockey, and Mexican food. Hate golf and hate when the cheese on pizza gets cold.
ScoringChance217: That is the most random information you could've given me.
Me: That's the way my brain works. Perks of having ADHD.
Me: Your turn.
ScoringChance217: I'm a man as well. Also in my late-twenties; also like hockey. Asian food is my favorite. I agree, golf is pretty boring. But I don't mind cold pizza.

I knew he'd be into hockey. His username gave it away. A *scoring chance* is a hockey term.

Me: Got any mental illnesses like me?
ScoringChance217: Sorry, no. Extra point for you, I guess.
ScoringChance217: But I do have a ton of daddy issues. That should count for something.
Me: Ah, point for you then.
Me: My family is awesome.
ScoringChance217: Lucky you.
ScoringChance217: Why are you on this app?
Me: Looking for something more than a casual hookup.
Me: What about you?
ScoringChance217: Can I be honest?
Me: Always.
ScoringChance217: I don't really know what I'm doing here. I want to find something... find someone... but I don't know what to do once I find it.
Me: What do you mean?

ScoringChance217: I haven't come out yet.

My stomach drops with disappointment. I don't want to get involved with another person who isn't going to be loud and proud about being with me. It felt awful when Kellerman kept me in the shadows during college.

Me: What's holding you back?
ScoringChance217: The same thing that holds so many people back. Fear of judgment.
Me: So, you'd rather upset yourself than upset the people around you?
ScoringChance217: It sounds shitty when you put it that way.
Me: Sorry not sorry.
Me: It's the truth.
ScoringChance217: You're right.
Me: Have you even been with a man before?
ScoringChance217: Yes, as well as women.
ScoringChance217: I know what I like, and I know what I want. Just figuring out the other stuff as I go.
Me: It's kind of like ripping off a bandaid. Once you do it, it's over, and you can finally start living your life.
Me: The people who truly love you won't care, and the ones who don't will see themselves out like the trash always does.
ScoringChance217: I like your mentality.
Me: You've seen my pictures. I think you like more than my mentality 😉
ScoringChance217: I do. Your body is very sexy.
Me: Send me something. I'd like to see you.
ScoringChance217: What do you want to see?
Me: Whatever you're comfortable with showing me.
ScoringChance217: *insert picture*
ScoringChance217: This good?

I stare down at my phone, eyes wide and lips parted.
Olive skin and cut abs fill my screen. The stranger has his hand wrapped around the base of his cock, but it cuts off so I can't see its entirety.

Me: Damn.
Me: Will you show me more?

Me: Or we can switch to a video chat.

There's a short pause before he responds, and I expect him to decline.

ScoringChance217: Okay, but I won't show my face.

I click on the call button, and wait for him to accept.

When the video chat opens, it's practically pitch-black in his room, aside from a dim light illuminating where his hand is wrapped around his cock.

"I've never done this before," he whispers, his voice raspy.

"You're doing just fine." I keep my voice low, to prevent the possibility of him recognizing it. "You have a really nice dick, by the way."

The silhouette is long and thick, but not *too* thick. I can barely make out the dark hair surrounding, but it seems neat and not overgrown.

He chuckles. "You do too."

I give myself a few strokes, showing it off to the camera proudly. "I want to hear you come. Will you jerk off for me?"

"Yes." He lets out a shaky breath. "Will you come with me?"

"Of course." I reposition myself on the bed, and adjust the phone to give him a better angle. "Since we matched, that means you like dirty talk."

"I do."

"I wish I could taste your cock in my mouth. Suck on your head, and run my tongue along it."

He groans. "Would you choke on it?"

"Is that what you like? You want to feel your cock hit the back of my throat?"

"Fuck, yes." His hand moves faster.

"Have you ever fucked a man before? Or been fucked by one?"

"Both."

His answer surprises me, and a loud moan slips free. "I'd love to bend you over and bury myself deep inside you. Fuck you from behind while I reach around and jerk you off at the same time."

The sounds of his hand slapping against his skin fills the room, mixed with his grunts of pleasure.

"But I wouldn't let you come. Not until you fucked me after. What position do you want to fuck me in, hmm?"

"On your back," he pants. "With your legs around my waist, your heels digging into my ass, and my hand around your throat."

My hips jerk at the thought of being choked by his massive hand. "God, I wish you were here right now. It'd feel so much better than my hand."

It's been so long since I've been with a man. I haven't wanted to since Kellerman and I parted ways four years ago. Focusing my attention on women helped bury the memories of him, and all that we were when we were together.

"I'm close," he warns. "Come with me."

"Not yet. Wait."

"Please." His voice cracks, and the sound of his desperation does something to me.

"Fuck, I like the sound of you begging."

He gives me more. "Please. Please, come with me. I need you."

Our hands move faster, our strokes sloppy and uneven as we moan louder.

Then I watch as spurts of cum spill out onto his stomach, over and over until he's sated. His deep moans push me over the edge, and then I unload onto my stomach, wishing I knew his name so he could hear it on my lips while I come.

Once I catch my breath, I tell him exactly that. "What's your name, stranger?"

But then he ends the call.

FRESHMAN YEAR OF COLLEGE

HAVE YOU EVER MET SOMEONE AND IMMEDIATELY KNEW YOU didn't like them?

It happens before he even opens his mouth. It goes deeper than the way he looks. It's a vibe I get, equivalent to Spidey senses. My body has this visceral reaction to a complete stranger, as if we knew each other in a past life, and I hated him then too.

I can't explain it, but the second I lay eyes on my college roommate, I know we're going to have a problem.

With short, coppery curls and pale, freckled skin, he beams at me as he strolls into our dorm room. "Hey, roomie."

He holds out his hand, and when my hand meets his in a firm shake, I lift my eyes to his. They're striking, a bright crystal-blue color. The skin around them crinkles as he smiles, and for a moment, my breath gets caught in my throat.

He's sunshine and confidence. Cool and unbothered. His face is open and unguarded, his demeanor laid-back and disarming. I surmise this instantly, like I do with all people—compliments of growing up with an unpredictable parent. People say not to judge a book by its cover, but my intuition has never been wrong.

I tear my eyes and hand away, returning to my open suitcase on the bare mattress.

"I'm Stephen McKinley." He tosses his suitcase onto the opposing bed and drops his duffle bag onto the floor. "I'm good with this side of the room. I'm not picky."

"I got here first. Didn't think it mattered."

"Yeah, man, it's cool. You gotta establish dominance and all." He laughs at his own joke and claps me on the back. "What's your name? Where you from?"

This guy has entirely too much energy. And he's touching me, in my personal space.

"Chance." I set my neatly folded clothes in piles on the bed, preparing to organize everything.

"Got a last name too, or do you go by one, like Madonna and Prince?"

I roll my eyes. "Kellerman."

"Where are you from, Chance Kellerman?"

I inch away from him and move to stand at the foot of the bed instead. "Brooklyn."

"Aye, a New Yorker. I'm from Cali." He flops onto the bed—*my* bed—knocking over one of my clothing piles. "What's your major?"

This guy is like an overgrown kid.

"Do you mind?" I yank the clothes out from under his large body. "You have your own bed."

"Sorry, man." But he doesn't move. He doesn't shut up either. "I'm here on a hockey scholarship. Gonna play in the NHL one day. You like hockey?"

A noise bubbles out of me, a mix somewhere between a humorless laugh and a groan, because of course he's a hockey player.

Hockey is just about the only thing I do like. I live, eat, breathe, sleep hockey, and have since I was a kid. It's my ticket out of this worthless excuse of a life.

"What position do you play?" I ask only because now I have to know.

"I'm a winger."

Same position as me. This should be interesting.

He lifts a pair of my boxer-briefs and dangles them off his index finger. "Guess that settles the *boxers or briefs* question. I prefer commando myself."

I snatch back my underwear and grit my teeth. "Get off my bed."

He chuckles, and like a clueless dog, he flips onto his back and stares up at the ceiling. "This is it, man. It's all about to happen. Our future is starting right now."

Nerves bubble in my stomach. All I've ever wanted was to be out of my house and on my own. I clawed my way to get here; some days I didn't think I'd make it. But right now, away from my home, away from my father...it feels like I can finally breathe.

Here, I can start over. I can be anyone I want to be.

Stephen stretches his arms overhead and his T-shirt rides up, revealing a sculpted set of abs. The dude is in shape. Broad shoulders, solid biceps, and prominent triceps, with veins running down his forearms, leading to massive hands. It's like the universe is tempting me—testing me to find out how I'll react to being in close proximity to a man this beautiful.

To make it worse, Stephen catches me staring, and he doesn't seem to mind. In fact, his flirty response leads me to believe he's into it.

"See something you like?"

Fuck. If I want to start over, I need to leave my past behind. Guard up, secrets buried, emotions off.

My eyes narrow as they snap to his. "Listen, we need to set some boundaries here. For starters, you need to get off my bed. You stay on your side of the room and I'll stay on mine."

He arches a brow. "You're going to be fun to live with, aren't you?"

"Up. Now." I yank him by his wrist, albeit a little too hard, and he stumbles toward me, his chest smacking into mine.

His scent invades my space, and for a brief moment, neither of us moves. His icy-blue eyes flick between mine, and it feels like he can see into me, see all of my truths.

I can't have that.

This is my chance to be someone else, to have everything I've ever dreamed of.

Stephen licks his lips. "What's Rule Number Two, Chance Kellerman?"

I shove him onto his side of the room. "Stay out of my way."

"Can you help me find a book?"

I smile down at the kindergartener blinking up at me with big, brown eyes. "Of course. Which book are you looking for?"

"It's about a lion." He holds up both of his hands and pantomimes claws. "Rawr!"

I tap my chin while I think. "I might need some more details than that. Do you know what the story is about?"

He goes into a seemingly endless monologue about a lion and a mouse and a forest, and a bunch of other details that I'm not sure where they came from because they most-definitely are not in the book he's talking about.

I walk around my desk and hold out my hand for him to take. "Come on. I think I know exactly where your book is."

I lead him to the fiction section where the larger picture books are, and scan the shelf until I spot the spine I'm looking for. "Is this it?"

He gasps and bounces on his toes. "That's it!"

"Ryan," his teacher warns. "Lower your voice in the library."

He covers his mouth with his tiny hand while his eyes flick up to mine. "Sorry, Ms. King."

I give him a pat on his shoulder. "It's okay, Ryan. Enjoy your book."

"Thanks for helping me."

"Anytime, kid."

I head back to my desk just in time to see my phone lighting up with an incoming call. My heart leaps into my throat at the sight of the number on the screen.

I spin around and hold up the phone to my ear. "Hello?"

"Hi, Ms. King. This is Avery's principal, Mr. Sturges."

"Is everything okay?"

"Avery is healthy and safe." He pauses, and I close my eyes waiting for him to continue. "But we caught him trying to cut class this afternoon. I have him here in my office."

I stifle a groan and press my palm against my chest. "I'm so sorry, Mr. Sturges. Can I talk to him, please?"

"Of course."

After a pause, Avery's voice comes through the speaker. "Hi, Aunt Presley."

I heave a sigh. "Are you alright?"

"Yeah, I'm fine."

"What class were you trying to cut?"

"Gym."

My stomach clenches. "Thought so. Have you told Mr. Sturges why you were cutting gym?"

"No."

"Well, someone there needs to know what's going on."

"Please, no." His voice sounds desperate. "You promised."

"I know I did, but you can't keep cutting gym every week. You're going to fail and have to take it over in summer school. Who the hell wants to take gym over the summer?"

"It'd be better than taking it with all these other kids."

He has a point, and now I realize that's exactly his plan.

"Are you mad?" he asks.

"No, of course I'm not mad. I just wish you would let me help you."

"It'll only make it worse."

"I know, I know." I was a kid once. I remember how cruel high schoolers can be. "Put Mr. Sturges back on the phone."

"Love you."

"Love you most."

When the principal returns to the call, I choose my words carefully. "Look, Avery doesn't want me to tell you the truth about what's going on, so I'm going to be as cryptic as I can. Is there another elective he can take in place of gym? I'm sure you're aware of the things that can go in inside of a boys' locker room, and I don't feel like it's a safe environment for him."

"Ms. King, if there is something going on in my school, then I'd like to know about it. Are you saying there's a bullying situation?"

There's *been* a bullying situation since this kid started at that school, but I promised Avery I wouldn't say anything to anyone, and I'm a woman of my word.

"I can neither confirm nor deny that, sir. However, I'm asking—no, I'm begging—can you please find a different option for Avery? There has to be something you can come up with to help. You know what our family has been through, and high school is hard enough without the boy's parents."

I hate playing the *dead parent* card, but I'll protect my nephew at all costs.

Mr. Sturges lets out a long sigh. "I'll talk to the art teacher and see if there's anything she needs help with during fifth period."

"Thank you, sir. I appreciate your help."

"But Avery was still caught cutting class, so I'm going to have to discipline him for that."

"Yes, of course. Totally understandable."

"Though I suppose detention isn't the best spot for him under the circumstances," he murmurs. "I'll keep him in my office for thirty minutes after school. You can pick him up here in the office at 4:00."

"Not a problem. Thanks so much."

I toss the phone back onto my desk and let out a breath of relief.

Ryan's teacher and my best friend, Dominique, leans against my desk. "Everything okay?"

I run my fingers through my hair and let my hand fall at my side. "Avery got caught cutting gym."

She grimaces. "Those boys are still bothering him?"

I nod, curling my hands into fists. "I wish I could kick their teenage a— hi, Ryan. Are you all set with your books?"

He nods. "Were you just going to say a curse word, Ms. King?"

"No, not at all." I scoff, feigning innocence. "Cursing is bad. I would never, and you shouldn't either."

Dominique stifles a laugh as she turns around.

Ryan's eyes flick to my arms. "My mom says you have too many tattoos to work in a school. But I like them. They're pretty."

I plaster on a fake smile. "Thanks, kid."

I scan his books, and check out the rest of the class's books before their library period is over.

"We're still on for drinks after dinner tonight, right?" Dominique asks as she holds open the door for her class.

"Yes." My shoulders slump forward. "I need a girls' night like you have no idea."

"Janelle is so excited for Avery and Alyssa to come over."

I smile. "Alyssa already has a giant bag of games packed. And I told Avery I'd pay him to babysit, so he's also excited."

A little bribery never hurt anyone.

Dominique laughs. "See you later, boo."

Excitement courses through me. One night a month, my niece and nephew babysit Dominique's seven-year-old while she and I have a couple of drinks. It only lasts two hours max, but it's the one night a month I get to feel like myself a little bit. Not the legal guardian who spends all her free time doing laundry and cleaning up after two teenagers; not the young adult who was thrown into an unfortunate situation she wasn't prepared for and missed out on half of her college years; and not the prim-and-proper school librarian who can't say curse words or show off her tattoos without getting scrutinized.

I've had to repress so much of who I am, and forget about who I'd once wanted to be. And I'd make the same choices all over again if it meant being here to raise and protect my sister's kids. But I can't pretend that it hasn't been difficult.

So, tonight, I get to have a little fun.

Just one night.

"I ALWAYS FORGET HOW HOT YOU ARE."

I cough out an incredulous laugh. "Is that supposed to be a compliment?"

Dominique shrugs. "I'm just saying, you're all covered up like this innocent little school librarian. Then we come out and you're dressed up like *this*, and it takes me a minute to remember you're a fucking smoke show."

"Sometimes I forget how hot I am too." I gesture to my tits. "Seriously, do you know when these babies last saw the light of day aside from in the shower?"

She pokes my cleavage. "Such a shame. They're so perky."

I glance down at her index finger touching my boobs. "And this is the most action I've gotten in an embarrassingly long time."

Dominique laughs before lifting her martini to her lips. "That's your own fault. You know you can have any guy you want within a ten-mile radius."

I'm shaking my head before she even finishes her sentence. "I can't deal with that right now."

"I know it'd be hard when you're home with the kids every night, but you know I'd watch them if you wanted to go on a date every once in a while."

"I know you would, and I appreciate that."

"But...?"

"But..." I wipe at the condensation on my glass. "I haven't met anyone who really does it for me."

It being that spark. That connection.

"You've only been out with a few guys in the last four years. You have to give yourself more opportunities to find someone you click with."

I cringe thinking about the dates I've been on. The guys were very nice, and I knew I *should have* been interested in them, yet I felt nothing. No excitement. No butterflies. No true attraction.

And the sex was god-awful.

Dominique sucks her teeth. "Besides, you weren't going after the right guys. You don't like nice guys. You like 'em nasty."

I tilt my head back as a loud laugh rips from my throat. "I seriously regret telling you everything I did during my wild college days."

"Girl, those are my favorite stories. I never experimented in college, and I'd give anything to go back in time and have a little fun before meeting my husband and getting knocked up."

I did enjoy myself back then. Until it was cut short by the news of my sister's accident, and finding out that I'd become the legal guardian of her children. I went from getting baked, to bake sales; from toga parties, to school trips. I had to leave my carefree youth behind and become a responsible adult.

I also had to leave behind the two men I'm currently staring at on the TV hanging above us. McKinley and Kellerman toss their gloves and trade blows in the middle of the rink, blood pouring from both of their faces. The referee skates over and breaks them apart, forcing each of them into their respective penalty boxes.

Some things never change.

My body heats at the reminder of how many of their fights ended—with me wrapped between them in one of our dorm rooms.

Do they still fool around? Do they spend time together? Do they remember me?

I've kept tabs on the boys over the years they've played professional hockey. Maybe it's silly to hold onto a college fling, but sometimes the memories of our time together are the only things getting me through the lonely nights.

Dominique snaps her fingers in front of my face, drawing me back to the present. "You good?"

"Yeah, sorry." I clear my throat. "Was watching the game."

Though I've told my best friend about my polyamorous college experience, I never told her *who* it was with. Protecting Kellerman's secret, even now, means something to me.

Which is totally ridiculous, because he's probably long forgotten about me.

"I feel like I'm sitting here with Jeff. If there's a hockey game on, I'm completely invisible." Dominique suddenly sits up ramrod straight. "We should go to a hockey game together. Jeff's co-worker gets him free tickets all the time." She gasps. "And the guy is newly divorced. We should make it a double-date!"

I grimace. "No, no. You know I hate being set up."

Ignoring me, she pulls out her phone, no doubt texting Jeff.

I snatch her phone out of her hands. "Blind dates are so awkward. I don't want to sit there and have forced conversation with someone I don't know."

The bar erupts in cheers as the Goldfinches score a goal, surging ahead by two points. My eyes follow McKinley across the screen as he raises his stick over his head, wearing his signature cocky grin.

The grin he used to flash at *me*.

Longing seeps into my chest before I can stop it. And it's not just desire for a man I once knew. It's the fact that he and Kellerman are out there living their dreams, having everything they've worked for at the palm of their hands, and I'm...here.

I love my niece and nephew more than anything in this world, and I would never trade them for a different life. But my dreams were cut short when I lost my sister, and I can't help but think about what my life would be like if she were still alive.

"Can I be honest with you, Pres?"

I blink at Dominique before nodding. "Of course."

"I think you purposely sabotage your love life because you think you don't deserve to have anything good without your sister."

The corners of my lips turn downward as I avert my gaze. "Why did her life have to be taken? She was so young. She had everything."

"I don't know." Dominique clasps my hand. "But she'd want you to live your life to the fullest. And I don't think that's what you're doing. You go to work at a job you never wanted; you're playing a mom role you never wanted. You're not really *living*. You're just going through the motions."

I hike a shoulder, pretending like her words don't sting as badly as they do. "I don't know what to do about that. Maybe once the kids go off to college, I can focus on myself. But right now? I have a responsibility to them. To my sister. I have to take care of them. My wants and needs aren't a priority right now."

"You need to take care of you too, Pres. Take it from another mom." She squeezes my hand. "Please, just come out with us and meet Jeff's friend. If you don't like him, I'll leave you alone about dating."

I arch a brow. "You'll leave me alone?"

She rolls her eyes. "For, like, a month."

I laugh and my shoulders droop forward. "Fine. One double date, and that's it."

Who knows? Maybe this guy will turn out to be the love of my life.

THIS GUY IS *SO* NOT THE LOVE OF MY LIFE.

Jeff's coworker, Andrew, hasn't stopped talking about the stock market since we sat down.

Who wears a suit and tie to a hockey game?

I'd rather listen to Alyssa practice the trumpet than be a part of this conversation, and that says a lot because *fuck* is that kid bad at the trumpet.

Dominique keeps sending me apologetic glances, and whisper-yelling to her husband about his friend, as if it's his fault when this blind date was her idea.

But most of my attention is on the game, because the tickets Andrew got us?

Goldfinches versus Sharks.

After four years of secretly watching my ex-boyfriends through the safety of a television screen, I now have a front-row seat.

I hold my breath every time they whizz by, praying that they don't see me—or hoping that they do. I'm not sure which scenario I prefer. Would they even remember me? Four years is a long time, and with the throngs of women who throw themselves at professional athletes, I'd probably be just another face in the crowd by now.

Andrew's arm wraps around my shoulders as he pulls me closer to him, and the armrest digs into my ribs. "Jeff mentioned you're a librarian. Does that pay well?"

My eyebrows hit my hairline. "Uh, it's average as far as salaries go."

"Are you investing for your retirement?"

Jesus Christ. I'm never complaining about Alyssa's trumpet again.

Luckily, the Goldfinches score, so I use the opportunity to jump out of my seat with the rest of the fans. Andrew remains seated, as if he couldn't care less about the game, but when I glance at him over my shoulder, his eyes are zeroed in on my ass.

I drop back into my seat and pretend like I didn't hear his previous question, my gaze finding McKinley and Kellerman as they shove past each other on the ice.

Dominique's gasp startles me. "Oh my god, look. You're on the KissCam."

My stomach seizes as I glance up at the jumbotron above the middle of the arena. Sure enough, my face is plastered on the screen, next to Andrew's in the middle of a red heart.

I laugh as I shake my head, trying to signal that we're not a couple, and we're not going to kiss. But Andrew grabs my face with both hands and pulls me toward him.

I push both of my palms against his shoulders, trying to get out of his strong hold. "Andrew, no."

The crowd chants, "Kiss him! Kiss him! Kiss him!"

"Ah, come on." He waggles his eyebrows as he overpowers me. "Just one kiss for the camera."

"I said no." I grip Andrew's wrists in a futile attempt to pry him off of me.

The cheering of the crowd drowns out my grunts as I say *stop* again.

"You're embarrassing me," Andrew whispers, yanking me toward him.

Then there's a loud bang on the glass in front of us.

Andrew jumps and drops his hands, blinking up at the menacing dark gaze staring back at him.

"Get your hands off her," Chance shouts through the glass.

Stephen crashes into Chance as he skids to a stop beside him. His crystal-blue eyes bore into mine as if he's looking at a ghost.

I suppose he is. I'm a ghost from his past.

"Presley," he mouths, fogging up the plexiglass.

My gaze bounces between him and Chance, and my heart leaps into my throat with the weight of both of their stares on me. Time stands still, the loud arena fading away into the background as my vision blocks out everything around us.

I swallow past the dryness in my throat, and muster a feeble shrug.

Hey, fellas. Long time no see.

Dominique's grasp on my forearm pulls me out of the fog, and the boys are yanked back into the game by each of their teammates so the game can continue.

"What the hell was *that*?" Dominique asks.

"I...I don't know." I shake off the shock, and shoot a glare in Andrew's direction. "No means no, asshole." Then I whip around to Jeff. "Will you switch seats with me?"

"Of course." Jeff rises from his seat, and I move to the seat farthest from nonconsensual-Andrew.

Dominique watches me as I bury my nose in my phone, pretending to check to see if the kids messaged me. "Two professional hockey players just slammed against the glass to rescue you from the KissCam, and one of them knew your name. So, again I ask: What the hell was that?"

"Can we talk about this later?" I whisper, eyes darting around to see if anyone is still staring at me. "I'm about two seconds away from bolting out of here and dying in the parking lot from embarrassment."

My cheeks burn at the thought of a student or their parents witnessing me get face-raped on TV.

"We will most definitely be talking about this later," she whispers back.

But I can't focus on the rest of the game. I blink as if it'll clear my vision, as if it'll wipe the image of them staring back at me from my mind.

They saw me.

They remembered me.

My heart surges with foolish hope, for what, I have no idea. A lot can happen in four years—a lot *did* happen to me in four years—and I guess I always assumed they didn't spare me a second thought once I left them. Especially after *the way* I left.

After the game ends, we slowly shuffle our way through the crowd. Drunk fans cheer and get rowdy as they funnel into the parking lot, but it all sounds like muffled chatter to me. It feels like I'm underwater, submerged in my memories.

Until I hear my name.

I spin around, and I'm faced with two painfully beautiful hockey players, looking like they're fresh out of the shower with damp hair. Stephen is shirtless—because of course he is—wearing a pair of gray joggers, and Chance is dressed in all-black, always trying to hide inside his hoodie.

They're like yin and yang, the light and the dark. And somehow, I fit between them for a little while, soaking up the best of both worlds.

"What are you...where have you..." Stephen shakes his head. "You're here."

My hands shake as I tuck them into the pockets of my coat. "Hi."

Chance folds his arms over his chest, his hardened expression giving off his usual I-couldn't-care-less vibes, yet he's here, standing in front of me instead of in his locker room.

Stephen inches forward. "It's so good to see you, Presley."

I offer him a small smile. "Is it?"

"Of course, it is. I didn't think I'd ever see you again." He pauses. "Do you live here, in Jersey?"

"She lives down Beaker Street," Dominique blurts out from behind me.

My head whips around to glare at her.

Stephen grins and shoots her a wink. "Good to know."

"I'm the best friend." She holds out her hand, and he gives it a firm shake. "Dominique."

"Pleasure to meet you, Dominique."

She offers her hand to Chance, but he remains unmoving like a statue, dark eyes boring into mine.

"No? Okay, then." Dominique drops her hand and moves to stand beside her husband. "Another time maybe."

Stephen rolls his eyes. "Don't take it personal. He's a dick."

That snaps Chance out of his trance. "Fuck you."

Stephen grins. "See?"

I can't help the chuckle that escapes me. "Just like old times."

Before my brain can register what's happening, Stephen rushes forward and engulfs me in his embrace, squeezing hard and lifting me off the ground. "It's so fucking good to see you again, pretty girl."

"Oxygen," I choke out, tapping his shoulder.

"Shit, sorry." He drops me back down and holds me out at arm's length. "I'm just happy to see you."

"I'm happy to see you too." My gaze flicks over his shoulder. "And you."

A muscle in Chance's jaw twitches. "Nice to see that you're okay."

I don't miss the undertone in his words.

He was worried about me.

Of course, he was. I left without an explanation, completely ghosting the two of them.

I step around Stephen's giant body, and move toward Chance. He doesn't budge, but he lets me unfold his arms and step into his chest. I raise my hands around to the back of his neck, and hug him.

"I'm sorry," I whisper.

Slowly, his arms come around me, and he holds me. His body practically vibrates against mine, years of anger, hurt, and confusion rolling off him in droves.

Why did I think my leaving wouldn't affect them the same way it affected me?

People around us have noticed the two hockey stars, and we've garnered a small crowd.

"Can I have your autograph?"

"Can we take a picture?"

"Philly sucks!"

I pull back, and clear my throat. "You guys should head back inside before it gets crazy out here."

Stephen holds out his hand, palm facing up. "Give me your phone."

I dig into my crossbody bag and unlock my phone before handing it to him. He saves his number, and presses the phone to his ear, waiting until he hears several rings before hanging up.

I take it back and hold it out to Chance. He didn't ask, and it's a bold assumption, but I blink up at him and wait nonetheless.

And he makes me wait.

Stephen scoffs. "Just give her your number, shithead. Stop acting like you don't want it."

Chance snatches my phone, angrily thumbs his number onto the screen, and hands it back to me. But he doesn't call his own phone the way Stephen did, leaving the ball in my court. Then he turns and disappears through the crowd.

Stephen leans down and presses a kiss to my cheek. "Talk soon, pretty girl."

Warmth envelops my chest, sending little tingles out to the rest of my body. I have to bite my bottom lip to stop myself from grinning like a loon.

Dominique squeals and drags me by my elbow to Jeff's car. "Bitch, you better start talking."

I slide into the back seat, and heave a sigh while we wait for Jeff as he talks with grabby-hands-Andrew outside.

My head falls back against the headrest. "Remember how I told you I was with two men in college?"

Dominique spins around in the passenger seat to look at me. "*Those* were the two men?"

I nod and squeeze my eyes shut.

"Holy shit. You banged not one but two professional hockey players?"

"They weren't professional hockey players at the time."

"What was with the tall, dark, and broody one?" she asks, arching a brow.

A small smile tugs at the corners of my lips. "He's mad at me."

"What did you do?"

I scrub my hands down my face. "When I got the call about Allie's accident, I dropped out of school and moved to New Jersey to be with the kids."

She nods, already knowing this part of the story.

I grimace. "I didn't tell the boys what happened, or where I was going. I kind of just...left."

She gasps. "Presley! Why?"

"What was the point? They were about to get drafted into the NHL, and it's not like we would've been together after college." I hike a shoulder and let it fall. "I had to let them go, and cold turkey was the only way for me to do it."

I was devastated over the loss of my sister, and terrified at the thought of raising two kids on my own. I couldn't ask the boys to stick by my side through all of that. Not when they were at the cusp of major success. They deserved to achieve their dreams.

And look at them now. I couldn't be prouder.

Jeff gets into the car, and twists around to look at me. "I'm so sorry about Andrew."

I wave him off. "It's fine. It's not your fault."

His eyes flick between me and his wife. "Did I miss the whole conversation about what happened with those hockey players back there?"

Dominique pats him on the shoulder before tugging on her seatbelt. "I'll fill you in later, baby."

I lower myself onto the edge of my niece's bed and brush her brown hair away from her face. "I did. Did you have fun hanging with Janelle?"

Alyssa offers me a sleepy smile as she bunches up one of her many fleece blankets and rests her cheek against it. "I like babysitting."

"You're really good at it."

"I think I want to be a mom someday. Or maybe I'll just work in a school with little kids like you."

I tuck her comforter around her. "You can be anything you want to be."

"Did you always want to be a librarian?"

I swallow the truth and offer her something close enough to it. "I love books, so what better place to be than surrounded by them all day?"

"What book are you reading right now?"

I can't exactly tell my ten-year-old niece that I'm reading a why-choose romance where the heroine gets railed by four dudes at the same time.

"Uh, it's a love story."

She grins. "You always read love stories. What's this one about?"

"Well, it's about a woman who falls in love with more than one man at the same time. And she has to figure out what she's going to do about it."

Alyssa's eyebrows lift. "Can you love more than one person like that?"

"I think so. Love doesn't have a limit, and it looks different for everyone."

She hums as her eyes droop closed. "Have you ever been in love?"

My chest squeezes. "I think I was. But I was in college, so I was young."

She peels open one eye to look at me. "Do you think you'll ever get married?"

I let out a soft chuckle and lean down to press a kiss to the top of her head. "You always have so many questions."

"Mom used to call me inquisitive."

"She was right. Maybe you'll be a reporter one day."

Her smile fades. "I miss her."

"I do too." I glance at the picture frame sitting on her nightstand, tears stinging my eyes the way they always do when I think about my sister. "Make sure you always love your brother, okay? He's going to be your best friend in life."

"Like Mom was yours?"

I nod.

Allie wasn't just my big sister. She was my very best friend. The one I'd call whenever I needed help or advice. When she died, I couldn't call her to get me through it. I was alone. And it was the hardest thing I've ever had to go through. It'd always been us against the world growing up. When our father left and Mom had to get a second job to make ends meet, Allie was there by my side, helping me with homework and making sure I was fed and taken care of. Then when Mom died the summer before I left for college, Allie made sure that I still went, and helped me with some of the tuition.

She's the reason I am where I am today, the reason I'm the person I am today, and I owe it to her to make sure her kids have the best life they possibly can.

"Goodnight, Aunt Presley. I love you."

I press a kiss to the top of Alyssa's head and whisper, "Love you most."

I peek into Avery's room after I close Alyssa's door, but he's already passed out, so I head to my bedroom down the hall.

I can busy myself with work and the kids during the day, but nighttime is when the loneliness creeps in. My thoughts and memories—of my sister, of McKinley and Kellerman, of the life I once had, of how I'm doing a shit job at raising these kids—take over my mind, making it hard to fall asleep.

But after coming face to face with the boys tonight, knowing I have their numbers at my fingertips, makes it that much worse.

Why would I call them? What would I even say? We're in different phases of life now. Our college fling is long over. How would they fit into my life?

I shake my head and laugh at myself. Why would I think they'd even want to be part of my life?

While I lie on my back and stare up at the ceiling, my phone vibrates with a text on the nightstand.

STEPHEN MCKINLEY

Sweet dreams, pretty girl.

Butterflies flit around my stomach.

I scoot up to sit against the headboard, staring down at the text.

What do I say? Why did he ask for my number in the first place? My heart thumps a furious rhythm in my chest.

But my mind quickly snuffs out the tune.

I set the phone back on my nightstand and try my best to fall asleep.

FRESHMAN YEAR OF COLLEGE

THE FIRST PRACTICE WAS TORTURE.

I loved every second of it. Hockey is a grueling sport, and I thrive on the feeling of pushing my body to its limits.

Heading back to the dorm for a much-needed shower and nap, I make my way through the exit.

"Kellerman." Stephen jogs after me. "Hey, Kellerman. I know you hear me."

I glance over my shoulder, not slowing my stride. "Yeah, everyone in a ten-mile radius can hear you."

He yanks my elbow when he reaches me, forcing me to spin around and face him. "What the fuck is your problem?"

I shake him off me. "I don't have a problem."

"Why didn't you tell me that you're a winger too? I told you I played hockey the other day, and you said nothing about being on the team."

I hike a shoulder and continue walking. "Does it matter?"

"Of course, it matters," he says, keeping up with my fast pace. "We're roommates *and* teammates. We're practically brothers now."

I cough out a laugh. "Don't be ridiculous."

"You know, you're kind of a dick."

I roll my eyes. "And you're kind of annoying."

Stephen laughs like I complimented him. "I'm gonna make you love me, Kellerman. You watch. We're going to be the best of friends before you know it."

I give him a side-long glare. "You're my competition, not my friend."

Everyone on this team will be vying for a spot in the NHL when the scouts come around, and I'll be damned if I let anyone get in my way.

His head jerks back. "No, we need to have each other's backs. That's how a team works."

I shake my head, and hold myself back from popping his positive little bubble. It's obvious he lives in a world filled with rainbows and sunshine. He doesn't know how ugly people can truly be.

And there's a small part of me that's happy about it, knowing he hasn't been tainted by the cruelty of the world. I hope he stays like that forever.

Stephen lowers his voice. "Hey, man. You shouldn't run out of the locker room as soon as practice is over, by the way. That's where we all bond and become a real team. What's that about?"

My teeth gnash together, and I ignore his intuitive question.

"You know, if you're into dudes, it's cool. I'm—"

"I'm not into dudes," I snap, way too quick and way too loud.

"I'm just saying, you don't need to be ashamed of it if you are."

A sardonic laugh escapes me. *Yeah, right.*

"I'm bi." He hikes a shoulder. "It's not that big of a deal."

My feet falter, but I recover quickly. I steal a glance at him out of the corner of my eye, in shock at how nonchalant he is with his confession, as if he just told me he likes both french toast and waffles.

My mind wanders to my father, and all the hateful things he'd have to say about my new roommate; all the ugly things he's said about *me*; all the ugly things that happened inside my high school locker room once word got out.

I shake my head. "I'm not gay."

Stephen nods, but the knowing look he gives me tells me he sees right through my front.

And I fucking hate it.

He caught me off-guard the day he walked into our dorm. For some reason, I'd imagined my roommate would be a quiet, studious biochemist, or a goth loner without any friends. I wasn't prepared for someone who looks like he stepped off a Hollister billboard with the charisma to go along with it.

To add insult to injury, I'll be spending all my time with him on the ice. There'll be no escaping him. And I *need* to keep my distance from him.

Because Stephen McKinley is the embodiment of everything I can't have.

"W‌HY DO YOU KEEP LOOKING AT YOUR PHONE?"

My eyes shoot up to the tiny, curly-haired little girl staring up at me. "Just checking to see if anyone texted me."

Giuliana leans over my arm, glancing down at my blank screen. "Is it a girl?"

I chuckle as I slip my phone back into my pocket and lift my niece onto my lap. "You're a very smart little girl, you know that?"

She rolls her big brown eyes. "I'm not a little girl anymore, Uncle Mac. I'm four now, 'member?"

I smack myself in the forehead with the palm of my hand. "I'm such an idiot. How could I forget?"

She giggles. "You're not an idiot."

I wrap my arms around her and she nuzzles against me. "I love you, kid. You know that right?"

"Yup. And I love you. You're the bestest uncle in the whole world."

"Make sure to tell Uncle Trenton and Uncle Jason that next time you see them."

She giggles again. "That's not nice."

"Hey, just so you know, I don't have to be waiting for a girl to text me. I could be waiting for a man. Men can like men, and women can like women."

She lifts her head and looks into my eyes. "Like Aunt Celeste and Aunt Kourtney?"

I nod. "Just like them."

"How will I know if I like girls or boys?"

I adjust us to sit up on the couch. "Well, I don't think you should look at it from a perspective of *girls or boys*. I think you should look inside someone's heart, and see what you feel for them. It doesn't matter what they look like on the outside."

She purses her little lips while she thinks about that for a moment. "What if I love dogs?"

I toss my head back and laugh. "Humans can't marry dogs. You have to be in the same species."

Her eyebrows furrow. "But I love Ellie."

Ellie's head perks up from her dog bed across the room.

"You can love Ellie, but you can't be *in love* with Ellie. Those are two different things."

Giuliana nods. "So, are you waiting for a text from a girl or a boy?"

Both.

Either.

The whole weekend went by without a response from Presley. I texted her the night of the game, after Chance and I saw her on the KissCam. At *my* game. I rarely pay any mind to what's going on in the crowd, but it was impossible not to glance up at the jumbotron while everyone was screaming about that douchebag's hands all over my girl.

My girl. Fuck. I can't even get a text back from her, yet I'm calling her *my* girl.

But what are the odds that the three of us were in the same place at the same time? It's like the universe threw us together again, after all this time.

Even Kellerman looked shocked as shit, and he never emotes. For some reason, I thought he might text me too. Reach out to talk about how crazy it was that we saw Presley.

I thought I'd get *something*. Anything. From either of them.

Yet here I am with nothing.

"*Hellooo.*" Giuliana pokes my chest with her index finger. "Boy or girl?"

I heave a sigh. "Girl.

"What's her name? Who is she?"

I chuckle as she questions me rapid-fire like she always does. "Her name is Presley. I went to college with her. She was my girlfriend for a couple of years, and then one morning I woke up, and she was just gone."

Giuliana's eyes widen. "Where did she go?"

"I didn't know. She was just gone. But the other night at my game, I saw her."

Giuliana gasps. "You saw her?"

I nod. "She was there, and I tried to talk to her, but we didn't have a lot of time. I asked for her number, and I texted her, but I haven't heard back from her. I know I'm getting ahead of myself, and reading too much into it. She could be married for all I know—fuck, did she have a wedding ring on? I didn't even think of that possibility."

Giuliana clicks her tongue against the roof of her mouth. "You said the f-word."

"Shit, did I?" I scrub my hand over my face. "Shit, now I just said shit. Don't tell your dad. I'll give you twenty bucks."

Her eyes narrow. "Make it fifty."

Can't even be mad at the kid. I'm training her to be a hustler.

"Deal."

"Do you love her?" she asks.

"I used to love her very much."

And if my beating heart is any indication, I still do.

"Used to...?" Giuliana scrunches her nose. "You can stop loving someone?"

"No, you can't." Alex strides into the living room, and scoops his daughter into his arms. "Love is forever once you let someone into your heart."

She glances down at me. "Then why did you say you *used to* love Presley?"

I rub the back of my neck. "I guess because I loved the person she was back then, and I don't know who she is now."

Giuliana rests her head against Alex's shoulder. "I think she'll text you back."

My eyebrows lift. "You do?"

She nods. "You're the bestest uncle in the world. And if you miss her, she probably misses you too. I miss you when you're not around."

My heart squeezes inside my chest, and I push off the couch so I can snatch my niece from my best friend. She wraps her arms and legs around me like a koala, and I hold her tight.

"You're the bestest niece in the whole world, and I love you so, so much."

"Love you too, Uncle Mac."

"Time to brush your teeth, baby girl." Alex takes Giuliana from me again, and sets her on the floor. "I'll be in to tuck you in after I say goodbye to Uncle Mac."

Giuliana scampers into the hallway with Ellie hot on her heels.

Alex gives me a wary look. "Are things that bad, you need advice from a four-year-old?"

I chuckle. "She gives good advice."

He smiles as he glances toward the hallway "She does."

"How's she doing with Aarya living here?"

He rolls his eyes. "She loves it. The two of them started ganging up on me."

"You've got a lot of female energy in this house, my man." I slap his shoulder. "You're officially outnumbered."

He blows out a heavy sigh through his lips. "It feels wrong deceiving her like this. Getting her hopes up, letting her get attached to Aarya when she's not going to stay here in the end."

"Don't worry about the end right now. Focus on what's right in front of you."

He grunts. "What's right in front of me is a drop-dead gorgeous woman who I can't have."

"By your own choice." I widen my eyes. "She has made it crystal-clear that she'd be down for a tumble in your sheets. I don't know how you're turning that shit down. I'd be all over that Middle Eastern princess if I were in your shoes."

Alex glares at me. "You know why I'm turning her down, and it's not for lack of desire. Trust me. She's not making it easy."

I laugh. "I know, I know. You're doing the right thing. I don't want to see you get a broken heart over a fake marriage arrangement any more than you do."

He pinches the bridge of his nose. "I take it Presley still hasn't responded?"

I shake my head. "Nope."

"Give it time, man."

Time. I've spent the last four years wondering where she went and what happened to her. Maybe she didn't think of me at all. Maybe I'm deluding myself by waiting for a message from her. Maybe she moved on.

Maybe everything the three of us had only meant something to me.

"God, these females have us fucked up, don't they?"

Alex lets out a humorless laugh. "You're not kidding."

I OPEN MY PHONE AND PEEK AT STEPHEN'S MESSAGES FOR THE fourth time today.

STEPHEN

Good morning, pretty girl.

STEPHEN

It was so good to see you Friday night.

My stomach coils itself into a giant knot.

No one is as persistent as Stephen McKinley. Ignoring him is useless. I know this, yet I can't bring myself to respond to any of his texts.

"Just answer him and put the poor guy out of his misery."

My shoulders jump. "Jesus, Dom. You scared me."

Dominique gestures to the little silver bell hanging above the doorway. "That's because you're too busy fantasizing about your hockey boyfriends."

I glance around the library, making sure there are no kids lingering in the nearby stacks. "I just don't know what to say to him. Like, what's the point of talking to him?"

Her dark brows shoot up. "The point? Ask your vagina. I can hear her crying from here."

I roll my eyes. "Be serious, Dom. Think about it: He's a pro athlete. What does he want with me?"

"Maybe he's looking for closure. I'm sure he'd like to know why you disappeared so abruptly from his life."

I chew my bottom lip while guilt gnaws at my insides. "You think that's what it is?"

"You won't know until you find out." She slides my phone closer to me on the desk. "Just text him."

Heaving a sigh, I lift my phone and type out a text.

ME

Hi, Stephen. It was really good to see you too.

His response is instant.

STEPHEN

I'd love to see you again.

I hold my phone up so Dominique can see his response. "Now what?"

She grins. "Now you set up a time and place to meet up."

The dismissal bell rings before I can offer her an excuse as to why I can't hang out with my ex-boyfriend, and we head outside to our afternoon duties.

After the parking lot clears out, I head to my car and drive to pick up my niece and nephew.

Monday through Friday, I run around like a chicken without a head. Alyssa is split between field hockey and band practice, while Avery takes private art lessons, which means I'm driving them to and from their extracurricular activities and trying to fit in some time to cook a healthy, balanced dinner when we get home.

I don't know how my sister did it, to be honest. Being a single mom is no joke, but she did it with a smile. Never a complaint. She was Super Mom, and the best big sister too. I strive to be like her every single day, though I know I fall short.

This wasn't supposed to be my life, but I'm trying my best.

"Who's that?" Alyssa asks as we finally pull up to the house later that evening.

My gaze follows hers out the passenger window as I roll to a stop beside the curb, and my foot jerks on the brake pedal.

Oh my god.

Chance sits on the top porch step, dressed in all-black with his hood up.

Waiting for me.

Avery, my nervous nelly, glances at me from the passenger seat. "Do you know who that man is?"

I nod, swallowing past the dryness in my throat. "He's...an old friend. Someone I went to college with."

Avery's green eyes narrow. "Did you know he was coming over?"

"No, but it's okay." I force a smile. "Come on, I'll introduce you."

Alyssa is out of the car in record time, ever the social butterfly and always down to meet new people. "What's his name, Aunt Pres?"

"Wait, 'Lyss." Avery grabs her backpack as she tries to dart past him, yanking her backward. "He's a stranger. Stay by me."

Alyssa rolls her eyes. "He's Aunt Presley's friend."

Avery glances at me with his unsure gaze again, undoubtedly recognizing the fact that I'm caught off-guard. Reading people is my boy's superpower, perks of being quiet and observant.

I hoist myself out of the car and sling my work bag over my shoulder, lifting my gaze to the man in question.

Chance rises from the porch as we approach, stuffing his hands in the pockets of his hoodie, and I don't miss the way his eyes dart to the kids with curiosity.

"Hi, Chance."

His obsidian eyes meet mine, and it suddenly feels like there isn't enough oxygen outside. "Hey."

"Hi!" Alyssa bolts up the stairs to stand in front of him. "I'm Alyssa. This is my brother, Avery. Why are you here?"

So bold. I freaking love her.

I cough out a laugh. "I think you meant to ask if he would like to come inside."

Her cheeks redden. "Sorry. Would you like to come in? We're making tacos tonight."

Chance's gaze flicks between the three of us before he shakes his head. "Sorry, I shouldn't have come."

He tries to jog down the stairs, but I reach out and grip his arm. "Chance, wait."

Despite the fact that it's only been four years, and Alyssa is nine-years-old, it wouldn't make sense for him to assume these are my kids. But he doesn't know if there's a man in my life, or anything about my life, for that matter, so he's running like the skittish cat he is.

"I didn't realize...I thought..." He sputters over his words.

"Chance, these are my niece and nephew."

Realization settles in, and his shoulders visibly drop like he's relieved at that information. "Oh."

I fight the smile tugging at the corner of my lips. "Why don't you come in so I can get them settled?"

He nods, and takes my work bag off my shoulder. I'm not even sure he realizes he's doing it. That's how he always was, doing little things to take care of me in his own quiet way.

Once we're inside, the kids kick off their shoes and head into the dining room to get started on homework.

Chance stands awkwardly in my kitchen, glancing around at the room.

I turn to face him and lift my eyebrows. "So, you found my address."

"Your friend the other night said you lived on Beaker Street. Wasn't hard to find you."

"And you wanted to find me because...?"

He heaves a sigh before his eyes settle on mine. "You didn't call me."

"I didn't know I was supposed to."

"I gave you my number."

"But you didn't take mine."

"Hence me finding you."

I roll my lips between my teeth to suppress a smile. "What is it you came here to say?"

He runs his fingers through his thick dark hair, his hood falling off with the motion. "It's been four years..."

I nod, waiting for it.

"You just left." He pauses, eyes searching mine for an answer. "And now you're here, and I just need to know what happened."

Guilt twists my stomach. I lean over and peer into the dining room, and Avery and Alyssa's heads snap back down to their homework.

Eavesdropping little sneaks.

I lower my voice and step closer to Chance. "My sister passed away. She named me as the children's legal guardian. I was a mess, and I didn't know what to do. I know I should've said something to you and Stephen; I should've said goodbye before I left. But honestly? It would've been too hard."

Hurt flashes in his eyes. "You lost your sister, and you didn't think you could talk to me about it?"

I hike a shoulder, toying with the hem of my blouse. "It was a lot. I had to be here for these kids, and I had to figure things out."

"You didn't need to do it by yourself."

"You would've tried to help, and you were both so close to having everything you ever dreamed of. I didn't want to stand in your way."

"You *were* my way." His jaw clenches as he steps forward into my space. "I—"

"Aunt Presley?"

Both of our heads turn to Alyssa standing in the doorway. "Are the tacos going to be ready soon? I'm hungry."

I press my palm to my forehead, completely forgetting about the chopped meat in the fridge that needs to be tossed into the pan. "Yes, I'm sorry. I'll get them started now."

Her green eyes flick to Chance. "Do you like tacos?"

He clears his throat as he nods. "I do."

"You should stay. Aunt Presley never has boys over."

I choke on my spit, and Chance smirks like he's pleased at that notion.

I bury my face in the fridge, collecting the meat and peppers before setting them on the counter.

"Where are your pots and pans?" Chance asks.

I bend down and pull out a pan from one of the lower cabinets. "You don't need to—"

He gently nudges me aside, and sets the pan on the stove before reaching for the package of chopped meat. "Do you want to get changed into something comfortable? I can handle the tacos."

My mouth flaps open and closed as I stand there staring up at him.

He leans in and presses a kiss to my temple. "Go. I've got this."

What is happening right now?

I bolt up the stairs and throw on a T-shirt and sweatpants, and that's when I hear the doorbell ring.

"Aunt Pres," Avery's voice calls up to me. "There's another man standing on the porch."

Another man?

I run downstairs and skid to a stop in front of the door. Peering through the peephole, my stomach drops to the floor.

No fucking way.

"Are we having a party?" Alyssa asks.

"No, go back inside and finish your homework."

Neither of the kids move.

I inhale a deep breath and swing open the door.

"Hi, pretty girl."

With a groan, I yank Stephen's wrist and pull him over the threshold.

I'm going to kill Dominique.

Stephen's eyes narrow as he gazes over my shoulder, spotting Chance in the kitchen. "What's *he* doing here?"

"I could ask you the same question."

He holds his arms out wide and grins. "I'm here to see you." His smile drops when he spots the kids standing beside me. "Oh, fuck. You have kids?"

Alyssa gasps at the sound of the curse word.

I wrap my arm around her shoulders and pull her close. "This is my niece, and that's my nephew."

"Cool." He waves at them. "Hey, guys. I'm Stephen McKinley. I play for the Goldfinches. You might've heard of me."

"I haven't," Avery says flatly, and I stifle a laugh.

But Alyssa's eyes light up. "I love hockey! I play field hockey."

"That's awesome." He kneels down to get eye-level with her. "What position do you play?"

"Attacker."

Stephen holds up his palm for a high-five. "That's badass."

Alyssa's wide eyes dart to mine.

"Watch your language," Avery tells him.

My little man of the house.

Stephen covers his mouth with his hand. "Sorry about that, bud."

"Finish up your homework." I guide the kids back into the dining room, and glance at Stephen over my shoulder. "You, kitchen. Now."

Chance's nostrils flare when Stephen steps into the kitchen behind me. "What are you doing here?"

"Same as you, it seems." Stephen reaches around him and pops a pepper slice into his mouth. "I came to talk to my girl."

Chance grunts. "*Your* girl?"

I snap my fingers in front of their faces. "Listen to me, and listen good. You can't just show up at my house. I have a life. I have kids to take care of. If I'm not calling or texting you, it doesn't give you an open invitation to stalk me."

Chance keeps his eyes on the meat as he seasons it, and gives me a curt nod.

Stephen plants his hands on his hips and lets out a long breath through his lips. "Look, I'm sorry for barging in like this. But I've been going crazy since I saw you at the game the other night. I've wondered what happened to you for years, and now you're standing in front of me. I can't believe it."

Without warning, he wraps his arms around me and pulls me in for a hug.

This man has always worn his heart on his sleeve. It's the thing I love most about him. He says what he feels, and he means what he says. He's never ashamed of who he is—and he shouldn't be. He's one of the greatest people I've ever known.

I sink into his embrace, and inhale the familiar scent of his cologne. Tears sting my eyes as reality sets in.

My boys are back.

They're *here*.

And I know they're not really *my* boys, but to me, it feels like they always will be.

I pull back and drop my gaze, trying to hide the evidence of my emotions.

But Chance's fingers tip my chin until I'm looking into his eyes. "Do I get one of those too?"

I slip my arms around his midsection, squeezing him as his arms come up around my shoulders. His tight muscles relax against me, and he lets out a long sigh.

Where would we have ended up had I not left them junior year? What would've happened to us when they got drafted to the NHL and we inevitably parted ways? It's a question I've wondered for years, if I made the right choice.

I never expected to see them again, let alone to have them standing in my kitchen.

And I can't help the excitement bubbling under the surface.

By the time dinner is over, Stephen has us all doubled over with laughter—even Avery.

The kid doesn't smile much, but when he does, it's a brilliant one that could rival the sun.

"Can you come to my field hockey game on Friday?" Alyssa asks.

I hold my hand up to interject. "Oh, I don't think they—"

"I have a game this Friday," Stephen says. "But I'll have your Aunt Presley send me your schedule, and I'll see when I can come watch you."

Alyssa beams, but my stomach twists with unease. These kids have been through a lot, and I'm hesitant to introduce new people into their lives, especially if they aren't going to be permanent.

"Okay, guys. Upstairs and get ready for bed." I point my index finger at Alyssa. "You have to do your twenty-minutes of reading tonight, plus the twenty you owe me from last night."

She grumbles. The kid hates reading, and it's literally like a knife to my chest every time she says it.

Who hates reading?! It's blasphemy.

Avery hops up from the table. "Rock, paper, scissors to see who has to shower first?"

The duo scampers into the hallway, yelling about *best out of three*.

I blow out a long breath through my lips, and lift my eyes between Stephen and Chance. "Well, now you see what I've been busy doing for the last four years."

Stephen shakes his head. "You're incredible for doing this on your own."

Chance nods. "I just wish you would've told us."

I roll my eyes. "Come on. You two were getting drafted into the NHL. I was here helping two kids grieve the loss of their mother, while trying to grieve the loss of my sister at the same time."

"And...?" Chance's dark brows pinch together. "You think I wouldn't have come running to help you?"

"That's the point. I didn't want to ruin your chances at the life you have now." I pause, emotion lodging itself in my throat again. "I'm so proud of you both. You've made your dreams come true."

"Regardless, the universe pushed us back together again." Stephen's hopeful blue eyes stare into mine before he turns to Chance. "The three of us."

I gesture between them. "Have you two been—"

"No." Chance's reply is instant and final.

They haven't been together...since the three of us were?

"He's still hockey's mysterious bachelor." Stephen's voice drips with disdain. Even after all this time, he's still bitter about the fact that Chance keeps his sexuality hidden from the world.

Chance rolls his eyes and rises from his seat. "It's getting late. I should get going."

"And still running from the truth," Stephen sing-songs.

Chance's jaw clenches as he flips him off. "Always a fucking pleasure."

I stand and walk him toward the front door. "Thanks for taking over dinner tonight."

Chance turns to face me when he gets to the door, his dark eyes roaming over my face. "Thanks for letting me in."

I reach up and brush his dark strands out of his eyes. "I know I hurt you when I left, and I'm sorry, Chance. I just thought it would hurt less that way."

He catches my wrist and presses my palm to his cheek, closing his eyes as he leans into my touch. "It hurt all the same."

I realize that now.

I pull back my hand and let it drop at my side. "I hope you can get closure now."

"Closure?" Something flashes in his eyes as they narrow. "You think that's what this is?"

I hike a shoulder. "What else would it be?"

We can't have what we once shared. Not again. Not after all this time. Not when I'm raising two children who need me. Our lives are so different now.

Stephen steps up beside us, and leans down to press a kiss to my temple. "Pretty girl, this is just the beginning."

They're out the door before I can say anything, before I can ask...

What does that mean?

Freshman Year of College

"Nice work tonight, Kellerman."

The team cheers and taps their sticks against their lockers.

My cheeks burn, but I tip my chin. "Thanks, Coach."

Even I have to admit, I played a hell of a game. A fire has been lit under me since I started playing on this college team. Being away from my father has breathed new life into me, and this team is proving to be more like family than my father ever could be. Every game, I'm working towards my dream, propelling myself closer to building the life I want.

I won't let anything stand in my way.

"There's a party at the Alpha house tonight." Stephen nudges me as we head out of the locker room. "Come out with the team so we can celebrate."

I'm about to shake my head and tell him no like I always do, but he cuts me off, tossing his arm around my shoulders as we walk. "They're starting to ask why you never come out with us, and I can only defend you for so long."

"I never asked you to defend me."

"That's the thing about friends—they don't have to ask. They just do it."

"Never said you were my friend, either."

Stephen chuckles. "You need me as your friend. Trust me."

We're still walking with his arm around me when I hear my name.

I whip around, coming face to face with my father, and ice fills my veins.

I shake off Stephen's arm, putting space between us. "Dad, what are you doing here?"

His eyes are bloodshot, and there's a familiar sway to his stance. "I came to see you play."

I had no idea he was out of jail, though I guess ten years is possible with good behavior.

His glossy gaze flicks to Stephen, so I step in front of him to keep his attention on me. "You need to get the hell out of here."

Dad scoffs. "You're a tough guy, now? All grown up."

"Yet you're still the same old nasty drunk."

Must've hit the liquor store the second he got out.

"You think I don't see what you're doing here?" He moves toward me, slow like a lion stalking his prey. "Running away to college so you can act like a fa—"

"Dad!" I cut him off before he can complete the derogatory term he's called me most of my life. "You need to walk away from me or so help me God, I'm going to—"

He lunges forward and shoves me against the wall. "What, huh? You're going to what?"

Stephen yanks my father by the back of his neck and tosses him several feet away.

"Stephen, stop." I try to push past him to get to my father, but the menacing look he gives me stops me in my tracks. Gone is the carefree, happy-go-lucky guy I've come to know over the last several months.

"Your son told you to leave," Stephen practically growls. "I suggest you listen. He doesn't want you here, which means I don't want you here either."

My dad smirks at me. "You gonna let your fairy boyfriend talk to me like this?"

Without a second thought, I slam my fist into my father's face. He falls backward, unsteady on his feet, and crashes onto the floor. I kneel over him and punch him again and again.

"I'm not a little kid anymore. You can't control me, and you can't put your hands on me. Now it's your turn to see what it feels like to be helpless while your own flesh and blood beats the shit out of you. I should kill you, right here!"

I black out in a rage, years of suppressing my father's abuse now breaking like a dam and spilling out of me.

Until Stephen's hands wrap around my biceps, hauling me up. "Enough, Chance. Enough."

His calm, deep voice rolls over my skin, snapping me back to reality. My chest heaves as I stare down at my father groaning on the floor.

Fuck.

Emotion lodges in my throat like a thick ball. No one has ever seen the ugliness my father is capable of, aside from me, my mother, and a handful of local cops. I feel vulnerable and embarrassed. Exposed. Stephen wasn't supposed to see any of that.

I have to get out of here. But before I do, I bend down and dig into my father's coat pocket, pulling out his key ring and separating the key fob from the keychain before tossing the rest back to him. Then I spin around and storm down the hallway.

"Chance, wait." Stephen jogs to catch up to me, but I don't slow down.

"Leave me alone," I toss over my shoulder. "You shouldn't have gotten involved."

"Are you kidding me?" He yanks me by my arm and spins me around to face him. "You're mad that I stuck up for you?"

"I didn't need you to!" I don't know why I'm doing this. My hands are shaking, my skin vibrating. But I can't stop the words from tumbling out of me. "That shit you just saw? That's my life, and it's none of your business. I didn't ask you to step in."

"You didn't need to ask me," he shouts back. "That's what friends do. They have each other's backs, and they're there when shit gets ugly."

"When are you going to get it?" I look him dead in the eyes. "We're not friends, and we're never going to be friends."

He should walk away from me and never speak to me again. Hell, he should punch me in the face for the way I'm acting after he defended me to my father.

Instead, Stephen pushes into my space until we're nose to nose. "I can see that you haven't had a great life up until now, and it's pretty obvious you don't have a lot of friends. So, you can keep trying to push me away all you want, but I'm not going anywhere. You're stuck with me. If someone disrespects you, I'm going to say something. Every. Single. Time. And if you don't like it, that's too damn bad."

The sincerity in his eyes calms something in my jagged, dysfunctional heart. He's not looking at me with judgment, and he's not asking me to talk about what he saw between me and my father. He stuck up for me without a reason to. He could've easily stayed back, stayed quiet, and let me handle it. I don't understand it, but fuck if I don't like how it feels to have someone on my side for once.

He leans closer, and grips the back of my neck. "You played a great fucking game tonight, and we are going out with the team to celebrate. You are going to forget that your father was even here—in fact, do yourself a favor and erase him from your memory completely. But if you don't come out? I'll sit in that damn room with you, bored out of my fucking mind, and you know I'll annoy the shit out of you, so you might as well just come out."

I swallow past the burning in my throat, and stuff down all the words I wish I could say to him. "You really are so annoying."

He grins and smacks the back of my head. "Let's go get shitfaced."

"Where is he?"

Principal Sturges holds up his hands to stop me as I charge into the main office. "The nurse is checking him out. Ms. King, I think you need—"

"What I *need* is to see my nephew." I dart around him and storm in the direction of the nurse's office.

"I was going to say, I think you need to tell me more about the kids who are bullying Avery."

My shoes skid to a stop, and I glance back at Mr. Sturges. "Thought you were going to tell me to calm down."

He grimaces. "I have a wife. I know better than to tell a woman to calm down."

I blow out a breath and run my fingers through my hair. "I'm sorry. I just don't know how to help him. He doesn't want to be a snitch, and I know that'd only make things worse for him. But I can't stand by and watch him get hurt like this. I'm out of my depths here. I don't know what else to do."

I came running as soon as I got the call from Mr. Sturges that Avery had been hurt. Luckily, my boss let me cancel my last library class and leave early.

"I called the counselor, Mrs. Landry. She's in there with Avery now. She'll be able to offer some helpful advice, as she has a lot of experience with situations like this." Mr. Sturges lowers his voice. "But I need to know who the boys are. I have a school to run, and this kind of behavior is unacceptable. It's my duty to put a stop to it."

I nod. "I'll talk to him."

I peek my head into the room, and spot Avery sitting in the chair beside Nurse Nancy's desk. When he turns his head toward me, holding an ice pack over his right eye, I swallow down the bile climbing up my throat. I need to stay calm, for his sake.

But when he lowers the ice pack and I see the swollen, bruised skin around his eye, I lose all my cool.

I kneel down in front of him and pull him into my arms, squeezing him tight. Tears sting my eyes. "Are you okay?"

His voice is muffled against my shoulder. "I'm okay."

"What happened?" I pull back and cradle his face in my hands. "Was it the same group of boys again?"

He nods. "They followed me into the bathroom. Two of them held me back while the other one hit me."

Those little shits.

The woman sitting beside Avery leans forward and holds out her hand. "Hi, Ms. King. I'm Monique Landry, the school counselor."

I shake her hand, blinking back the tears. "Hi."

"I've been talking with Avery, and he said this has been going on since September."

"He hasn't wanted to disclose who the students are, because he's afraid they'll come for him even harder if he gets them into trouble." I glance at Avery. "But we've tried it your way, and now it's time to try a different tactic."

Monique nods. "It's common for students to retaliate after they get in trouble for their actions. But Avery, it's their actions that got them into trouble—not you. You have every right to stand up for yourself and put a stop to this."

"They won't stop." Avery's voice is flat. "They're never going to stop."

He's not wrong. From what I've seen growing up, the only thing that'll stop a bully in his tracks is when someone bigger and stronger puts him in his place. But that's not Avery.

Monique turns her attention to me. "I explained to Avery that we can't lose hope. Things can always change; things can always get better. He's not alone in this."

"No, you're not alone." I squeeze his knee. "We're going to figure out a solution together."

I just don't know what that solution is.

When I pull up to the curb at home, Alyssa flies out of the back seat. "Chance is here!"

I can't help the way my heart skips a beat at the sight of him sitting on my porch, but my head falls back against the headrest with a groan. After everything with Avery today, I don't have the energy for my love life—or lack thereof.

"Looks like he brought dinner," Avery says beside me.

"Thank God, because I was *not* in the mood to cook tonight."

Avery's eyebrows pinch together. "You don't have to cook every night, you know."

"It's important to me to make sure you and your sister are eating healthy foods." I hike a shoulder. "Your mom hated fast food."

He's quiet for a moment. "We don't expect you to be like mom."

"I just want to do right by you guys. I want to do right by her." My bottom lip trembles as I struggle to keep it together. "Sometimes it feels like I'm failing."

"You aren't failing. I'm really glad we have you, Aunt Pres."

A lone tear rolls down my cheek and I lean over the console to wrap my nephew in a hug. "Thanks, kid. I'm really glad I have you too."

He gestures out the window. "Let's go save your friend from Alyssa."

I chuckle, and some of the tension rolls off my shoulders.

Alyssa pops up when I get to the bottom of the stairs. "Aunt Presley, Chance brought us Thai food. There's shrimp and noodles and vegetables. And he said he would listen to me play the trumpet after dinner."

Avery scrunches up his nose. "That's because he doesn't know how awful you are at it."

Alyssa plants her hands on her hips. "That's not kind, Avery."

"Be nice to your sister." I hand Avery the house key as I lug my work bag up the stairs. "Go inside and set the table."

The kids head into the house, and my eyes trail up Chance's tall frame until I'm met with his dark gaze. "You really didn't have to—"

"What happened to Avery's eye?"

I let out a long exhale. "Some kids are bullying him at school."

"And they put their hands on him?"

I nod.

He crosses his arms over his chest. "What is the school doing about this?"

"Avery doesn't want to rat out the kids bothering him. He's worried it'll make them mad."

"So, you're just going to sit back and let it keep happening?"

My chin jerks back. "I'm not *letting* anything happen. But I don't know what the hell I'm doing here, and I don't know how to help him. I'd always call my sister for help when I needed advice, but she's not here so I'm alone, and I'm fucking this all up, and I just don't know—"

Chance wraps his arms around me and swallows me in his embrace. My tears soak into his sweatshirt as they spill out. His palm presses against the back of my head, holding me against his warm body like he's trying to shield me from everything.

"You're *not* alone," he whispers.

Four years ago, I was thrown into a life I had no clue how to manage. I still don't. It never gets easier. As the kids get older, a new kind of danger presents itself, and it's different than the last one. Just when you think you have a handle on the first little fire, another one starts up somewhere else. I'm doing my best, but my best doesn't feel like enough.

I need help.

Chance pulls back just enough to look into my eyes, his thumbs coming up to swipe at my tears. "Let me talk to Avery, and we'll come up with a plan so that no one will ever lay a finger on him again."

My chest aches at the reminder that Chance was once in Avery's shoes. Only, it wasn't a punk-ass kid putting his hands on him. It was his own father. On top of that, Chance lost his mother at a young age too.

Maybe Chance is the perfect person to help Avery navigate this situation.

I stretch up on my toes to reach him and press a kiss to his cheek. "Thank you for being here. And thank you for dinner."

He slides my work bag off my shoulder and slings it onto his own. "Anything for you, Presley."

I stamp down the butterflies swarming my stomach as we step inside the house.

The kids have already ransacked the food. Chance makes me a plate before making one for himself, and he takes the empty seat beside Avery.

Avery keeps his head down, keeping his bruised eye turned away from us.

"Do you know how to defend yourself?" Chance asks.

No lead up to the conversation; he dives right in. That's how Chance is. He doesn't speak much, but when he does, it's about something important.

Avery shakes his head. "Wouldn't matter anyway. There are three of them and one of me."

"Doesn't mean you have to take all three of them at once." Chance dabs the corner of his mouth with a napkin. "Go for the leader. There's always a leader."

"Austin." Avery's eyes dart from me to Chance. "He's the leader, and the other two are his minions."

Chance nods. "After dinner, I'm going to teach you how to throw a punch."

Alyssa's eyes fly to me. "Can he teach me too?"

I clasp her hand. "Another time. Let Chance focus on Avery right now."

Maybe my sister wouldn't want her kids learning how to fight. Maybe it's wrong to teach them. But I refuse to let anyone cause harm to my niece and nephew. If I can't punch this Austin asshole in the face myself, then I'm sure as shit going to let Avery do it.

"We don't start fights," Chance says. "But we can be ready for them."

Something flashes in Avery's eyes, and he sits up a little straighter in his chair.

"Were you ever bullied?" Alyssa asks.

Chance nods. "The boys at my high school used to beat me up in the locker room every day before practice."

Avery's eyebrows shoot up. "The boys on your team?"

He nods. "Yup."

My heart hurts for him. I know how much he hates talking about his past, but I appreciate him talking to the kids about it.

As soon as they finish eating, Chance takes Avery into the basement. Alyssa insists on following, and I'm curious too, so we end up sitting on the couch to watch.

Chance holds up his fist in front of Avery. "Make a fist like this. Never tuck your thumb inside, or you'll break it."

Avery balls his hands into fists, and when Chance holds up his palms, Avery throws a couple of punches.

"Step into it," Chance says, demonstrating with a punch into the air. "Put your body weight behind it, and don't lock your elbow."

He shows Avery how to block his face, and dodge an incoming attack. The more he learns, the more confident my nephew appears. There's a new determination behind his eyes that wasn't there an hour ago.

Halfway through the lesson, Chance reaches behind his neck and pulls off his sweatshirt, leaving him in a plain black T-shirt. I catch a flash of his incredibly muscular torso as his shirt rides up with his sweatshirt before he tugs it down, but that flash is all it takes for my skin to heat.

I remember what this man looks like without clothes on; what he looks like crawling on top of me, settling between my thighs; what he looks like when he comes.

My chest heaves with shallow breaths, and I remove my own hoodie.

Chance arches a brow, no doubt reading me like a book. "You okay over there?"

My cheeks burn. "It's just getting a little warm in here."

Chance smirks before returning his attention to the lesson.

Avery does everything Chance shows him, and even I learn a few things that I didn't know about throwing a punch. It breaks my heart that Chance had to learn all this in order to defend himself in his own house, whether it be from his dad or from his many different foster parents after his father was put in jail, but I'm so grateful that he's here right now to help.

At eight o'clock, I tell the kids it's time to take showers and get ready for bed.

Before Avery darts upstairs, he throws his arms around Chance's waist and hugs him tight. "Thank you for helping me."

Chance heaves a long sigh and rests his chin on top of Avery's head. "Anytime."

"Do you think..." Avery pauses, pulling back. "Do you think we could do this again sometime?"

My chest aches. Chance's eyes flick to mine before answering. "Of course, if that's okay with your aunt."

Avery graces us with a wide grin, and I swallow a gasp at the sight of it. He hasn't smiled much since he lost his mom, and it has been my mission to put one on his face any chance I can get.

Alyssa says goodnight to Chance and bounds up the stairs, leaving me alone with him.

I wring my hands in front of my body. "I can't thank you enough for helping Avery tonight."

He reaches out and covers my hands with his. "He shouldn't have to go through this alone, and neither should you."

I nod, glancing down at our connection. "I've been doing it alone all this time."

"You chose to." I can hear the resentment in his voice when he says it.

"You're living your dream." I hike a shoulder. "Look how wonderful your life is."

"None of it matters, Presley. It never did. Not when it came to you."

His words sink into my chest, wrapping around my heart.

"Did you even miss us?" he asks, his voice quiet, and I don't miss the fact that he's asking about Stephen too.

"Of course, I did." Tears sting my eyes, and emotion thickens in my throat. "I hated not being a part of your lives. I watched every one of your games just to get a glimpse of you, trying to hold onto the memories. It killed me to lose you, but—"

Chance walks me backward and presses me against the door, his large hands coming up to cradle my face. His dark eyes are wild as they bounce between mine, his chest heaving with shallow breaths.

"I would've given it all up to help you. You didn't have to go through that alone. You didn't have to push me away. And as long as I'm breathing, you will never be alone again. Do you understand?"

A tear rolls down my cheek as I nod, swallowing a sob.

He brushes it away with his thumb. "Use your words, Pres. Let me know that you hear me when I say that I'm here for you now."

"Yes," I whisper. "I understand."

"Good." He presses his lips to my cheek, centimeters from where I really want his mouth to be. "I'm going to take care of this bullying problem. Then you're going to let me know what else you need help with, and I'm going to take care of those problems too. And when you're back on your feet and you feel like you can breathe again, we're going to have a conversation about what you want in life—for *you*, not for the kids, and not for anyone else."

"W-why?" is all I can ask, because my tears are threatening a flood, and I can't trust my own voice.

Why is he helping me?

Why does he still care after all this time?

"Because I've missed you too. And I don't plan on going back to a life without you in it."

Presley's eyes widen when she sees me.

She didn't expect me to show up.

She should know better than that. Then again, it's been a while since we've been together. I'll have to remind her of who I am.

I lower myself onto the bleachers beside Presley, and hand her a to-go cup. "Half decaf, half hazelnut creamer. Hope that's still your favorite."

Her mouth pops open in surprise as she takes the cup from me. "I can't believe you remembered that. Thank you."

I lean over her and hand Avery a matching cup. "Not sure if you like hot chocolate, but got you one because it's a superior beverage that everyone should be drinking."

He tugs on the brim of his hat before taking the cup. "I do. Thanks."

A blueish-purple splotch mars the skin under one of his eyes, and my stomach drops. "I hope the other guy looks worse," I say, gesturing to his eye.

He swallows as he glances around at the families sitting nearby. "Everyone's staring at you."

"Let 'em stare. I came here to see our girl play." I wave at Alyssa who's playing defense across the field, and she waves her stick in the air.

"*Our* girl, huh?" Presley shakes her head, but I spot the slight tip of her lips and take that as a win.

"How was your day today, pretty girl?"

"Good."

I note the sadness in her tone despite the smile she pastes on her face.

"What's up with the black eye?" I whisper so Avery can't hear me.

"Tell you later."

"So, you're a school librarian, huh?" I nudge her with my shoulder. "Sounds like one of my fantasies."

"Lower your voice," she hisses.

I press my lips against her ear and whisper, "This better for you?"

Her body shivers before she shoves me away. "No."

I grin and return my attention to the field. Alyssa stands there looking like a badass with her goggles and mouthguard, but her stance is all wrong and she's holding the stick in the wrong places.

"What days are you free this week?" I gesture to the field. "I'd like to give 'Lyss a few pointers."

Presley's eyebrows shoot up. "Aren't you busy? You have a big game coming up this weekend."

My chest warms at the fact that she knows my game schedule. "Not too busy to make time for my girls."

"I don't understand the two of you," she murmurs.

Two. Me and Chance. "He's been to your house again, hasn't he?"

She nods.

Jealousy streaks through me, but something else is there as well. Something that makes me feel like I've missed out on not just time with Presley, but with Chance. With the both of them, together.

"What's to understand?" I lean my elbows on the seat behind me. "We missed you. Isn't it obvious?"

"Yes, but we're not in the same situation we were in." She turns her head to look me in the eyes. "This isn't college."

"That doesn't change a thing."

She purses her lips. "It changes everything."

The opposing team gets possession of the ball, charging toward Alyssa's goalie. I jump to my feet and cup my hands around my mouth. "Stop them! Get in there, Alyssa!"

One of the kids winds back to make her shot, but Alyssa jumps in front and smacks the ball away. One of her teammates runs it back down to the other side of the field, and the crowd cheers. Alyssa's head snaps over to me and she lifts her stick over her head in celebration.

"Woo! That's my girl!" I clap as I lower myself back onto the bleachers. "She's a natural."

Presley laughs, checking her phone to make sure she got the play on video. "She's my spirit animal."

I pull out my phone and snap a couple of pictures so I can show Alyssa later. A few small adjustments to her stance, and she'll be unstoppable.

"I'm going to get closer so I can get some better pictures," Avery says as he stands.

Presley squeezes his hand. "Thanks, kid."

Once he's out of earshot, I ask the question that's been on my mind since I met these kids. "Where's their father?"

Presley hikes a shoulder. "Off traveling somewhere with his flavor of the month."

My brows pinch together. "Does he ever see them?"

"He'll send money for the holidays, but he stopped making time to see them years ago." She rolls her eyes. "My sister divorced him when the kids were little, so they're used to it by now."

Disdain for a man I've never met courses through me. "How could he walk out on them? I've only just met them and I want to be around them as much as I can."

Presley's eyes glisten in the sunlight as she keeps her gaze on the field. "Not everyone has as big of a heart as you do."

"Tell me what happened to Avery's eye."

She blows out a long breath before she speaks. "He's getting bullied at school."

My eyebrows shoot up. "He got beat up?"

She nods. "Chance came by the other day and gave him some pointers on defending himself, but I don't know what else to do."

"Are these kids getting expelled? What is the school doing about it?"

"The principal is letting Avery skip gym and take an extra art class instead. But Avery is worried that the kids will retaliate if he snitches."

"They could. But that doesn't mean we do nothing about this and let him get his ass beat." I reach into my pocket and pull out my phone. "I can get better security at the school. Or maybe he can go to a private school, one where he can focus more on art."

Presley covers my phone with her hand. "Stephen, no. I can't let you do any of that."

"Why not?"

"I don't want Avery to think that he should run away from his problems. I hate that he's getting hurt, and hopefully the principal will be able to put a stop to it, but he needs to learn how to overcome problems like this in life."

I let out a frustrated sigh. "I don't like that plan."

"Me either." A humorless laugh escapes her. "I don't know what the hell I'm doing here. I'm so far out of my depth."

"Hey, you're doing a fantastic job with these kids." I rest my hand against her thigh and squeeze. "They're so lucky to have you, Pres. And I'm lucky to have you back in my life again."

She chews on her bottom lip as she lifts her eyes to mine. "What if *friends* is the only capacity I can be in your life?"

It's not, but I'll play along. "Then I'm going to be the best friend you've ever had."

She smiles, relief smoothing out her features, as if she was worried that I wouldn't want her any way I could have her.

Presley assumes that because of her new lifestyle as a guardian, as an elementary school librarian living in suburbia, she can't also have the kind of relationship that the three of us once had.

But that's where she's wrong.

This loneliness inside of me has been there since I lost two of the most important people in my life. I haven't been able to find anyone who makes me feel the way it felt to be in love with Chance and Presley.

With Presley back in the picture, maybe the three of us can have a second chance.

And maybe it could be forever.

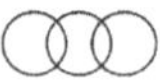

"So, you stalked her."

"I didn't *stalk* her. She sent me Alyssa's game schedule, and I showed up." I point at my sister. "That's called an invite."

Chelsea rolls her eyes from across the table. "I don't understand how you're just okay with her now after dropping you like that. Don't you remember how heartbroken you were when she disappeared?"

I nod, talking around the lump of food in my cheek. "I do. But now that I know what happened, I can forgive her and move forward."

"I think what she did was very selfless." Mom reaches over and squeezes my hand. "She put your and Chance's needs before her own, and that must've been extremely difficult with everything she was going through."

My eldest sister, Kathy, takes a sip of iced tea. "I agree. She chose to grieve her sister's death by herself, and to take care of two kids by herself, all while still being a kid herself."

Chelsea hikes a shoulder. "I get that, but I still don't know if I'd be so willing to open my heart to her again."

"Have you met your brother?" Dad asks with a chuckle.

"Maybe that's why you're single right now, Chels." Kathy arches a brow. "You need to let some forgiveness into that stone-cold heart of yours."

Chelsea lets her fork fall with a clank against her plate. "No, the reason I'm single is because Darren is a lying fucking piece of shit."

Dad and Kathy exchange knowing glances.

I clink my glass against Chelsea's. "You keep giving him shit, CC. If he truly loves you, he's going to stick around and keep fighting for you until you give in."

"A little groveling never hurt anybody." Mom grins at my father. "Isn't that right, dear?"

He shoots her a wink. "I'll get on my knees any day of the week for you."

Chelsea makes a gagging noise, and Kathy laughs.

With three of our sisters scattered around the country with their spouses and kids, Kathy, Chelsea, and I make it a point to see our parents for dinner once a week as the remaining siblings. Kathy is the oldest, married and living one town over; Chelsea is the second youngest, born a year before me, and still in medical school to become an anesthesiologist so she lives in the basement here at our parents' house.

All the siblings are close, each of us sharing different relationships with each other, but Kathy has always been my favorite. She's patient and kind with an even-keeled temperament. I know I can go to her with anything, and she'll give me advice with my best interest at heart.

"I want to know how things are going with Chance." Kathy arches a brow at me. "He still an asshole?"

"Yup." I laugh. "Honestly, I don't know how any of this is going to work. He's still in the closet; we've been fighting for years. And Presley has convinced herself that she can't have the relationship we once did. I'm just flying by the seat of my pants here."

"Invite them over for dinner," Mom suggests. "I'd love to meet them."

"It's still new, Mom." Chelsea shakes her head. "Give them some time before you start crocheting a baby blanket."

Her mouth drops open. "When are you going to let that go?"

Chelsea's eyes widen. "You made baby blankets for all six of your children before any of them had babies! How do you not see how crazy that is?"

Dad grimaces. "Don't say the C-word. That never goes over well."

"That reminds me," Kathy says, wearing a smirk that tells me she's only going to add fuel to the flame. "What did you do with my baby blanket? Since I'm not having kids, did you throw it away?"

"Of course I didn't throw it away."

"So, then where is it? Are you planning on giving it to someone else's baby instead?"

Mom hikes a shoulder. "What do you care? You're not giving me grandchildren. What does it matter to you if I gave it away?"

Kathy's eyes bulge. "Oh my god, you totally gave it to someone else."

Chelsea tosses her head back and laughs. "Eww, Mom. You regifted a baby blanket? That's so creepy."

"How is it creepy?" Mom's shoulders straighten. "I made it for a baby, and now a baby has it. What's the big deal?"

Kathy scrunches her nose. "You created it to the thought of my unborn child."

I shiver. "It sounds so dirty when you say it like that."

"Oh, to hell with you all!" Mom tosses her napkin down on the table. "I will not be shamed for wanting my grandchildren to be wrapped in the comfort and warmth of a blanket made by their grandmother."

Dad slowly rises from his chair, taking his empty dinner plate with him.

But Mom catches on. "Are you just going to run away and not stick up for your wife?"

Dad lifts his right hand in the air. "I gotta be honest...it was a little presumptuous, sweetheart."

She lets out a disgusted noise from the back of her throat. "Well, you know what? My existing grandchildren love my blankets, so I don't care what you people say."

"I'm just saying, it's not fair that I don't get a famous Patricia McKinley blanket just because I chose to not have children." Patty crosses her arms over her chest and feigns offense. "I'd like a blanket of my own."

"Or a scarf, at the very least," Chelsea adds.

My eyes widen. "Oh, could you make a pair of slippers? I'd love—"

"The three of you aren't getting shit!" She pushes back her chair in a huff, and storms into the kitchen with her empty wine glass.

And the three of us howl with laughter, while Dad tries to stifle his.

I look around the room, and I imagine what it'd be like to have Presley and Chance here with me. Kathy would love Presley, and I can picture Chelsea bickering with Chance. Dad would talk about hockey while Mom doted on Alyssa and Avery.

I can see it so clearly.

I can *feel* it. This time around feels different than it did in college. That was fun and carefree, but now? This feels like we could be at the start of building our future together.

I only hope they feel the same way.

Kathy nudges me with her elbow. "You happy, baby brother?"

"For the first time in a long time, I am."

Sophomore Year of College

"Would you put your clothes on?"

Stephen grins and plants his hands on his hips. "What's the matter, Kellerman? You getting turned on by the sight of my magnificent dick?"

I spin around and set down the to-go cup on his nightstand.

His dick is magnificent, but I'd never tell him that.

"Nothing wrong with admitting it," he continues. "I'm secure enough in myself to tell you that you've got a nice cock too."

I choke on my spit as my head whips around to glare at him over my shoulder. "Why are you looking at my cock?"

He shrugs like it's no big deal. "Like I said, it's nice. Nothing wrong with appreciating a nice cock when you see one."

My skin heats. "Yeah, well, maybe you should keep those thoughts to yourself."

"Why the fuck would I do that? You see something you like, then you should let them know. Life is too short to keep your feelings bottled up."

"Just shut the fuck up and get dressed."

But he doesn't shut the fuck up.

Nor does he ever.

"You know, that's your problem. You're stuck inside your own head, always worrying about what people will think."

I roll my eyes and pull on my jeans. "I don't care what people think."

We both know it's a lie, but Stephen doesn't call me out on it. "Another black coffee? You've had two today already. That shit's bad for you."

"It's not coffee."

He opens the lid on the cup and inhales. "This smells like hot chocolate."

"That's because it is." I sift through the shirts in my closet, keeping my back to him.

"Since when do you drink hot chocolate?"

I grunt. "I don't. It's for five-year-olds."

He pauses. "You got this for me?"

"I was passing the place you like, so I grabbed one for you."

For the last year, Stephen has pushed every single one of my buttons—some buttons I didn't even know I had—trying to get me to snap, to get me to blurt out something, to get me to tell him what he has somehow figured out, because he reads me like an open book.

Honestly? He's wearing me down. Aside from the fact that he's relentless, I'm starting to run out of reasons why I can't tell Stephen that I'm into men in addition to women. And why shouldn't I tell him? He's bisexual too. He won't judge me. He won't berate me, or shun me. If anything, it'd bring us closer together.

But therein lies the problem.

I'm scared of getting close to Stephen McKinley. He's charismatic and outgoing and lovable, and everyone gravitates toward him. I can't allow myself to give in to the temptation of him. And *fuck* am I tempted by him. How easy it'd be to get wrapped up in all that he is. But I'm not good enough for someone like him. We're too different.

He's joy, and I'm sadness. He's a symphony, and I'm silence. He's sunshine and I'm the rain cloud that ruins it all.

So instead, I push him away...at least, as much as I can for someone who sleeps in the bed next to mine, and plays on the same team as I do.

I yank a black T-shirt off the hanger, but Stephen steps into my space before I can pull it over my head. His fingertips graze over the humming-bird etched onto my skin just below my collarbone. "What does this mean?"

"My mother loved hummingbirds."

Stephen's eyebrows lift. "Loved?"

I nod once.

Stephen's fingers brush back and forth over the bird's wings, goose-bumps flying along my skin. "When did she pass?"

I swallow. "My father killed her when I was twelve."

His mouth drops open, and mine does too because I can't believe I just admitted that. I move to turn away, to hide from the truth I spilled, but Stephen doesn't let me get away.

He grips my shoulder. "What happened?"

I shake my head, not wanting to revisit that memory. "Let's get going. The team is waiting for us."

"They can wait." His eyes bounce between mine. "Tell me."

When we're this close, I can spot the different shades of blue swirling in his irises. It's like looking into the depths of the ocean, beautiful yet danger-ous, ready to pull me under.

I try to keep my voice even and not let the memory assault my mind. "My father was drunk one night, and my parents were fighting out in the driveway. He was heading to the bar, but my mother didn't want him to leave because he always came home in worse shape than he was when he left, and he got violent when he drank." I swallow around the ball of emotion lodged in my throat. "He got in the car and I ran into the street to stop him. I hated seeing my mother upset, so I thought everything would be better if I could just keep him from leaving." I pause, sucking in a breath before letting out the rest of the words. "He stepped on the gas pedal, and gunned it. My mom jumped in front of me, and he mowed her down. Dragged her under his car for half a mile before he realized what he'd done."

Tears well in Stephen's eyes. "She saved your life."

I shake my head. "She wouldn't've needed to if I hadn't run out into the street."

His eyebrows press together. "You can't seriously blame yourself for that."

I shove him back and move across the room. "Let's go. I don't want to spend the night talking about this shit."

Stephen stares at me a moment, rooted to the spot I left him in. I know he wants more out of me, but I've already said too much.

"I don't need your pity," I say.

He blinks away his emotion, and hikes a nonchalant shoulder. "Just wishing I would've beat your father's ass last year when I met him."

A small smirk tugs at my lips. "He's not worth it."

"No, but you are."

Affection warms my chest, pumping through my veins to the rest of my body.

I don't say anything.

I can't.

I'm too afraid of what might come out if I respond to Stephen's notion that maybe I'm worth a damn.

"Ladies, drop your panties. The Ospreys just walked in!"

I glare at the DJ across the room as cheers fill the air.

Frat parties aren't my thing, and they never will be my thing. But every once in a while, I have to appease my teammates and show face for a celebratory drink, which consists of me holding a Solo cup filled with disgusting keg beer, and pretending to sip on it throughout the night.

Nobody but Stephen knows about my father's alcoholism, so he's the only one who's aware that I'm stone-cold sober, and he doesn't give me a hard time about it like he does with everything else.

"Look at this place." Stephen's eyes bounce around the room at the potential hookups like he's a kid in a candy shop. "Take your pick, Kellerman. We've got the whole football team *and* the cheerleading squad."

I roll my eyes. "I'm here to spend a little time with the team, and then I'm out. I have—"

My gaze snags on a girl dancing with her friends on the other side of the room, and my brain erases all other thoughts.

Her dark-brown hair is in a messy bob, the shorter pieces falling over her eyes while the ends of her strands hover just above her shoulders. Her toned arms are covered in a myriad of tattoos, each one weaving into the other like it's telling a story; the mandala on her throat in particular catches my attention, along with the thin, sparkly ring dangling from her septum. Her tiny black tank-top says *Emo Girl* in big white letters, and ripped baggy jeans sit low on her waist, rounding out her rocker-girl appearance with black combat boots.

This girl is my fantasy come to life.

Apparently, she's Stephen's fantasy too, because he's staring just as hard as I am.

"Dibs," he murmurs.

I roll my eyes. "She's out of your league."

He scoffs. "No such thing."

Regardless of how good-looking Stephen is, he hasn't yet learned that you can't call dibs on a woman like *that*. You don't *own* a woman like that. *She* decides what she wants and who she wants, and you'd be wise to obey.

Stephen grips my elbow and pulls me across the room. "Occupy her friends."

I dig my heels in as we get closer. "I don't dance, man."

"You're my wingman. I need you."

This guy doesn't need a wingman. Women and men alike throw themselves at him.

The hazel-eyed beauty glances up as Stephen makes a beeline right for her, dragging me behind him. She wears a playful smirk on her lush lips as she moves her hips to the beat, waiting to see what he'll do.

Stephen releases my arm and slides up behind her, his body moving in sync with hers. He whispers something in her ear, and her shoulders shake with her laughter.

I'm about to spin around, ready to disappear from the crowded dance floor. Stephen gets the girl, and I'll sneak out of the party and go back to my dorm alone.

But then her gaze shifts to me.

With Stephen's hands sitting on her waist, she reaches out and her fingers wrap around my wrist. "Where do you think you're going?"

I dip my head so she can hear me over the music. "Looks like you've got a dancing partner."

She arches a brow. "Who says I can't have two?"

"I don't dance."

She smiles, and her hand slips around to my back, pulling my body closer to hers. "That just means you haven't danced with the right woman yet."

Holding me against her, her hips sway and mine follow. It feels awkward at first, my insecurity blaring in my head. But then, Stephen takes my hands and places them on her waist. His fingers trail up my arms, his light touch setting a blaze along my skin, and settling on top of where her hands are resting on my shoulders.

The three of us are sandwiched together. Connected. My eyes dart around the room, looking to see who's watching us.

But no one is. Everyone here is halfway to drunk, enjoying themselves.

So why can't I do the same?

She tips her head back and rests it against Stephen's chest as she gazes up at me. "This isn't so bad, is it?"

My fingertips squeeze her hips. "No."

Stephen's hand leaves my left shoulder and moves to her chin, tilting her face to the side. She closes the distance willingly, and presses her lips to his.

Possession rips through me—whether it's because he's kissing her, or she's kissing him, I have no idea. I stop moving, stricken as I watch their tongues snake out and wrap around one another. I should go. Leave them to themselves, and leave this stupid party.

But then she turns her head and presses her lips against mine.

Her lips are soft and pillowy, and they open for me instantly. There's a hint of cinnamon on her tongue from Stephen's gum as it snakes into my mouth in search of mine.

I glance up at Stephen, my mouth fused to hers, and I don't miss his hungry gaze, his hooded eyes watching me. He licks his lower lip before he takes it between his teeth, and that subtle move makes my dick jump. He dips his head a fraction of an inch, teasing me with the thought of him joining our kiss.

Until the beauty between us pulls away from my mouth, panting. "Let's take this somewhere else."

She says it to both of us. She wants us, together.

But it snaps me out of my trance, and I step back like a bucket of cold water has been dumped on my head.

What the hell am I doing?

I turn away and leave them standing there.

"WHAT'S THE PLAN? WE CAN'T EXACTLY GO IN THERE AND KICK the shit out of a bunch of kids."

I rub my palms together as I grin at my teammates. "No, but we can scare 'em."

Alex shoots me a warning glare. "Seriously, what's the plan?"

I turn my attention to Kellerman. "This was your idea. How's this going down?"

"We make our anti-bullying speech. We give a spotlight to Avery, letting everyone know that he's our friend who invited us today." Chance crosses his arms over his chest. "Then the principal will remind the students of the consequences of bullying at school, and the coaches will let their teams know that any athletes caught causing problems will be kicked off their teams. Hopefully, that sends the message."

I have zero tolerance for bullying. Athletes are supposed to be role models and leaders. They shouldn't be the ones instilling fear in the rest of their school.

"Remind me why *he's* here?" Jason arches a dark brow in Kellerman's direction.

It does look strange, having him here when he's not one of the Goldfinches. And I can't tell my teammates that I used to fuck someone on our rival team—not because they wouldn't support me, but because Kellerman is hellbent on hiding what we had.

Kellerman's jaw clenches. "I'm friends with Avery's aunt."

Alex nods, and claps him on the shoulder, ever the peacemaker. "It'll look great having two rival teams here, coming together for a good cause. Show the kids that if we can get along, so can they."

That's why Alex is our captain. He's level-headed and understanding, and can swallow his pride for the greater good of the cause.

The gymnasium fills with students while we wait to be introduced.

Principal Sturges takes the microphone and quiets everyone down. "We have some very special guests with us today. I hope you'll give them a proper Rebels welcome." He pauses for dramatic effect, and then he announces us into the room. "Our very own Jersey City Goldfinches, accompanied by Philly's Chance Kellerman."

The students erupt with surprised cheers, and we enter the booming gymnasium.

I lock eyes with Avery, sitting in the front row like we requested. He's wringing his hands in his lap, and his eyes are wide. He said he doesn't want to be called up to the podium with us, but he's aware we're going to point him out to everyone to thank him for inviting us here.

I'll admit, I've never been shy. I don't know what anxiety feels like, and I was never the loner kid growing up. He has more in common with Kellerman, and fuck if that doesn't make me feel jealous. But I want to show him, and Presley, that I'm here for them.

I shake the principal's hand, and take the microphone from him. "Ramtown Rebels, how are we doing today?" The students cheer again. "We're here today because our good friend Avery King invited us. Does everyone know Avery?"

The students look around the room, their heads whipping left and right until Principal Sturges walks over to him and points him out. Avery lifts a meek hand to wave to everyone, his cheeks tinged with a deep red as students clap to thank him.

"As some of you might know, us hockey players get into fights on the ice. The game is intense, and our emotions run high. I'm sure you've seen me get into it with this guy a few times." I pause, turning to face Kellerman. "But fighting on the ice is a lot different than fighting off the ice."

I didn't rehearse a speech. I really didn't think too much about what I was going to say. I just want to be real with these kids, and make an impact on them.

"Fighting off the ice happens in the real world where there are real consequences. There's no referee to stop it, no penalty box to cool off in for a couple of minutes. The things you say and do to other people will affect them for the rest of their lives. So, be a leader. Be a friend. Be someone who makes people feel good, and make them remember you for the difference you've made in their lives."

I hold out the mic to Kellerman. He stares down at it like he's looking to it for answers before he speaks. He's never been the best at talking, but when he finally decides on what he wants to say, he makes it count.

His words have always mattered to me.

"I was in high school. I know how hard it is. You have all this pressure on you to figure out what you want to do with the rest of your life. Keep your grades up; get into a good college so you can get a job; please your teachers, please your parents; try to find where you fit in. You've got all this pent-up frustration, but you're just a kid, and all you want to do is have fun."

He pauses as several students clap and shout in agreement.

"And while you're trying to keep your head above water, real-life crashes into you. Depression. Anxiety. Maybe your parents get divorced. Maybe you lose a loved one. Maybe you struggle with addiction. Maybe your family can't afford to put food on the table, or a roof over your head. Maybe you're confused about your sexuality or your identity. Every single one of us is struggling inside. We're all fighting hard battles every single day. But instead of coming together and supporting one another, we take it out on each other."

The room falls quiet.

"Bullying other kids doesn't fix your problems. It won't take your pain away. It doesn't make you strong; it makes you weak. You think it makes you look tough, but it only shows how much you're hurting inside. My father beat on me every single day, and I can promise you—I didn't look at him with respect. I looked at him with hatred."

Pride swells in my chest, and I reach out to lay a hand on Kellerman's shoulder in silent support, knowing how difficult it is for him to talk about this, let alone in a room filled with strangers.

"So, what I'm asking you—the reason we're here today—is to show kindness and compassion to one another. Be a person who people look up to. Help others when they need it." He glances at me over his shoulder. "And let them help you, because it's okay to need help sometimes."

Emotion clogs my throat as he hands me the mic, and I hand it off to Alex because my voice will give me away.

All I ever wanted was to help Chance; to help him be his true self; to help him break free from the shackles of his father.

To help him feel worthy of love.

He never truly gave himself to me or Presley. Physically, sure, but his heart was guarded then.

Would it be any different now?

After the assembly ends and the children head to their next classes, Principal Sturges allows Avery to stay behind for a few pictures.

The kid lost both of his parents—one who left him by choice and one who was taken too soon. I can't imagine the weight of emotion he carries on a daily basis. It kills me to know that punk-ass kids are making life even harder for him.

Avery and Alyssa are extensions of Presley; they have a piece of her coursing through them. I'd do anything for her, which now means I'll do anything for them too.

And judging by the way Chance holds on tight to Avery as he hugs him goodbye, I'd say he feels the same way.

The coaches of the football, baseball, and soccer teams have their students stay behind in the gym so we can have a deeper conversation with them. They ask us questions, mainly about what it's like playing a professional sport, and then I leave them with a little reminder at the end.

"You should be the leaders of this school. The protectors; the ones to look up to. Do you want to be remembered as the guy everyone wanted to be with, or be? Or do you want to be remembered as the asshole who picked on kids who didn't deserve it?" I shrug. "You're not going to get any dates by beating on people. It's a major turn-off. It doesn't make you look tough; it makes you look weak."

Chance adds more. "And if you ever want a shot at going pro, then you'd be wise to remember that. Big organizations aren't looking for trouble-makers who make them look bad, or players with nasty attitudes. Having passion is different than having a temper."

The rest of my teammates nod in agreement, and it seems like the students are truly listening to us.

I clap Principal Sturges on the back. "I'm going to be signing out Avery for the remainder of the day."

Avery's eyebrows shoot up. "You are?"

I wrap my arm around his neck. "Me and the guys have something fun planned, and we want to hang with you."

The other kids gasp and murmur, and I grin wide.

Good. Let them see Avery spending the day with a professional hockey team while they schlep back to class.

Principal Sturges clears his throat. "Only people on the approved list can sign out students."

"Guess I'll have to get on that list then." I slip my phone out of my pocket and search for Presley's number. "Will a verbal confirmation from Avery's aunt suffice for the time being?"

The principal nods. "Yes, that should be fine."

Avery's cheeks push up into his eyes as he smiles.

And I don't miss the smirk on Chance's lips as we head to the main office.

"Best day ever!"

I laugh at Alyssa's excitement as she steers the stationary car in the arcade. She's well-behaved and respectful, but she's full of life and bounces off the walls with energy. I didn't know her mother, but she reminds me a lot of Presley—the version I met in college.

It breaks my heart to see this subdued version of her, knowing the pressure and pain she's had to endure these last few years. I'm determined to fix that, to give her anything and everything she and the kids need to feel carefree and secure.

And I know Chance feels the same.

Affection warms my chest as I watch him and Avery playing Skee-ball across the room. Chance doesn't give himself enough credit. He never has. He has so much love in his heart to offer, and Avery brings out a softer side of him. It's easier with kids than it is with adults; you don't have to worry about judgment or vulnerability. They're honest and blunt, and they're funny as hell.

My mind wanders, and I imagine the five of us living in Presley's house. A family. I can see it so clearly, and possession rips through me. I've been told I can be *too much*, and move *too fast*. But I can't help the way I feel. When my heart is set on something, I will stop at nothing to have it. And what's the point of putting it off anyway?

Life is too short to hold yourself back from happiness.

With Presley's permission, we took the kids to the boardwalk down the shore. The place is nearly empty, being that it's a cold winter day during school hours, so we have the place to ourselves.

"When was the last time you came down here?" I ask.

Alyssa scrunches her nose. "When my mom was alive. I was little."

I ruffle her hair. "Littler than you are now?"

She shoots me a dirty look. "I'm not little."

I chuckle. "You're right. I'm just teasing."

She's quiet while she steers the video game. "Thanks for taking us here. I can't believe Aunt Presley let you take us out of school for this."

I lean on the empty car next to her. "Well, school is important. I can understand why she doesn't want you to skip."

"Yeah." Her eyebrows pinch together. "We don't even do stuff like this on the weekends."

My eyebrows lift. "Really?"

"We'll go to the movies every once in a while, or to the mall. Places around the neighborhood." She shrugs. "She's worried a lot."

"Worried about what?"

"I don't know. It's like she doesn't want to have fun because she feels too nervous." She side-eyes me before flicking her eyes back to the game. "I think she's lonely."

My heart sinks. "Oh, yeah?"

"Yep. She doesn't have any friends besides Ms. Dominique, and she doesn't have a boyfriend or a husband like all my friends' parents." Her car crashes into a roadblock, and she growls as she tries to spin it around. "She spends all her time with me and Avery. I mean, I know we're awesome, but she's an adult. She should be doing adult things."

I sigh as I blink up at the ceiling. "She cares about you guys a lot. She just wants to make sure you're taken care of. That's what parents do; they put kids before their own needs."

"Well, I don't think I could ever be a parent. If I want to do something, I don't want an annoying kid to stop me."

I bark out a laugh. "What if your kid isn't annoying though? What if he or she is like you?"

She thinks on it a minute. "I don't know. We'll see."

I love this kid.

When everyone gets hungry, we stop at the pizzeria next door to the arcade. I strategically sit next to Avery so I can question him about some of the things Alyssa said.

"Okay, Ave'. Real talk for a minute." I lean my elbows on the table. "How's your aunt doing—and not the *I'm fine* bullshit she tells you."

He heaves a sigh far too heavy for a teenager. "She's doing a lot for us, working and driving us everywhere. I feel bad. If I could afford a car, I'd be able to drive myself around and help out with Alyssa more, but..." He shrugs.

"When do you get your license? Are you taking Driver's Ed classes?"

He nods. "I can drive with an adult when I turn sixteen if I get my permit."

I make a mental note to get him a reliable car when he's ready.

"What are some things she needs help with around the house?" I take out my phone and click on my notes app. "I can take care of the landscaping when the winter is over. Is there anything that needs to be fixed inside?"

Avery widens his eyes as he nods. "There's a bunch of stuff on her to-do list on the fridge, but she's always too tired to get to it."

"Can you take a picture of it and text it to me later?"

"Sure." He arches a brow. "She's not going to like us going behind her back like this."

I hike a shoulder. "She'll get over it once she sees all the work we get done."

"You'll let me help?"

"Why do you sound surprised?"

"I don't really know how to do anything."

"So, you'll learn. I learned how to do lots of stuff from my dad growing up."

He glances down at his plate. "Guess that's why I don't know how to do anything."

Sadness tugs at my heart. I pat him on the back. "I'll teach you. Don't worry about it. I can even pay you. You can be like my apprentice."

He coughs out an incredulous laugh. "Yeah, right. Aunt Presley will never go for it."

I lean in and lower my voice. "It'll be our little secret."

"And your funeral," he whispers.

He's probably not wrong.

I PUSH THE BUTTON ON THE HANDLE, AND THE UMBRELLA OPENS above me.

Making a run for it, I dash across the parking lot to my car. Only, the spot is empty when I get there.

My eyebrows pinch together. That's weird. I could've sworn that I parked on the end of the last row when I arrived at school this morning.

My head whips around, searching for my car. I dig into my coat pocket for my keys, but my fingers hit nothing but the inside of my pocket.

What the fuck?

A black town car pulls up in front of me, and an older man with salt-and-pepper hair jogs around the front bumper holding up a large black umbrella. "Ms. King, I'm here to escort you to the spa."

My chin jerks back. "Uh, what?"

"I can assure you that your car has been safely delivered to your home. I've been instructed to pick you up and take you to get a massage at four o'clock."

"Instructed by who?"

The man smiles. "Mr. McKinley."

My chest tightens. "He planned this?"

"Yes, ma'am." He swings open the back door, and gestures for me to get inside. "Come in and get out of the rain."

"Sorry, please just give me a moment." I slip my phone out of my purse and click on Stephen's name before holding it up to my ear.

"Hey, pretty girl," he answers.

"Don't pretty girl me. There's a strange man standing in front of me telling me to get in his car. As a woman, you can understand my hesitation. What is going on? Where's my car? And how did you get my car keys?"

He chuckles. "That's Carl; he's my driver. He's going to take you to get a massage."

"But I have to pick up Alyssa from school. Her field hockey practice got cancelled because of the rain and—"

"We've already taken care of that. I've got her with me right now. Say hi to your aunt, 'Lyss."

Alyssa's cheery voice blares through the phone. "Hi, Aunt Presley!"

My eyebrows shoot up. "First grand theft auto, and now kidnapping. What's next on the agenda?"

Stephen laughs again, like this is totally normal behavior. "Enjoy your massage, pretty girl. We'll see you at home."

The call ends, and I'm left blinking down at the screen in disbelief.

Carl clears his throat. "Ms. King, come on inside. I have the heat on. Wouldn't want you to catch a cold."

I snap the umbrella closed, and slide into the back seat of the car.

The door shuts behind me, and Carl scurries around to the driver's side. He glances at me in the rearview mirror as he climbs inside. "How was your day, Ms. King?"

My head falls back against the seat as I laugh. "Like any other day, up until now."

His eyes crinkle as he smiles. "I've heard good things about this spa. You'll have a very enjoyable afternoon."

I shake my head as I stare out at the rain. "And how many women have you driven around for Mr. McKinley, Carl?"

"I assume you mean the ones not blood related?"

I smirk. "Exactly those ones."

"None, Ms. King." He pauses, his eyes flicking to mine in the mirror before returning to the road. "And if I may add, I haven't seen him this excited in a long time."

Worry seeps into my gut. "I was afraid you'd say that, Carl."

Stephen McKinley doesn't do anything in half measures. He's all in, balls to the wall, giving two-hundred percent of himself. He moves with the force of a barreling train.

But I can't give him what he's hoping for. I can't be a pseudo-mom *and* be in a poly relationship. How would that even work?

Visions of the three of us living in my sister's house with Avery and Alyssa flash through my mind. Chance and Avery painting in the dining room while Stephen runs around the backyard with Alyssa; me moving around them in the kitchen as Stephen chops vegetables and Chance stirs a pot of sauce; the three of us snuggling under the covers as we fall asleep at night.

My skin warms at the memory of how it felt to be loved by the two of them. The way they treated me, the way they cared for me.

Longing grips my heart in a vice. I've missed them. I miss the way they made me feel, and I miss the person I was with them. And now that they're back, I can't help but want it all back again.

Maybe it'd work behind closed doors—and that's a big maybe with two children—but it definitely wouldn't work on the outside. I can already hear the things other parents would say about us. The way they'd judge us, and keep their children away from mine. And that can't happen. My responsibility is to those kids, and I won't let anything stop them from having the best lives.

I have to shut this down. Stephen and Chance need to know that we can't be what we once were.

No matter how deeply I crave it.

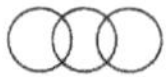

The aroma of sauteed garlic and onions fill the house as soon as I step inside.

But it's the sound of people that take me by surprise.

I creep through the hallway and spot Stephen, alone with several large men, sitting on my couch, shouting over a video game as Alyssa howls with laughter, playing right in the middle of them. Judging by their size, I assume they're Stephen's teammates who attended the assembly at Avery's school today.

Inching further into the house, I peer into the kitchen. Avery stands beside Chance at the stove, listening intently to whatever Chance is explaining to him. Something about flavors and temperatures.

In the dining room, four women sit around the set table, sipping glasses of wine.

Before I can sneak back into the hallway and dart up the stairs to change and make myself look presentable, the redhead makes eye-contact with me.

"Oh, hey." She stands and rounds the corner of the table with her wine glass. "You must be Presley… and wondering what we're all doing in your house."

I laugh. "Correct on both accounts."

She wraps an arm around me and pulls me in for a hug. "I'm Celeste, one of Jason's wives. This is our wife, Kourtney," she gestures to a pretty brunette who waves from her seat at the table. "This is Cassidy, Trenton's wife." A curvy brunette with a warm smile raises her hand. "And this is Aarya, Alexander's wife." Another dark-haired beauty shoots me a wink.

I give everyone a big wave. "Hi, ladies. Uh, I'm assuming your husbands are all Goldfinches?"

Celeste slaps her forehead. "Duh, you've never met them before. Yes, they're the giant dudes in your living room playing video games like five-year-olds."

These women are stunning, as different as they all look. My brain tries to keep track of who Celeste said they were each married to. "I'm sorry, did you say you and Kourtney are both married to Jason?"

Celeste beams. "We're a threesome. We've been best friends since high school. It's a whole thing. I'll tell you the story sometime."

I arch a brow, completely intrigued by this news. A real-life poly relationship. It's like the universe heard my thoughts earlier, and is showing me that it's possible.

"So, what's going on between you and Mac?" Celeste asks. "I'm going to need all the details because up until today, I had no idea you existed."

Kourtney laughs as she stands and places her hand on Celeste's forearm. "Why don't you let the poor woman get settled before you start interrogating her. She hasn't even put her things down yet."

I'm literally standing in the middle of the room holding a dripping wet umbrella and two large work bags.

Alyssa pops into the dining room. "Aunt Presley, you're home! Come into the living room. You have to meet the team. We're playing NHL 24 and I totally kicked their asses—" She freezes and clamps her hand over her mouth. "Their butts. I totally kicked their butts."

Damn Stephen and his potty mouth.

Stephen joins us, and scoops my things into his hands, leaning in to press a kiss on my cheek. "Hey, pretty girl. How was your massage? Are you feeling relaxed now?"

I let out a sardonic laugh. "I was, up until I walked into a house party that I didn't know about."

He grimaces. "Yeah, sorry about that. I should've told you. But the kids invited the guys over for dinner, so I figured it would be a great way for you to meet the WAGs too."

Avery comes into the room carrying a large pot filled with red sauce. "Hey, Aunt Pres. Chance showed me how to make marinara sauce. It's just about ready."

My head swirls with everything going on. I suck in a deep breath. "Great. Let me go get changed and I'll be right down."

I dart out of the room and bolt up the stairs to my bedroom. Sinking onto the edge of the bed, I close my eyes and run my fingers through my hair.

It's not that I mind having everyone over. They all took the time out of their busy schedules to help Avery today, and I'd love to be able to personally thank them. But for the last four years, I've been on my own raising these kids. I haven't had a break, or time to do anything for myself. Today was the first time I didn't have to pick them up from school, or worry about dinner —and to top it off, I got a fucking massage at a spa.

Where's my car, by the way?

There's a soft knock on the door before it cracks open, and Chance's dark eyes meet mine. "You okay?"

I blow out a long breath through my lips. "I'm good. Just taking a second to digest everything."

He closes the door behind him and lowers himself to the mattress beside me. "I'm sorry for ambushing you like this. You know how hard it is to stop Stephen when he gets an idea in his head."

I smile. "I sure do."

Chance reaches out and tucks a strand of my hair behind my ear. "Did you enjoy your massage at least?"

"I did." My eyes bounce between his. "That was your idea, wasn't it?"

"I didn't want you to have to worry about anyone for once. I wanted you to have a moment for yourself." His fingers linger on my ear, tracing it and then skimming down along my jawline. "I want to take care of you in all the ways I wasn't able to for the last four years."

I close my eyes and lean into his light touch, and his palm cradles my face. "I appreciate it, but you don't have to do any of this."

"I know I don't have to." His thumb skims along my bottom lip. "I want to. I want to be here for you. I want you to lean on me."

Chance has always wanted to be wanted. He needs to feel needed. He's the caretaker, the fixer. He spent his childhood trying to pick up the pieces of his father's mess and protect his mother. Her death weighs heavily on him, and I think a part of him will forever feel like he couldn't do enough to save her, so he tries to make up for it in everyone he meets. I could kill his father with my bare hands for the way he fucked with this man's head. How could someone this amazing never feel good enough?

I want to show him that he is.

Lifting my eyes to his, mine fill with tears. "I'm so glad you're here."

Here, meaning back in my life.

He dips down and rests his forehead against mine. "I'm not going anywhere, rebel."

My heart constricts at the sound of the old nickname, and I can't help but let out a sardonic laugh. "I'm not a rebel anymore. Haven't been for quite some time."

"It's still a part of you. You just haven't let her out in a while."

He must be right, because the only thing I can think about right now is feeling his lips on mine. That would be reckless and foolish. I need to keep the lines clear between us, keep the boundaries set.

We can be friends, and nothing more.

But when Chance pulls back to gaze into my eyes, my heart beats a furious rhythm. My body betrays me, desperately seeking a physical release to ease this yearning.

Chance's hand slides down to my throat, his fingers tightening around my neck just like he used to. "Do you miss me, rebel? Do you think about all the things we used to do together? All the ways I made you feel good?"

Wetness pools between my legs, and my nipples harden.

He leans in and swipes his tongue across my lips, and a low moan escapes me.

"Have you been with anyone else since you left us?" he asks. "Has anyone else touched this beautiful body?"

I wish I could give him another answer, one that wouldn't make me look so pathetic, but I can't lie to him. I shake my head. "No," I whisper.

He groans like that pleases him. "This body must be desperate for affection."

I can't think straight with his grip on my throat, and his dark eyes boring into my soul.

"Will you let me relieve some of this tension?" His free hand slides underneath my shirt, and his fingers dance along my stomach. Goosebumps fly over my skin, and I clench my thighs together. "I can take care of this ache for you."

Oh, I know he can. Every nerve ending in my body lights up at the memory of just how good this man can take care of my body.

But the sounds of the kids downstairs pull me from my lust-filled haze. I shake my head and scoot away from Chance, putting space between us so I don't pounce on him like a dog in heat.

"I...I can't." My eyes drop to my lap in shame. "I'm sorry."

Chance reaches out and tips my chin, bringing my eyes back to his. "Don't you dare apologize for it. If you're not ready, then I can respect that. You set the pace, and I follow."

My bottom lip trembles. "I don't want to give you the wrong impression, Chance. We can't just go back to the way things were between the three of us."

"Why not?" Stephen's voice startles us both as he stands in the doorway. "Why can't we try again?"

I sweep my arm out, gesturing to the floor. "Those kids downstairs? They rely on me. It's up to me to keep them safe. Avery's having enough of a hard time as it is. I can't draw more attention to our family."

Stephen crosses his arms over his chest. "We can take it slow, and see where it leads. One day at a time."

I point between the two of them. "You two can barely stand to be around each other. How do you expect this to work, hmm?"

Chance arches a brow. "Are you saying you'd consider it if Stephen and I were on better terms?"

I rub my palms against my thighs. "I'm just saying, you can't snap your fingers and make everything perfect for us. This isn't a fun college fling. This is the real world, and I have my family to think about. I'm not the rebel who used to get high and fuck two guys at the same time without a care in the world."

"Maybe not, but this version isn't you either," Stephen says, walking toward me. "You're not happy. I can see it in your eyes. You're tired, and stressed, and you've been exhausting yourself trying to do everything on your own. You're stifling yourself, and you think it's what you need to do for the kids, but you're not setting a good example for them."

I scoff. "Excuse me? I'm doing the best I can, and I think I'm doing a pretty damn good job given the situation."

Chance stands up, facing Stephen. "Hey, I don't think this is helping right now."

"Fuck you too, man." Stephen's face reddens as he speaks. "The both of you might be okay with hiding who you truly are, and denying yourselves of the things you want, but you're only hurting yourselves in the end. And those kids? They need some fun in their lives. They need you to show them it's okay to let loose a little, and enjoy life. Do you want them to grow up and look back on their childhood and remember how stressed you were trying to juggle everything and hold it all together?"

Tears stream down my face. "No, I—"

"I had to listen to Alyssa tell me how lonely she thinks you are, and how Avery wishes he could help out more because he knows how stressed you always are."

My mouth flaps open. "What?"

Stephen nods. "They see you, Pres, no matter how hard you try to hide it. They see how much pressure you're putting on yourself."

I flick my eyes to Chance, and he nods in confirmation before dropping his gaze.

Fuck.

"I don't know what I'm doing," I blurt out. "I don't know the first thing about raising kids, and all I want is to do right by my sister. But I'm not her, and I keep falling short."

Chance steps forward and wipes my tears with his thumbs. "Maybe that's your problem. Maybe you need to stop trying to make up for her being gone, and just be yourself. Those kids love you as their aunt. Stop trying to be a perfect mom, and just be you. Love them; be there for them; and have a little fun with them every now and then. That's what kids need."

"Your sister left them with you for a reason," Stephen says, lowering his voice as he inches closer. "She knew you better than anyone else, and she knew they'd be in the best hands with you—the exact person you were four years ago."

A sob escapes me. "I don't know how to be that person in this new life."

"We can help." Stephen smooths his palm down my back. "Maybe that's why life threw us back together. Maybe we can be what the other needs."

Chance looks just as scared as I feel. Being together would mean that he has to admit to the world that he's bisexual. And that wasn't something he was ready for four years ago. I don't know where he stands now, or where any of this will lead.

But I lift my hand to his cheek, reassuring him as much as myself. "One day at a time, right?"

His chest expands with his deep inhale. "One day at a time."

I shouldn't be here.

I glance around the table at Stephen's friends, everyone talking comfortably with one another—Stephen at the forefront of the conversation, as usual. He's outgoing and personable, always making everyone laugh with his antics.

Presley is in the same boat as I am, meeting these people for the first time, yet she doesn't seem as uncomfortable as I feel. She's easy to get along with, and can adapt to any situation. Even Alyssa fits right in, asking questions and laughing along with the strangers she just met.

I nudge Avery with my elbow. "What was your favorite part of your day?"

He thinks on it while he chews, and then he swallows. "Seeing Austin's face when he saw me getting signed out of school to hang out with you guys."

I smirk. "That felt pretty cool, huh?"

"Yeah." He sips on his water. "I don't know if it'll make a difference, but it made me feel better than them for a day."

I shift in my seat to face him. "Hey, you should feel better than them *every* day—and not just because you got to rub some pro athlete friends in their faces."

"It's okay." Avery pushes the food around in his plate. "I know I'm not. They're bigger, stronger, cooler."

I tip his chin to bring his eyes to mine. "What people look like on the outside means nothing. It's what's in their hearts—how they treat people when they have nothing to gain—that shows their true character. You're smart and creative and kind; you look out for your sister and help your aunt. You're a good person, Avery. Don't let a bunch of asshole kids make you feel less than. You're better than they could ever hope to be. Do you understand me?"

His eyes dart around the table as it falls silent, everyone's attention now on us, and his cheeks redden. "Yes, I understand."

Presley dabs at the corner of her eye with her napkin. "I didn't know you felt like that."

Avery shrugs. "It's not something I like to talk about."

But he talked about it with me.

Pride swells in my chest, especially when Presley reaches under the table and clasps my hand.

Here I am, giving Avery advice to boost his confidence, yet I'm thinking that I don't fit in with this group, wishing I could be more like Stephen. But if I weren't exactly the person I am, maybe I wouldn't have been able to form this connection with Avery.

And I wouldn't trade it for the world.

Celeste—the only one whose name I remember because she's so loud and bold—leans on her elbows and gestures between Presley, Stephen, and me. "So, how do you three know each other again, college?"

Presley clears her throat. "Uh, yeah. We met at a party, and we were inseparable for a while after that."

Celeste watches us from over the rim of her wine glass. "And neither one of you tried hitting on Presley?"

Stephen chuckles. "Oh, we definitely did. We—*ouch*!" He glares at Presley across the table. "What was that for?"

Her eyes dart to the kids. "So sorry. I didn't realize that was your leg."

I try to help smooth things over. "We both had a crush on Presley. I think that aided to our rivalry."

"Do you have a crush on her now?" Alyssa asks, wide eyes blinking between the three of us.

Stephen and I glance at Presley, letting her take this conversation where she feels it should be around the kids.

"We're just friends," she says quietly. "It's been a long time since we've been in each other's lives, and we're getting to know each other all over again."

But Alyssa doesn't let it go. "You said you were reading a book where a girl fell in love with two people at the same time, and I asked you if you were ever in love, and then you said you were in college." Her keen eyes dart to me and Stephen. "Were you in love with *them*?"

Jesus, this kid is sharp.

Avery chokes on his water, and slaps his chest as he sputters.

Celeste grins. "Yeah, Pres. Were you in love with these two back in college?"

Presley looks mortified, so I jump in before Stephen says something he shouldn't in front of the kids. "Hey, Celeste. I'm new here. I don't know the story about how you, Kourtney, and Jason got together."

Alyssa nods fervently. "See, Aunt Presley? You can be married to two people at the same time, just like them."

"Drop it, 'Lyss," Avery chimes in.

Her bottom lip juts out. "What? I'm just saying, it's possible. And I like Stephen and Chance. They help when they're around, and Aunt Presley smiles a lot more."

Presley rubs her temples. "Let's save this conversation for another time, okay? We can have a girl talk before bed."

Alyssa beams. "Promise?"

"Promise, promise."

Celeste finally takes control of the conversation. "Kourtney, Jason, and I were best friends in high school. Kourtney was dating Jay at the time, but then they broke up after we went away to college."

"She broke up with me," Jason interrupts. "I did not want to break up, for the record."

Kourtney leans in and presses a kiss to his cheek. "But we found our way back to each other, and that's all that matters."

"Kourtney and I, uh, got together in college." Celeste glances at the kids, no doubt tiptoeing around the inappropriate parts. "Then I got hired to do PR for Trenton in Seattle, so I left and Kourtney stayed behind."

Presley winces. "That must've been hard being so far away from each other."

Celeste nods. "But then Trenton got himself into a bit of drama, and got traded to the Goldfinches, so I came back here and got reunited with Kourtney and Jason."

"You're welcome," Trenton says, raising his beer.

"And that's when he met me!" Cassidy beams at Trenton's side.

"Wow." Presley looks around the table at everyone. "You're all inter-woven into each other's lives. It's like everything was meant to be just to bring you all together."

"Much like you three." Alexander gestures to us. "Seems like you were brought back into each other's lives for a reason."

"That's exactly what I said." Stephen clinks his beer bottle against Alexander's, and swings his gaze to me. "Can't fight fate, no matter how hard one might try."

I've fought to keep my feelings for Stephen hidden for years, and hidden my sexual orientation for even longer.

But sitting around this table with such open-minded, accepting people —especially with a healthy, loving polyamorous trio like Celeste, Kourtney, and Jason—I'm starting to wonder if it's time I come out of hiding.

What kind of hypocrite does it make me if I can't heed the advice I'm giving Avery? If he can learn to believe in himself, and stand up to his bullies, then I should be able to learn to embrace the man I truly am.

For Avery.

For Presley.

For Stephen.

And for myself.

Sophomore Year of College

Fuck, yes.

With my fist closed around my cock, I pump myself in slow, punishing strokes.

While Stephen stayed at the party with the bombshell we danced with, I'm alone in my dorm room, jerking off to the thought of what could've been if I gave in to them.

She wanted us both, it was clear. And Stephen was millimeters away from kissing me.

I was millimeters away from letting him.

Precum leaks out of my tip, as if my dick is weeping at the loss of the opportunity to be inside both Stephen and the gorgeous girl. My body hums at the memory of the way her mouth felt against mine; the way Stephen watched us. And forget about the way his tongue stroked hers when they kissed, his eyes on mine.

I pick up the pace, fucking myself to the thought of them.

Until the door bangs open, and they're both standing in my doorway.

Fuck.

There's no hiding what I'm doing. I'm on top of the covers, lights on, dick in my hand. I slip myself back inside my boxer-briefs, wincing at how painfully hard I am.

"Don't stop on our account," the girl says, wearing a playful smirk on her lips. "Looked like things were just about to get good."

I roll my eyes and search for my sweatpants on the floor before pulling them on. "I'll be back in an hour. That should give you two enough time."

"We didn't come here to fool around, just the two of us," Stephen says, stepping in front of me and blocking my exit. "We came here for you."

My hands curl into fists at my sides as I try to stop myself from reaching out for them. I was just about to come before they walked in, and my head hasn't cleared from the lust-filled fog yet.

"Were you thinking of us?" the girl asks. Hazel eyes blink up at me as she trails her fingertips along my arm. "Were you imagining your dick was in my mouth? Or his? Or were we fucking?"

My control is slipping, and I need to get out of here before I do something I can't come back from.

"Don't run from this," Stephen whispers. He reaches out and slowly uncurls my fist until he can lace our fingers together. "I know you want me just as badly as I want you."

My dick strains against my pants, like it's reaching out for them, begging me not to let this moment go.

But that's all this is—a moment. How would Stephen and I go back to being friends after this?

And *friends* is all we ever can be. I won't let us get ruined by the ugliness and hate of the world. I've seen firsthand what happens to people like us.

"Stop overthinking it." The brunette rises onto her toes and wraps her hands around the back of my neck, pressing her body against mine. "I want you both. You think you can be good boys and share?"

I shiver against her. "I'm an only child. I never learned to share."

She sucks my bottom lip into her mouth and bites down before she releases it. "I can teach you. You'll see how much fun it is."

She drops to her knees, and I'm helpless against her as she drags down my pants and boxers in one quick motion. My cock springs free, bobbing in front of her face. She gazes up at Stephen, and tugs him down beside her.

Fuck me. Looking down at the both of them on their knees for me, Stephen gazing at my cock like he's hungry for it, I'm harder than I've ever been.

I'm not thinking straight. This needs to stop.

But before I can protest, she sucks me all the way into her mouth, wrapping her tongue around me. She hums, dragging me out and taking me inside again. Stephen's eyes stay locked in on my cock, licking his lips and leaning closer to her mouth. She takes one of his hands and slips it inside her pants.

Stephen groans. "You should feel how wet she is, Chance."

She takes me further into her mouth, moaning as her hips rock against Stephen's fingers.

"Fuck," I hiss, trying not to fuck her mouth and come too soon.

Then she pops me out of her mouth, and holds out my dick for Stephen.

I should stop this. I should pull away. We can't cross this line. We can stick to sharing her, and not give in to each other.

But Stephen's eyes lock with mine as he leans forward and slides his tongue along my dick, and any semblance of fight drains from my body.

Fuck it.

I've fantasized about this moment for the last year.

Instead of pushing him off me, I lift my hand and grip the coppery curls at the top of his head, forcing myself inside his mouth and setting the pace. He breathes through his nose, and lets me fuck his face the way he knows I need to be in control.

"That's it, Stephen," I whisper. "Let me shut this mouth up for a while. God, you always talk so much, I've wanted to fill it with my cock since the day I met you."

He whimpers, reaching into his own pants to relieve his ache.

My beauty bends down and wraps her tongue around my balls, and my toes curl into the carpet. I'm not going to last, but I don't want this moment to end. The second I spill my release, the spell breaks and I'll fall into post-orgasm clarity.

I'm not ready to stop yet. I haven't nearly had my fill of these two.

I yank Stephen off of me, and pull him by his hair until he's standing. We dive for each other's mouths in a crushing kiss. He grips onto my jaw, holding me like he's afraid I'll pull back. And I should. But his scent surrounds me; his arms wrap around me; and his taste is on my lips. I can't go back now. Stephen McKinley is etching himself into my bones, pouring himself into my blood. After tonight, he'll be my oxygen, and I won't know how to breathe without him.

Yet I can't seem to care at the moment.

I reach for her, needing her close, and she joins us so we're a mix of lips and tongues and panting moans. She's the catalyst. The conductor. The one who made this all happen. I don't know her yet, but I vow to. Something in her calls to me, and I want to show her that I can be whatever she needs me to be.

I break the kiss and lift her into my arms, turning to lay her on my bed. "What's your name, baby?"

"Presley," she whispers.

I yank off her shoes while she unbuttons her pants and shimmies them down her hips. Stephen pulls them off the rest of the way and tosses them along with her top into a pile with his own clothes.

I lean on my elbows and settle between Presley's thighs. I can smell her sweet arousal, the wet spot soaking through her red thong letting me know how turned on she is.

I glance up at Stephen who's watching over my shoulder. "Bet she's got a pretty pussy. What do you think?"

He kneels beside me and toys with her nipple while she squirms underneath us. "I bet you're right. Why don't you have a taste and let me know how good she is?"

I pull her panties to the side and admire her glistening skin. "God damn, you're perfect."

Presley's hand slides through my hair to the back of my head, and she lifts her hips, bringing herself closer to my mouth.

I chuckle at her impatience. "What's the matter, baby? You need me to make you feel better? You look like you're aching, all swollen and wet."

She moans as I drop a few light kisses to her clit. "Please, Chance."

I drag my tongue along her from bottom to top, swirling around her clit before making my way back down to repeat the motion. "Mmm, fuck. You taste incredible."

Her moans fill the air, and Stephen swirls his tongue around her nipple while I lap at her, spreading her legs wider so I can feast.

Stephen kisses his way down to where my mouth is, and I shift over so he can join his tongue with mine. It's erotic, stroking his tongue at the same time as her pussy, the taste of her mixing with the taste of him.

It's intoxicating.

I sit up on my knees and Stephen takes over, kneeling in my spot on the bed while he works her over.

"Slip a finger inside," I instruct.

Stephen inserts his middle finger, and Presley bucks off the mattress, letting out a loud moan.

"Yes, more," she pants. She lifts her eyes to mine. "Please."

I arch a brow. "Tell me what you need, Presley. Use your words."

She grips onto Stephen's hair and looks me straight in my eyes. "I want you both inside of me. At the same time."

I dig into Stephen's nightstand, knowing I'll find everything I need, and pull out a couple of condoms and a bottle of lube. I roll one onto Stephen before rolling one on myself.

"On your back," I tell him. I caress Presley's face as I lean down and kiss her. "You're going to ride him. And once you're dripping, when you've soaked his cock, that's when I'll fuck this tight little ass of yours. Sound good?"

Panting, she scrambles on top of Stephen. "Yes."

I watch as she sinks down onto Stephen's dick, inch by inch, letting herself get used to his size. He holds onto her hips, but he lets her set the pace until she's ready.

I kneel behind her, letting my hands roam over her curves and trailing my fingertips over the artwork along her arms. I lick her neck and she moans, circling her hips in a steady rhythm.

I watch them as they fuck, my cock throbbing for its own release.

But my dark thoughts begin to creep in.

How happy they could be together, just the two of them.

They don't need me.

I don't deserve them.

Presley reaches back for me, her eyes looking into mine as if she can see that I'm struggling. "Kiss me, Chance. Kiss me, and then fuck us."

Unable to deny her, I part her lips with my tongue, and kiss her deeply. She's fire and passion, and sexy as hell. I lose myself in our kiss, falling deeper into the point of no return.

"You ready, baby?" I nip her bottom lip as I pull back. "Are you ready to take the both of us?"

"Yes," she says on an exhale. "I'm ready."

I gently push her back until her chest is pressed against Stephen's, leaving her perfect, plump ass in the air for me. I squeeze the bottle of lube, drizzling it over her backside.

"We're going to start off slow." I rub my thumb around the rim of her hole before adding a bit of pressure. "You let us know if you want to stop, understand?"

She moans and grinds against Stephen.

"Words, Pres." I tilt her chin until she's looking at me over her shoulder. "I need you to understand that you can stop us at any time."

"I understand." She swallows, looking between us. "I want this."

I pump my thumb in and out of her while she rocks on Stephen's cock. She moans loud, and drops her forehead against his while I open her up.

She's so tight, and with Stephen's cock filling her from the front, this is going to feel incomparable to anything I've ever felt.

I blow out a steadying breath, and lube myself up before pushing the crown of my cock against her ass. My eyes flick to Stephen to find him watching me with rapt attention.

Nerves and worry crawl into the darkest parts of my head, but I stamp them down.

Not now. I'll deal with the aftermath in the morning.

I breach Presley's entrance, going as slow as I can to make sure she's okay while I fill her up.

She gasps. "Oh, my God."

Stephen kisses her hard while I bend down and suck on her neck, lighting her up everywhere we can until I'm fully inside her.

"How do you feel, baby?" Sweat lines my forehead as I use all of my restraint to stay still until she tells me to move.

"So full." She pushes back against me. "You're both...it's so much."

Stephen smirks. "Our pretty girl likes being filled up by two cocks."

I pull out just as slow, and push my way back inside. Stephen groans, wiping the smirk right off his face. "I can feel you fucking her."

"How much do you wish it was you, hm?" I pull out and drive back inside Presley, her hips bucking against me, begging me for more. "How many nights have you thought about it? You know, you think I'm asleep when you jerk off in the middle of the night, but I stay awake listening to you."

Stephen grins. "I know you're not sleeping. I do it to torture you. I want you to hear the way I sound when I come to the thought of you."

Fuck. Me.

Leaning down, I sandwich Presley between us and capture Stephen's mouth. He holds onto the back of my head while he kisses me, groaning into my mouth as he drives into her.

Stephen's cock rubs against mine through Presley's tight warmth, and the three of us fall into a rhythm. We put our focus on Presley, bringing her to the brink of ecstasy until she comes.

"That's it, baby." I grip her throat and talk her through it. "Break apart on our cocks and let us hear you."

With her head thrown back and her eyes squeezed shut, she comes loud and hard; uninhibited and wild.

Our little rebel.

The three of us are connected, Stephen and I sharing this intimate moment while Presley tethers the both of us. For the first time, it feels like I belong; like I'm part of something; like I'm meant to be exactly where I am.

And now that I've got it, I don't want to lose it.

I smile as I watch Avery's face light up in wonderment.

Aarya, Alexander Krum's wife, waves her arm around the gallery. "Stay as long as you'd like. I'd offer to show you around, but if you're anything like me, you'll want to explore on your own."

Avery nods. "Thank you, ma'am."

Aarya scrunches her nose. "Jesus Christ, kid. Don't make me feel old. Just call me Aarya."

He chuckles. "Sorry."

I rest my hand on his shoulder. "Do you want me to walk around with you?"

He shrugs. "If you want to."

That's teenager code for no.

I shoot him a wink. "I'll be around if you need me."

Aarya and I stare at Avery's back as he practically bolts away from us.

"Thank you for inviting us today."

Aarya turns to face me. "Mac said Avery is really into art. Is he taking lessons?"

"Mac?"

"Sorry, that's what the guys call him. I'm not used to calling him Stephen."

I smile. "Hockey guys and their nicknames. It's hard to keep up."

"I just make my own." She shrugs. "I have a long list of cake names for Alex."

"He's Krum Cake, right?"

She nods. "I've called him Cupcake, Pound Cake, Bundt Cake, Carrot Cake—you name it."

I toss my head back and laugh. "That's amazing. You should add Shortcake to the list."

"Genius. He'll hate that one."

"To answer your question, yes, Avery has been taking art lessons. I'm not sure if he realizes his full potential, but he's incredibly talented."

Aarya hums. "Artists usually don't know the extent of their talent."

It's going to be up to me to push him, to show him just how high he should aim for.

She flicks her long, dark hair over her shoulder and folds her arms over her chest. "So, I gotta ask since the kid isn't here: What's happening between you and Stephen?"

I slip my hands into the back pockets of my jeans and shrug. "Nothing since college."

Her dark eyes narrow as her red lips turn up into a smirk. "Does *he* know that?"

"What do you mean?"

"Come on, you know him. Everything he does is balls-to-the-wall, two-hundred-and-ten percent. That's why they call him Mac—because he hits you like a Mack truck."

That's him, alright.

Aarya nudges me with her shoulder. "I'm not good with small-talk. Give me the juicy details."

I chuckle. She's honest and to the point. I think I love her.

"I'm sorry to disappoint, but there aren't any juicy details to give." My eyes bounce around at the artwork on the nearby walls. "I can't give Stephen what he wants."

Aarya tilts her head. "And what does he want?"

"A relationship."

She's quiet as she watches me, and doesn't fill the space with unnecessary chatter.

I gesture to Avery as he wanders around at the far end of the gallery. "I have to focus on the kids. They've been through a lot, and they need a stable life and a guardian they can count on. I can't get thrown into the mix between star hockey players."

"Hockey players, plural?"

Oh, shit. I swallow. "You know, the life of hockey players in general."

"I get it. I wasn't prepared for all of this either. Their lives are so different. All that money; they can do anything they've ever dreamed of."

"Exactly. Their lifestyle isn't exactly compatible with a single parent living in the suburbs of New Jersey."

"Mac's great with kids though." Aarya smiles, and it seems like she's recalling a specific memory. "He's the best uncle to Giuliana, Alex's kid. He's got a big-ass mouth, but his heart is even bigger."

I grin. "He does have a big-ass mouth."

It's part of the reason I fell in love with him in college. He says what he feels and doesn't hide anything or hold back. He'll never lie, and you always know where he stands. And Aarya's right—he's great with kids. He'd be the perfect man to get into a relationship with...if our situation was a simple relationship.

My heart aches, longing for two men I can never be with. Not in this lifetime.

A man appears from one of the hallways to the left. "Aarya, can I see you in my office?"

"Sure, Carter." Aarya turns her back to him and rolls her eyes. "If you'll excuse me, I have to go. Make sure you see me before you guys leave."

I step toward her with my arms out, but she holds up her hands and backs away. "Oh, I don't do hugs."

I chuckle. "No hugs, got it."

"Alyssa, did you fart again?"

She giggles from the back seat.

"Ugh." Avery pinches his nose and opens the passenger window. "What the heck did you even eat at that sleepover?"

"Pizza, ice cream, and Cheetos."

I glare at her in the rearview mirror as I crack my own window. "All three of those things have cheese in them. You made an atomic bomb of dairy in your poor belly."

"You think this is bad?" Her eyes widen. "You should've smelled what I did in Sheena's bathroom last night."

Avery gags. "You're lactose intolerant, you little gremlin. You're not supposed to eat that much dairy."

Alyssa shrugs like it's no big deal. "I guess Milk Duds are out of the question at the movie theatre, huh?"

"Yes," both Avery and I exclaim.

I chuckle to myself. "Your mom had the worst gas. I remember when we were kids, our mother made her hang her ass out the window on the ride home from dinner."

The kids crack up with laughter. "She was lactose intolerant too, right?" Avery asks.

"She sure was, but that didn't stop her." My eyes flick to Alyssa's in the mirror again. "You remind me so much of her sometimes."

The car fills with silence, each of us thinking about our own memories with their mother. As painful as it is to talk about her, I don't want her to be a taboo subject. The kids should think and talk about their mother often, and feel comfortable asking questions. It helps keep her memory alive for them, especially Alyssa since she was young when my sister died.

"Aunt Pres, can I ask you a question?"

"Of course, 'Lyss." I slow to a stop at a red light and glance over my shoulder at her. "What's on your mind?"

"How come all of your friends are married, but you're not?"

"Jesus, Alyssa." Avery pinches the bridge of his nose. "You can't ask things like that."

"Why not?" Her eyes dart from her brother to me. "That wasn't rude, was it? I didn't mean it to be rude."

I pat Avery on his shoulder to settle him down. "It's okay. I know you didn't mean it like that."

She shrugs. "I couldn't help but notice it when I looked around the table the other day when the team came over, and they all had wives with them. It got me thinking, and even Dominique is married, so, how come you're not?"

"Real talk, kid, I haven't had time to date anyone to even have the possibility of getting married."

"Because you've been taking care of us," she says.

"Well, I've just been busy, you know? When your mom died, I had to get a job and take online courses to finish my degree at the same time. It was a lot to juggle. And now, we're so busy with work and school and sports, I don't really have the energy to go out and date." The light turns green, so I glance at Alyssa in the mirror. "How come this is on your mind?"

"Well, I was thinking that Stephen isn't married either. So, if you were lonely, maybe you guys could date each other."

"Chance is single too," Avery mumbles.

I can't help but laugh. "You saying you want me to date one of those guys?"

"Or both." Alyssa pauses. "Stephen's friend has two wives, right? So, that means you could technically have two husbands."

Avery turns his head to look at me. "Is that possible? Can you really have two spouses at the same time?"

I heave a sigh, totally not ready for this conversation. But they're asking, and I want them to get the correct information from me instead of their friends or whatever the media portrays. "In the eyes of the law, no, you can't marry two people at the same time. Jason is married officially to Kourtney, but they bought a ring for Celeste, and they act as if they're married. They're in a polyamorous relationship. *Poly* means more than one."

I pause, letting that information sink into their brains.

"Why doesn't the law allow you to marry more than one person?" Alyssa asks. "If you love them, you should be able to marry them."

Out of the mouths of babes. "Right now, the world isn't a completely accepting place. A lot of people living in our country don't have the same rights as everyone else. Hopefully one day we will."

Avery chews his bottom lip. "If you dated both of them, would that mean that Chance and Stephen...would be together, as well? Like boyfriends?"

I bite back a smile as my keen boy connects the dots. "Chance and Stephen are what you call bisexual. They date men as well as women."

"Do you want to date them, Aunt Presley?" Alyssa asks. "Do you like them?"

I click on my blinker, and turn left into the movie theatre parking lot. "Can I tell you guys a secret that not a lot of people know?"

Once I pull into a spot, the kids unclip their seatbelts and Alyssa moves to sit on the center console. Nerves eat at my stomach, but I know this is an important conversation to have with them. My sister would want her children to be open-minded and accepting of everyone's sexuality and orientation. She had the biggest heart, and I want her kids to follow in her footsteps.

"When I was in college, I dated both Stephen and Chance. That's how we know each other, from school."

Alyssa's mouth hangs open. "You were in a polygon with them?"

Avery barks out a laugh. "Polyamorous, not polygon, you twit."

I point at him, trying not to laugh myself. "No name-calling. Be nice."

Alyssa frowns. "You know what I meant."

I clasp her hand and give it a squeeze. "I was in a polyamorous relationship with them. But that was a long time ago, and things are different now."

"How so?" Avery asks.

"Like I said before, I'm busy and don't have time to date. I love having Stephen and Chance around as friends, but I don't think we'd be able to manage a relationship like that again."

Both of the kids look down at their laps.

"Why?" I ask, venturing into the subject further. "Is that something you'd want for me—for us?"

Alyssa nods. "I like when they're around. They're fun, and they help you so you're not so stressed."

Guilt tugs at my heart. "I've been pretty stressed, huh?"

"It's understandable," Avery says quickly. "We should step up and help more."

I shake my head. "No, no. You and your sister are doing exactly the perfect amount of help. You go to school, get good grades, and you do your chores. I'm the adult—I deal with everything else." I cup his face. "Don't you go worrying that amazing brain of yours about it, you hear me?"

He nods.

"And you." I turn to Alyssa. "There's more to life than finding a husband. We're strong, independent women who don't need no man!"

She giggles. "Okay, fine. But for the record, I really like having Stephen and Chance around."

I smile. *I do too, kid.*

I do too.

"Let *The Very Manly Book Club* commence."

Trenton glares at me. "We never agreed to calling it that."

I grin. "We never disputed it either."

"I'm disputing it now."

Alexander chuckles from his seat in the row behind us. "Let's just focus on the book. We don't have a long ride today."

My stomach churns at the reminder. We're on the team bus on our way to a game in Philly. It's the first game against Chance since we've been spending time together with Presley, and I'm unsure of what will transpire. It's no secret that there's bad blood between us, and the fans are used to seeing us come to blows on the ice.

What will it be like now that we're back in each other's lives?

Knowing Chance, it won't be much different. He's a stubborn fucker.

I smirk as I imagine his face when he sees Presley and the kids wearing black and yellow tonight. I sent Presley three tickets for tonight's game, along with three jerseys—with my name on the back of them, obviously. I'm dying to see my pretty girl wearing my number.

Jason punches my shoulder from the seat beside me. "Dude, are you listening?"

"Of course, I'm listening." I blink up at the guys. "What did you say?"

Alexander chuckles. "I said that I really liked the enemies-to-lovers storyline in this book."

Oh, yeah. The book. "Me too. There was so much sexual tension. My dick was hard the entire first half of the story."

Coach turns around from his seat at the front. "Can you go five minutes without talking about your dick, Mac?"

"The max I can give you is three minutes, Coach."

He mutters something about headphones as he turns back around.

"I liked this one a lot," Trenton continues. "It reminded me of how Cassidy and I met when I moved into her apartment building."

Jason laughs. "You mean when you were slamming your door and pissing her off?"

Trenton holds up his hands, feigning innocence. "I wasn't slamming anything. She was the one singing power ballads at the crack of dawn."

I reach over and ruffle his thick hair. "And we all know how much you need your beauty sleep."

He slaps my hand away. "You could use some beauty sleep, you ugly fuck."

"Your mom didn't think I was ugly last night."

"My mom's dead, you moron." Trenton lunges for me, but Alexander grabs him and holds him back.

"Enough, children." Alex shakes his head. "My four-year-old is more mature than the both of you."

"She's smarter, too," Jason chimes in. "Do you know what she told me the other day? She said that babies are born with three hundred bones in their bodies." He shrugs. "I didn't believe her. The human body has two-hundred-and-six bones. But I Googled it and sure as shit, she was right."

Alexander groans. "She's obsessed with babies. She wants a sibling so badly."

"You should give her one." I wink. "Make sure that wife of yours knows she's not going anywhere."

He smirks, but bites his tongue. No one outside our friend group knows about his fake marriage arrangement with Aarya. His grandfather is an evil piece of shit, and is the only reason Alexander asked Aarya to marry him when they barely knew each other. But I've seen the way they are when they're together, and I'd bet my entire salary that they're going to be each other's happily ever after in the end.

I rub my palms together. "Now, let's get to the good part and talk about those sex scenes." I flip open to one of the red tabs in my book. "I particularly loved when he fucked her on her desk."

Jason leans over. "What are all those things sticking out of your book?"

"They're like mini-sticky notes." I thumb through the pages to show him. "Red is for the sex scenes; blue is for the scenes that made me cry; yellow is for my favorite parts; and pink is for the romantic scenes."

His eyebrows jump. "Why did you do all that?"

I hike a shoulder. "I like to keep track of everything as I read. Then I can go back to those scenes when we discuss it."

Trenton leans over and snatches my book. "You even took notes?"

I grab it back from him. "Those are my private thoughts, thank you very much."

He shakes his head. "You have too much time on your hands. You need to get laid."

"Speaking of..." Jason side-eyes me. "What's happening with Presley and Kellerman?"

I blow out a long breath through my lips as my head falls back against the seat. "I don't know."

The group falls silent, waiting for me to elaborate. But I don't know what to say. I know what I want, but I don't know if that's even a possibility.

"Oh, shit." Trenton lets out a low whistle. "It must be serious. I've never seen you this quiet before."

Alexander watches me with those dark eyes of his. He's my best friend, the one who knows me inside and out. I haven't told him anything about my past with Chance; I never needed to. But now that he's back in my life, I know Alex can tell there's more to the story.

I clear my throat. "The three of us were...together, in college."

"Together," Trenton repeats.

"Like me, Kourtney, and Celeste, together?" Jason asks.

I nod. "Chance had it rough growing up, and his father made him feel like he couldn't be who he truly was. I knew he was attracted to me. There was always this spark between us, but he never let himself act on it. Not until Presley was in the picture. It was like she was this missing link, and she connected us in a way that neither of us could have."

Jason nods as he listens, and I know he understands me better than anyone. He, Kourtney, and Celeste are tethered together like what can only be described as soulmates.

"All the fighting on the ice makes sense now," Alex says. "You've got more than just animosity over a lost friendship."

Trenton leans forward, resting his elbows on his knees. "So, what happened between you?"

"It was amazing being with them for that year. But when Presley left, it broke us. We blamed each other, not knowing the real reason why she left. We were hurting and confused, and it was like we couldn't figure out how to be together without her. I tried, but..." I shake my head. "Chance isn't the best at communicating. So, we took all that pain out on each other."

"You still have love for them in your heart. And so do they, otherwise they wouldn't be entertaining any part of this." Alex rests his hand on my shoulder. "There's hope for the three of you to have something."

"Presley thinks we can't be together. Between the kids and her job at the school, she thinks it'd be too much; that people wouldn't accept them."

"Maybe at first," Jason says. "But look at what happened with me. I had the support of my team, and our fans. Not everyone will understand, but the good outweighs the bad. Love will always win in the end."

I believe that with my whole heart.

I just have to figure out how to convince Presley and Chance.

My eyes scan the glass when I skate onto the ice to warm up.

It doesn't take too long to spot Alyssa jumping up and down as she waves, wearing my jersey and a bright-yellow beanie.

"Hi, my 'Lyssa girl!" I tap my stick against the glass and she giggles. I do a double-take as my eyes flick to Avery, who's wearing a Philly jersey—Chance's Philly jersey.

I clutch my heart.

Avery smirks, dropping his chin as a smile breaks free.

I shoot him a wink to let him know I'm only busting his chops.

Figures, Chance sent them jerseys the same as I did.

I shift my gaze to Presley. A cream-colored sweater pokes out of her jacket.

She rolls her eyes, and I can't help but chuckle. There's no way she'd choose between us, and I love that about her.

"Enjoy the game, pretty girl," I shout through the glass.

I skate backwards, waiting for the pink blush to tinge her cheeks before spinning around and making my way towards my team.

Once the game starts, Chance is all over me. Each time I find an opening, he gives me a calculated shove, sending me into the boards. The refs aren't calling any penalties tonight, and it gives Philly the confidence to continue the cheap shots and brutal hits that they're known for. But it also allows me to fight back. Chance hasn't been able to take a shot the entire first period.

Each time we get close, he glares at me, but it's different this time. It's not just him wanting to throw a punch, not just his need to get by me for a goal. There's a burning intensity in his gaze, like he's silently promising something...*more*.

And fuck if I'm not going to provoke the shit out of him until he breaks.

Nearing the end of the second period, we're tied up 1-1. Alexander takes the puck into enemy territory while Chance and I race toward his goalie, me looking for an opening and him preparing to stop me. But I'm faster than him—always have been—and when Alexander passes me the puck, I take the shot before Chance can block it. The buzzer goes off, and I lift my stick in the air as I shout.

"Two-to-one, baby!" I skate around to Presley and the kids, and blow them a kiss.

Everyone's fired up in the third period. My chest heaves and my legs burn as sweat pours into my eyes. We're so close, I can taste the win.

Alexander moves the puck with ease across the ice, setting us up for a chance to score again. Then Ivanov comes in like a freight train. I fly toward him to protect my captain. This guy is known for the most ruthless hits in the game. I'm almost there when Chance shoves into me, derailing my plan. I see it happen in slow motion as Ivanov drops his shoulder, and sends Alexander crashing into the boards with a sickening thud.

The arena lets out a collective gasp, and my heart leaps into my throat.

I toss my stick and gloves to the ice when I reach Ivanov, and he does the same, grinning like the sick fuck he is. I'm going to make him pay for that illegal hit from behind, and wipe the damn smile right off his face.

I throw the first punch without hesitation before Ivanov can get his fists up to block it. Blood pours from his nose as he throws a jab in my direction. I dodge it, and hammer him with another punch to the jaw before taking him to the ice and letting my fists fly with unrelenting focus.

I'm a happy-go-lucky guy until you fuck with my family.

When the refs finally tear me off of him, they send Ivanov into the penalty box.

I skate over to Alex, and tap my helmet against his. "You good?"

He nods. "You know I always get back up."

By the end of the period, we win 3-1.

"Get a leash on that animal of yours," I call to Chance as we skate by each other.

I don't know why I do it. It's like I *need* to make some kind of connection with him, even if it's a negative one. Any attention is better than none.

"You getting soft? This is hockey." He glares at me. "It isn't for the weak."

"That hit was illegal and you know it."

"Go have Alex wipe your ass after he's done wiping your tears."

I smirk. "Still thinking about my ass after all these years, Kellerman? I'm flattered."

"Fuck you," he spits.

"I dare you to."

I'm yanked back by my jersey. "Enough," Jason shouts. "Let's go."

I head to the locker room with fire in my veins and adrenaline coursing through me.

"Congrats on the win."

I wrap my arms around Presley. "See, you should've worn my jersey."

Presley rolls her eyes as she shoves me back. "Not when you're both playing."

"I know, I know. We'll have to figure something out though. Sew the two jerseys together or something. I think I read that in a book once."

Her eyebrows shoot up. "You read books?"

I scoff, feigning offense. "Yes, I read books. Romance books, as a matter of fact."

Alyssa scrunches her nose. "Aunt Presley reads those books."

I tap my index finger against her little nose. "What's with the face?"

"They seem so boring," Alyssa whines. "I would want to read a book with action."

I shrug. "Why not have both? There are plenty of books with epic battles *and* a love story. In fact, most epic battles are fought *because* of love."

Her eyebrows shoot up. "Really?"

"Girl, I am going to rock your world. Wait until you see all the cool books I have at my place."

Alyssa's head jerks up to her aunt. "Can we go to Stephen's house?"

Presley chuckles as she brushes a strand of Alyssa's hair behind her ear. "You can't invite yourself over people's houses."

"I didn't." She blinks. "He just told me to come see the books at his house."

Presley crosses her arms over her chest. "And since when are you interested in reading, hmm? I have to bribe you in order to get you to complete your reading log for school."

"School books are boring." Alyssa plants her hand on her hip. "Besides, you should be happy I'm taking an interest in reading now."

"Oof." I nudge Presley with my shoulder. "Wonder where she gets that sass from."

Presley scoffs. "I'm not sassy."

"You so are." I lean in close and press a kiss to her cheek, lingering by her ear. "And that's okay; I like you sassy."

She shoots me a glare, but it's undermined by the way her body shivers at my proximity.

I loved knowing she was in the arena watching me play tonight—even more so, getting to see her after a win. With the adrenaline still coursing through me, it's taking all my willpower not to pounce on her in the middle of this parking lot.

We're waiting for the team to pile onto the bus so we can head home. If I had my way, I'd be going home with Presley. I'm dying to hold her, to make love to her, to fall asleep with her in my arms.

Alexander spots us and makes his way over. "Hey, Alyssa. Want to check out our bus?"

Her eyes widen. "Do you have a bathroom on there?"

He chuckles. "We sure do."

She squeals and takes off running toward the bus.

Presley laughs as she shakes her head. "Never seen someone so excited to see a bathroom."

Without hesitation, I grasp her hand and tug her around the corner of the back of the bus, away from prying eyes.

Chance took Avery to meet some of his teammates in the locker room, so with Alyssa occupied, I get a few precious moments alone with Presley.

She comes willingly, and lets me cage her in. I slip my left hand into her hair, and grip her hip with my other hand. "I loved having you at my game."

Her eyes drop to my mouth. "I enjoyed watching you play."

I dip my head and nip at her jaw. "You always did enjoy *watching*."

Her lips part, her warm breath dancing along my mouth. "Stephen..."

"What's the matter, pretty girl? Talk to me."

"W-we shouldn't," she says, but she fists my hoodie and pulls me closer. "We can't."

"I disagree." I brush my nose against hers. "I think we can, and we should."

"You're not playing fair."

"Oh, I'm not playing at all, Pres." I close the tiny gap between us, speaking against her lips. "There are only two things I take seriously in this world: Hockey, and you. The sooner you realize I'm not letting you go, the sooner you can get on the same page."

She wraps her hands around the back of my neck, and I lift her into my arms, claiming her willing mouth. Her ankles lock around my lower back as I pin her against the back of the bus. My tongue surges inside, searching for hers. She lets out a sexy-ass moan, letting me know she's as ready and desperate for me as I am for her.

Four years.

I've gone four years without this woman, without the company of anyone who could compare. At least I've been able to keep in contact with Chance—as volatile as we are together. I haven't lost him completely, and the way he reacts to me lets me know that what we had still runs deep inside him.

But Presley was ripped from my life the way a band aid is ripped off a wound and disposed of, never to be seen again. Now that she's back, now that I see how perfectly she fits right back into my life, it's full-steam ahead.

Presley tears her mouth away from mine, gasping for breath while I lick a path down her neck. "The kids…"

"Are taken care of."

"And Chance…"

"Can decide if he wants back in or not."

She whimpers as I bite down on her neck, loving the way her racing pulse beats against my lips.

"I've missed this." Those three words are whispered so quietly, I almost miss them right before the bus roars to life.

Presley drops her legs and I set her down, steadying her as she snaps back into the present moment. She hits me with a look that looks like a mixture of desire laced with regret.

Don't regret me, baby.

We've barely even started.

So she's worried about the kids and Chance. I can handle them. I can get Chance to admit that he wants this—wants us, both of us—and everything else will fall into place. Nothing is stronger than love, and with that, we're unstoppable.

Once he caves, Presley will admit that she wants us too.

I already know what I want.

And I always get what I want.

Sophomore Year

"Where are we going tonight?"

Stephen's lips land on my neck as his hands trail up my arms from behind me. "I think we should stay right here tonight. Fuck the party."

My dick jumps at the idea. "I thought Presley was celebrating her friend's birthday."

"She is." His tongue traces my ear. "Doesn't mean we have to."

I turn my head and glance at him over my shoulder. "So, you want to stay in just the two of us?"

He leans in and captures my lips, his hand skating along the waistband of my sweats. "Would that be so bad?"

I catch his wrist, and spin around to face him. For the last two weeks, Stephen, Presley, and I have been going at it like rabbits—the three of us, together. I haven't fooled around with Stephen, or Presley for that matter, one-on-one.

Stephen's eyebrows press together, his crystal-blue eyes searching mine. "What's wrong?"

I shrug. "I don't know how this works."

"This works however we want it to work."

He says it so simply, as if a polyamory is as easy as making a peanut butter and jelly sandwich.

"Have you and Presley fooled around...without me?" I ask, unsure of how I'll feel if he says they have.

Stephen's hands come up and rest on my shoulders. "Is that what you're worried about? Being left out?"

I roll my eyes, even though that's exactly what I'm worried about. "I'm just asking."

"We haven't been together without you, but I'm sure we would if you weren't available. I think if the three of us are going to do this, then we should be able to explore what we feel whenever we want to." The corner of his mouth tips up to one side. "I do like you jealous, though."

I scoff. "I'm not jealous."

"You are, but that's okay." He slowly drops to his knees in front of me. "Let me reassure you that you have nothing to worry about."

I arch a brow as I look down my nose at him, feigning nonchalance. "And why's that?"

He tugs down my pants and my cock springs free, hard and ready for him. "Because I want you just as much as I want her, and I'm not willing to give you up."

My heart constricts in my chest. I don't have a response for him. I don't know what to say. I *want* to ask why.

Why does he like me?

Why does he care?

Why doesn't he want to be with just Presley?

Stephen's eyes stay locked on mine as he leans in and runs his tongue along my length. "You don't see it, but you will."

I let out a shaky breath. "See what?"

"The way I want you." He sucks on my crown. "The way I feel about you." He cups my balls. "The way I'm going to care for you."

My hips jerk forward, unable to endure his teasing. "I don't know if I'm ready for this."

I whisper the words into the quiet room like a hushed confession.

Stephen pushes off his knees and stands to his full height before me. He takes my face into his hands, and speaks against my lips. "I'll wait for you."

A lump forms in the back of my throat. "You shouldn't."

I'm broken.

Fucked up.

Unlovable.

I'm the opposite of all the best parts of Stephen McKinley.

"You're worth it, Kellerman." He nips at my bottom lip. "And when you're ready, I'll be here to tell you I told you so."

"Ah, I see." My arms wrap around his body, pulling him closer in spite of myself. "This is about you being right."

He chuckles. "No, this is about you getting out of your own way and realizing that the life you've had up until this point isn't the life you're destined for."

My heart hammers in my chest. "And what is it you think I'm destined for?"

"Love."

The word encompasses so much.

Loving myself.

Loving others.

Letting others love me.

I don't know how to do any of it. My greatest fear is that I'll end up exactly like the person my father told me I was, worthless and undeserving. I've buried myself in hockey, practicing so I could be the best and prove him wrong. But I haven't quite figured out how to be worth a damn in any other aspect of my life. I'm not fun and carefree like Presley. I'm not friendly and confident like Stephen. I'm not much of anything. Nothing that matters.

But gazing into the blue eyes looking back at me with such certainty, it's hard to deny him. I want the kind of life he's talking about. I want more than what I've had.

I want it with him. With them.

Instead of fooling around and making each other come, Stephen pulls me down onto his bed and lays his head on my chest. It's bigger than sex. It's more than a physical connection. It's intimacy. Trust. Vulnerability. And I don't fight it. It feels good to give in to him.

"The three of us are going to be something incredible," Stephen whispers. "Just you wait and see."

"This feels so creepy."

I scoff. "Are you kidding? This is fun. It's like a stakeout."

Chance rolls his eyes. "We're sitting in an elementary school parking lot essentially stalking one of the teachers."

"You always make everything so negative. You're such a grump."

If looks could kill, pretty sure I'd be dead with the way Chance glares at me. "Yeah, that's me. I ruin everything. How could I forget?"

Guilt slices through me like a knife. "I was just kidding. I didn't mean it like that."

"Yeah, you did." He sits back against the passenger seat, and shifts his gaze out the windshield. "And you meant it when you said the same thing four years ago."

"Look, I'm sorry about that. I'm sorry I said what I said. I didn't mean it. I was just hurting, and I took it out on you." I pause, trying to choose my words carefully so this doesn't escalate into a fight. "I was angry at you for pushing me away, and not fighting for us."

"Presley left us. How was I supposed to fight for someone who didn't care enough to say goodbye, or let us in on what was going on?"

"I get that, but you didn't fight for *us* either."

His jaw works under his skin. "You were better off without me. I would've only dragged you down. You were right to say what you said."

I tip my chin. "And now...?"

His eyes flick back to mine. "I don't know."

"You don't know, yet you're here." I take a chance and reach for him over the console, brushing my fingertips against his. "With me."

Chance's chest rises and falls with his shallow breaths as his eyes bounce between mine.

"You know what you want, you're just afraid," I whisper, lacing our fingers together. "Admit it."

His gaze drops to my mouth. "I'm terrified." His voice comes out like a hushed confession, and it hangs between us, igniting the energy around us.

I lean forward, and grip the back of his neck with my free hand, pulling him closer to me. "It'll be different this time around."

Chance's head dips, and he rests his forehead against mine. "How can you be sure?"

"No one is ever sure of anything." I close the gap between us and brush my lips against his. "You just have to have a little faith."

He nips at my bottom lip. "I've missed you so much. Being apart from you was the worst torture I've ever had to endure."

My heart swells. "You don't ever have to be away from me again. I—oh, look!" A flash of white goes past my car as a white SUV pulls into the parking lot. "That's her."

Chance adjusts the seat of his pants. "You're gonna have to give me a minute."

I toss my head back and laugh. "Okay, I'll give it to you; popping a boner in an elementary school parking lot is definitely creepy."

Are we stalking Dominique? *Technically.*

But is it for a good reason? *Absolutely.*

Presley has taken on two kids and a new life all on her own for the last four years. She deserves a break every once in a while, and what better way than to rekindle her love for her two ex-boyfriends?

Her two, super attractive, muscular, fine-as-fuck, soon-to-be-*current* boyfriends.

As Dominique parks a few spots down, we get out of the car and walk over to her.

"Why do teachers always carry so many bags?" I ask.

She spins around, a purse and two totes on her shoulders. "Jesus, you scared the shit out of me."

Chance jerks his thumb in my direction. "He has that effect on people."

I flip him off, and then quickly hide my hand behind my back. "Shit, we're near a school."

Dominique chuckles. "Nobody's here yet. Wait, what are you two doing here? Is Presley okay?"

"Presley is fine." Chance slips his hands into the front pocket of his hoodie. "We were hoping you could help us set up a nice kid-free night for her this weekend."

Dominique's brown eyes light up. "Oh, fuck yes. What do you need me to do?"

"Can you take the kids for a sleepover at any point this weekend?"

She nods. "We're free Friday night."

"Perfect." I rub my palms together as the plan forms in my mind. "Don't tell her we spoke though. I know you chicks have girl code and all that, but—"

"Fuck girl code." Dominique lifts her chin. "Our girl needs to get laid."

Yes, she does.

"Don't you worry about that." I shoot her a wink. "We're going to take good care of her."

"Love you, Aunt Pres."

"I love you guys. Have fun tonight." I give Avery and Alyssa one more quick hug before they walk outside to Dominique's car.

"Enjoy the quiet house to yourself tonight." Dominique winks. "I still think you should call up your boyfriends and have some adult time."

"I'm sure they're busy. It's Friday night."

"Neither team is playing tonight." She shrugs. "Just saying."

"And I'm not going to bother them on their night off. Plus, I have a shit-ton of laundry to do."

She scrunches her nose. "You're right. Laundry sounds *so* much better than taking two dicks at once."

My mouth drops open as I swat her arm. "I'm never telling you anything again. Get out of here."

Dominique's laughter follows behind her as she darts across the grass and hops in her car.

Closing the door behind me, I lean against it and let out a big sigh. I hate how empty the house feels when the kids aren't here, yet it's nice to get a break and not have to be on for the kids.

I give my sister so much credit for raising them on her own. I wish I was older when they were born so that I could've helped out more.

I throw the first load of laundry in, and head upstairs to take a shower. You know you're pathetic when the highlight of your Friday night is to take a long, steamy, *everything shower* without anyone in the house to disturb you or use up all the hot water.

Back in college, I was living it up, dancing on bars, dominating at beer pong, and yes, as Dominique so eloquently put it, taking two dicks at once.

My body reacts to the memory as I lather myself with soap. What I wouldn't give to go back to the time the three of us shared in that dorm room. Stephen's insatiable appetite, and Chance's dominating way; watching the two of them together was almost as hot as being the focus of their attention.

I unhook the shower head and pull it down, aiming the warm spray between my legs.

The boys are a bit older now, fuller in all the right places than the lean muscle I last saw them with. Stephen with his adorable freckles and curls; the dimples bracketing his killer smile; and captivating crystal-blue eyes. He gives off total golden retriever energy, making you laugh until your sides hurt. But when he gets you in the bedroom, sexy charisma oozes out of him, and he could sweet talk you into doing anything. He's fun and flirty, and has stamina for hours.

Chance is more reserved, more in control. He doesn't wear his heart on his sleeve, but oh when he lets you see it, it's the most incredible thing you'll ever witness. He's passionate, and loves deeply. Your pleasure is the only thing he cares about, which is what makes his dominant nature in the bedroom so mind-blowing.

God, I miss them.

Stephen's kiss last weekend moves to the forefront of my mind. I could've come right in the middle of the parking lot with the way he felt through his sweatpants, pressed against me and rubbing where I wanted him most. He ravaged my mouth, letting me know how much he wants me still.

My hips rock against the stream of water, chasing a release to the thought of the only two men I've ever loved. I've done this before, pleasured myself to their memories. But this time is different. Now, they're back in my life, and I'm not getting off to the memories of what we did. Now, I'm imagining all the new ways they can touch me, please me, and make me feel good. Now, I have to look them in the eyes, knowing I came to fantasies of them.

I let out a frustrated groan, and set the shower head back in its place on the wall.

I need to stop.

Nothing good will come of this.

I need to keep things platonic with them.

I don't step out of the bathroom until I've rinsed out my deep conditioning mask, and removed the hair from every orifice. Not that I have anyone to see my handiwork, but it makes me feel good.

Pulling an oversized tee over my head, I shimmy into a pair of cotton boy shorts and head down to the kitchen. *Fuck cooking.* I'm going to order a pizza tonight.

But the sound of the doorbell garners my attention before I can find the delivery menu.

I squint one eye and peer through the peep hole.

And my heart stalls out.

I peek through it again just to make sure I'm not hallucinating.

I swing open the door, and obsidian eyes meet mine.

"Chance, what are you doing here?"

He glances down at my bare legs—my very smooth and shiny bare legs, thank you—and arches a brow. "Do you often answer the door without pants on?"

I roll my eyes. "I checked the peep hole first. Come inside, it's chilly."

Carrying a shopping tote in each hand, he steps into the foyer. "I brought dinner. Heard you were on your own tonight."

I groan and slap my forehead with my palm. "Dominique called you, didn't she?"

"I can neither confirm nor deny." Chance carries the bags into the kitchen and sets them on the counter before turning to face me. "I might've heard that you were going to have the house to yourself tonight, and that you'd probably just order pizza because you wouldn't feel like cooking, so I figured I'd come over and cook you something better than pizza."

"Better than pizza?" I cross my arms over my chest. *Fuck, I'm not wearing a bra.* "That's doubtful."

"Hey." He pulls me into his arms and tilts my head back to look up at him. "I want you to enjoy this time without the kids. I know how rare it must be for you. I'm not trying to ruin that. I just want to cook you a nice meal, and if you want me to go, then I'll be out of your hair. I promise."

This man.

I rest my head on his chest, and let him engulf me in his embrace. His arms are solid, slightly bigger than they were in college. I can only imagine how good he looks now, on a professional athlete's training regimen. I squeeze my thighs together to suppress the building ache.

"God, you smell good," I murmur.

I should've made myself come in the shower. Then maybe I wouldn't be ready to hump his leg like a dog in heat.

His shoulders shake with his low chuckle. "Did you hear anything I just said?"

"Something about cooking me a nice meal." I hum, sucking in another lungful of his scent. "Sorry, I'm a little distracted at the moment."

"Imagine how I feel with the sexiest woman alive standing in front of me without any pants on."

I laugh. "Please. Nothing you haven't seen before."

"I've only seen it in my dreams for the last four years." His lips are at the cusp of my ear. "I still can't believe you're really here, in my arms right now."

I can feel the yearning rolling off of him in waves, crashing into my own desire. My brain short-circuits being this close to him. His voice in my ear, his arms around me, his lips mere inches from mine.

Torturing myself more, I lift my arms and run my fingers through his tousled hair. "I've missed you so much."

"Me too." He rests his forehead against mine, letting his hands skate down my ribs. He stops at my hips, being a gentleman even though my shirt is riding up, and I'm overcome by the notion of how much I don't want him to be a gentleman right now.

Stephen had a taste. It's only fair to let Chance have his, right?

My skin heats, my body coming alive, and it's more than the way I felt in the shower. I've deprived myself of physical touch from another for so long, it's as if my body is taking control right now, overriding the warning signals my brain is trying to send.

Slow down.

Don't go any further.

You shouldn't do this.

I helplessly try to stay in control, to keep my wits. But I know what this man can do to my body, the way he can make me feel, and the visceral need to have him pulls me under.

Maybe for one night, I can pretend like my choices don't have consequences. For one night, I can forget about being a parent and do something selfish. For one night, I can be the person I used to be.

"Why don't you go relax, and I'll let you know when dinner is ready," Chance whispers.

I lift my head a fraction of an inch, and brush the tip of my nose against his. "Forget about dinner, Chance."

His hands ball my T-shirt into his fists. "You're not hungry?"

I shake my head.

One of his hands comes up to rest at the back of my neck. "Do you want me to leave?"

I shake my head again.

"Then what do you want, baby? Use your words and tell me."

"You, Chance. I want you."

"You've got me." His lips brush against mine. "You've always had me."

"Kiss me." I nip at his bottom lip. "Please."

My plea is like the shot at the starting line. His fingers grip my hair at the base of my neck, and he tugs, jerking my mouth up to his. He devours me, kissing me with such need, such force, that it steals my breath. His tongue surges into my mouth and winds around mine. It's all-consuming, and all I can do is grip onto his shoulders, my feet barely touching the tile below.

He lifts me and plops me on the counter, and I wrap my legs around his waist, pulling his hips against mine.

A moan escapes me, but I can't find it in myself to be embarrassed for how needy I sound.

Chance has a bruising grip on my waist, grinding me against himself like he's just as desperate as I am.

And then the doorbell rings.

My eyebrows dip. "Who the hell...?"

Chance steps back, his eyes dropping to the floor as his chest heaves. "It's Stephen."

I tilt my head. "What?" I hop off the counter and stalk toward the door to peer through the peephole. "How did you know?"

Chance rubs the back of his neck as he comes to stand beside me, not saying a word.

A humorless laugh escapes me as I swing open the door. "I can't wait to talk to Dominique tomorrow."

Stephen smiles wide and holds up a bottle of tequila. "Happy Friday, pretty girl."

I roll my eyes, fighting a grin. "Let me guess: Dominique took the kids because she thinks I need to be thoroughly fucked, so you both came over to double-team me. Is that right?"

Chance shakes his head, starting to refute, but Stephen shrugs and says, "Basically."

A laugh tumbles out of me and I press my palm against my forehead. His honesty is refreshing. "I forgot how much I love your bluntness."

Like a happy dog, Stephen bounces into the house and plants a kiss on my cheek before shoving Chance's shoulder. "What's for dinner, Grumpy Gills?"

Chance glares at the back of his head. "What the fuck is a grumpy gill?"

I pat his shoulder. "It's from a kid's movie."

He rolls his eyes. "Of course it is."

In the kitchen, Stephen rummages through the cabinets. "Where are your shot glasses?"

"I don't have any." I hop up onto the counter, and point to the cabinet to my left. "I have wine glasses and Solo cups in there."

He pops open the tequila, and takes a swig directly from the bottle before passing it to me. "Limes and salt?"

"Limes in the fridge. Salt in that cabinet." I take a sip from the bottle, and close my eyes as it slides down my throat. "Damn, I haven't had this in such a long time."

Chance slices a lime and hands each of us a wedge. "How often do you get a kid-free night?"

I heave a sigh. "Not often. Sometimes they'll sleep at a friend's house, but most of the time I host the sleepovers. I try to get out once a month with Dominique, but it's pretty tame."

Stephen arches a brow. "Not like our college days."

I smile at the reminder. "Not one bit."

He steps between my legs, and tips my chin. "Stick out your tongue."

I do as he commands, and he sprinkles the salt onto my waiting tongue. Then he dips his head and strokes my tongue with his.

Oh, fuck.

Chance takes the bottle from my hand and gently tugs my chin away from Stephen. "Open." He tips the bottle, pouring tequila into my mouth.

I swallow and suck on the lime while he pours some into Stephen's mouth next. Forgoing the lime, Stephen grips the back of Chance's neck and pulls him in for a rough kiss.

It's been so long since I've seen the two of them together like this. Wetness instantly pools between my legs.

This is crazy. We should talk about this.

But I can't seem to get out of the way of the train speeding toward me.

I've missed them, missed this, missed being touched.

The last four years have been filled with stress and grief, and all of my focus has been on the kids. For tonight, I just want to be selfish and indulge in my favorite guilty pleasure.

I yank them by their shirts, and pull their mouths down to mine. Having them both back feels like a dream I don't want to wake from. It's like I've stepped back in time, and nothing has changed. It's just the three of us in love without any obstacles standing in our way.

"Do you want us, pretty girl?" Stephen pants against my mouth, his eyes tight like it's taking all of his strength to stop. "Because this is your night, and it goes how you want it to go."

I nod, throwing caution to the wind. "This is exactly how I want tonight to go."

Without another word, Stephen drops to his knees and reaches under my shirt, tearing my panties from my body and tossing them onto the floor. He licks a trail along my thigh before reaching for the salt and shaking it over my wet skin. Then he laps it up, and opens his mouth right below my pussy, like he's waiting.

Chance pours the tequila over me, and I gasp at the feel of the cool liquid over my heated, swollen clit. Stephen slurps it up, and then starts to feast on me.

I lean my palms back against the counter, and let out a loud moan. Chance grips onto my neck and hauls my mouth against his, his tongue surging inside and matching the pace of Stephen's licks. He slides his hand under my shirt and teases my nipples while Stephen sucks on my clit. His muffled moans only spur me on.

Stephen doesn't go down on me because he has to, or because it's a chore. He wants to be the best at everything in his life, and this is no exception. He studies me, learning every sound, every movement of my hips, every tremble in my legs, until he can bring me to my release with expertise. Stephen excels in every aspect of my body.

I hike up my knees, planting my feet at the edge of the counter, completely baring myself to Stephen. Then I grip his curls in my fist and grind my hips against his face.

Chance lets out a dark chuckle as he sucks on my bottom lip. "You're about to come, aren't you, baby? You're so desperate for it."

"Yes," is all I can chant as the pleasure mounts.

Chance kneels down, and then I feel his tongue join Stephen's. My senses are overwhelmed by the both of them, and my body relishes in the onslaught of pleasure. I place one hand on the back of each of their heads as I watch them between my legs.

I feel like a queen.

"Oh, my God." My orgasm racks my body, and my head falls back as I cry out.

It feels like it lasts forever, wave after wave of white-hot heat crashing into me. I haven't come this hard in so long—since the last time I was with them, no doubt.

The boys pull each other in for a kiss, my arousal glistening on their lips, before pushing to their feet to kiss me.

Chance scoops me up in his arms and stalks out of the kitchen, with Stephen hot on his heels. I'm carried upstairs and into my bedroom.

Chance lays me on the bed. "Take off that shirt and get on your knees, baby."

I scramble to do as he orders, watching the two of them undress each other. My heart pounds in anticipation, knowing full-well what's about to happen in this room.

I'm scared and ready at the same time.

What will happen tomorrow, in the light of day? No liquid courage, no house to myself. This can only be a one-night thing. I can't fuck two men at once with children in the house, and I can't devote time to a relationship, let alone a polyamorous one, while I'm raising them.

I almost laugh. Who says they'd even want a relationship with me? They can have any woman they want. There are thousands of women who'd jump at the chance to be with a professional athlete.

Why would they want to limit themselves to me? Certainly not now, in mom-mode, in this new diluted life in suburbia.

"Hey." Chance dips down and forces my eyes to his. "Stay with us, baby. Get out of your head."

They both crawl onto the bed on either side of me, sandwiching me between their gorgeous, hard bodies.

"Forget about whatever you're thinking, pretty girl." Stephen peppers my face with kisses. "We're here. We're together. We've found each other again. That's all that matters."

Tears well behind my lids, unexpected emotion bubbling to the surface. "I've missed you two so much."

They cradle me in their arms, Stephen's chest pressed against mine while Chance wraps around me from behind.

"We've missed you too," Chance whispers.

Stephen smirks. "And we're going to show you just how much."

A shiver runs down my spine.

Chance sits back against the headboard and fists his cock with his right hand. "Ride me, baby."

Chance is rarely selfish, always letting Stephen take what he needs first. But the way his obsidian eyes shine with unshed tears, it's clear that he needs this right now.

I sniffle as I sit up. "I don't have any condoms."

Stephen chuckles as he slips out of bed, and digs into the pocket of his sweatpants. "Don't you worry, pretty girl. I've got us covered."

He pulls out a long-ass strip of condoms and a bottle of lube, and holds them up the way a fisherman holds up his prize fish.

My shoulders shake with my laughter. "Think you brought enough?"

Chance yanks me over to him with an arm around my waist. "You better hope he did." He lifts me up by my hips and rubs me against his hard cock. "Because you're not getting any sleep tonight. We're going to fuck you in every way we've wanted to for the last four years."

"You're about to get four years-worth of fucking, pretty girl." Stephen tears open a condom and tosses it to me, then opens one for himself. "Hope you don't have any plans for tomorrow because you're going to be sore."

My pussy clenches at the thought, and a fire ignites inside me. It feels like an awakening; like the piece of me that has been asleep all this time just woke up from hibernation.

And she's hungry.

A smile spreads across my face. "Bring it, boys. Because for as long as you've been missing me, you've been able to get out your desires with other people. I haven't had anyone to have hot, meaningless sex with; I don't have people throwing themselves at me on a daily basis. I've got four years of pent-up frustration, so if I were you, I'd be scared right now because I'm about to pump you both until you're dry."

Stephen tosses his head back as he laughs. "There's our girl."

I roll the condom over Chance, and waste no time straddling him. "You ready for me, Grumpy Man?"

His hands fly to my hips with a bruising grip. "Use me, baby. Take what you need."

I sink down onto him, but stop halfway. "Oh, fuck. I forgot how big you guys are."

The burn hurts so good, and I take my time working myself onto him. Once I'm filled, I start to rock my hips, nice and slow.

Chance's hooded eyes watch where our bodies connect, his lips parted like he's in a trance.

Stephen comes up behind me, straddling Chance and nestling his erection against my ass as he moves with me. "He looks so sexy when he's turned on, doesn't he?" he whispers in my ear. "It's the only time he's not glaring at someone, or mouthing off about something."

Chance's eyes flick up to him. "Too bad I can't shove my cock down your throat right now."

"No, but I'd love to lick you clean after you come."

Chance groans, and it's now that I realize—these boys haven't been together since college either. Not only did they lose touch with me, but they lost each other as well. This is the first time all three of us have been together in years.

I reach behind me and rest my hand on the back of Stephen's neck. "Fuck me, Stephen. I'm ready."

Ready for the three of us to finally be connected.

His palm presses against my back, lowering me until I'm leaning over Chance. My nipples brush against Chance's chest as he continues fucking me. Stephen drizzles the liquid onto my ass, pressing his thumb inside. He pumps it in and out of me to stretch me open. I let out a low moan.

"You've missed this, haven't you? Yeah, you have. You miss being filled up like our dirty little slut." Chance caresses my face, gazing up at me like I'm a sweet angel, but his words prove otherwise. "We've missed you too, baby. We've been dreaming about this perfect pussy for years. Every time I jerked off, I thought about you, about the three of us—all the depraved things we've done together."

"Oh, fuck," I whimper. I forgot how turned on I get by listening to him talk like this.

Stephen replaces his thumb with his crown, and I feel myself spreading open for him. My body stills as I close my eyes, breathing through the initial discomfort. Stephen pours on more lubricant.

Chance captures my mouth and thrusts his hips up to distract me, bringing me closer to the edge while Stephen takes his time working into me.

I'm so full, so filled up with both of these men, and I love it. "Chance... Stephen... yes."

"That's it, baby." Chance watches over my shoulder as Stephen moves faster inside me. "Fuck, Stephen. I feel you."

"I can feel you too." Stephen grunts as he drags himself out, and then plunges back inside. "This feels so good."

The three of us move as one, our breaths, our bodies, our heartbeats. Nothing but the sound of skin slapping together fills the room; we're too overwhelmed to speak.

I fall over the edge, and come hard, crying out for them. They hold me while my body trembles. It's a release of everything I've buried deep—all the grief, the pain, the yearning, the stress, and the heartbreak. I let go of it all.

Chance comes next, with Stephen right behind him. These big, strong, beautiful men surrender themselves to me, to each other.

As we lie wrapped in each other's arms, panting as our racing hearts calm down, I allow myself to believe that this could be real. That we could be what we once were. That we could be together again.

In the light of day tomorrow, I'll see the harsh reality. But for tonight, just tonight, I pretend that it's the three of us against the world.

Junior Year

"Of course, aliens are real. Are you kidding?"

Stephen scoffs. "If they were, we'd know about it. There's no proof."

My eyes narrow. "The proof is in the logic. There are billions of galaxies, each containing billions of stars—and probably even more planets we haven't discovered. It's statistically likely that life exists elsewhere in the universe."

Presley leans her elbows on the table. "The government probably knows about it, and covers it up."

"Exactly."

Stephen lifts his cup of hot chocolate to his lips. "There's no way. I don't believe it."

I roll my eyes. "It's close-minded to think it isn't possible."

"I'm the opposite of close-minded." He spread out his arms wide on either side of him. "My mind is as open as they come."

"Open and *empty*," I mutter.

Presley giggles as she threads her fingers through my hair. "You're such an Aquarius, my grumpy man."

"What does that mean?"

Her back straightens as her eyes widen with excitement. "Have you never read about your zodiac sign?"

I shake my head, and she looks to Stephen. "What about you?"

"If I don't believe in aliens, then I'm definitely not believing that someone's birthday can tell you all this bullshit about them."

Presley gasps as she scrambles for her phone. "I'm about to blow your minds."

Stephen lowers his lips to her neck. "I have something else you can blow."

"Behave." She laughs as she digs her elbow into his ribs. "Okay, Chance. You're an Aquarius. *You seem detached and aloof because you prioritize logic over emotion; you're independent and don't like to be told what to do; and you're extremely intellectual.*"

I lean back in my seat as I think about everything. "Okay, that sounds about right."

Stephen rolls his eyes. "Come on. You don't think there are other people in the world with different birth months who have those same exact qualities?"

Presley smirks. "Let's read about Leo, shall we?"

He crosses his arms over his chest. "Go for it."

"*Leos are known for their vibrant personalities.*" She widens her eyes at Stephen. "*They have strong self-assurance; they're very generous; they have magnetic personalities.*" She shoots him a look again. "*They're deeply loyal, passionate, optimistic, and dramatic.*"

He scoffs. "I am not dramatic."

I toss my head back and laugh. "Says the man who announced he was having a *coffee catastrophe* the other day because he woke up late and didn't have time to grab his usual coffee before class."

Presley holds her index finger up in the air. "And I offered to bring it to you while you were in class, to which you said that it wouldn't be the same because you always pet the barista's service dog..."

"And then you said the dog was going to think you abandoned her," I finish.

His eyebrows pull together. "Dogs are creatures of habit. She expects me at the same time every morning."

"Dogs can't tell time!"

Presley throws her head back as she laughs. "Come on. The description of your personality is pretty spot-on, baby." She presses a kiss to his cheek. "And that's okay, because those are all the reasons why I love you."

He grumbles as he nuzzles her neck.

I tip my chin. "Read yours, rebel."

Presley's thumbs fly across her screen before she clears her throat. "*Geminis are dynamic and versatile. They're adaptable; communicative; playful; and persuasive. They are known for their curiosity, as well as their social nature.*"

Stephen nods. "You are very social. Look at what you put together today."

My chest expands with pride. Presley organized a gathering for LGBTQ students so that they could connect with one another on campus. She worked on it for weeks, and though I'm not one for socializing, it was pretty awesome to see just how many queer students are here; how many people are just like the three of us.

Presley types some more, and I lean over her shoulder to get a glimpse of what she's reading. "The thing I love most about the zodiac is the way we are connected through our signs. Listen to this: *Leo and Aquarius are considered polar opposites.*" She holds up her phone to show us a circle containing each of the zodiac signs, with Leo and Aquarius on exact opposite sides. "*But this dynamic can actually create a powerful connection between them. Much like air breathes life into fire, air sign Aquarius breathes life into the fire of the Leo. They balance each other's needs, and have a strong magnetic attraction.*" Presley sets down her phone, and claps each of our hands. "So, you're basically written in the stars."

I lock eyes with Stephen. "You always say you believe in that destiny mumbo-jumbo."

He nods as he leans across Presley and cups my face. "The three of us are meant to be. We're meant for forever. I know it."

"The universe knows it too," Presley whispers.

It's funny how the idea of aliens seems more believable than being destined for love. But I keep my thoughts to myself. With the two of them looking at me the way they are, it's hard to argue.

I'll believe in anything they want me to.

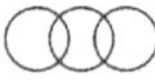

Stephen wraps an arm around Presley's waist as we get to our dorm room. "You had a big day today. You deserve a foot massage."

She hums. "That sounds like heaven right now."

I turn the doorknob and swing open the door, letting them walk into the room first.

Presley gasps, and Stephen's feet falter behind her. "Oh my God. What is this?"

I smirk as I slip my hands into my pockets and lean against the door to close it behind me, watching their reactions.

Stephen's head whips around to look at me. "You did this?"

"You mentioned you didn't end up going to prom because you got sick, and I never wanted to go...so I figured we could have a re-do." My eyes flick to Presley. "With our girl."

Presley's eyes bounce around from the string lights hanging from the ceiling to the glittery *PROM* sign I hung on the wall. Dozens of tea light candles dance around in the dimly-lit room. I take out my phone and hit play on the playlist I created, and a soft melody begins to play.

"This is..." She shakes her head. "I can't believe you did this."

Stephen's mouth flaps open and closed. "I can't believe you used glitter."

I roll my eyes. "It was an instant regret. I'm still finding specks of it on me."

He chuckles, and tugs me close. "Can I have this dance, boyfriend?"

I arch a brow. "Boyfriend...? That's presumptuous."

"You don't do all this," he waves his arm around the decorated room, "for someone who isn't your boyfriend."

I snake my arm around Presley's waist and pull her into our embrace, and the three of us start to move to the music. "Does that make you our girlfriend?"

She beams up at me. "It better."

"I've never been a boyfriend before."

"I think you're going to be the best boyfriend ever." She lets out a contented sigh and rests her head on my chest.

My gaze lifts to Stephen, and his crystal-blue eyes shine. "Thank you."

I bite back a smile.

Anything for these two.

I smile as Presley stretches her arms overhead, her eyes still closed as she wakes up.

"Good morning, pretty girl." I lean in and press my lips against her cheek. "I forgot how adorable you are when you wake up."

She groans, and buries her face in my chest. "Don't look at me."

I chuckle as I wrap myself around her warm body. "I love looking at you with your crazy hair, and your eye boogers."

"Don't forget the drool on her chin," Chance mumbles from the other side of the bed, his arm thrown over his eyes to shield himself from the sunlight streaming through the open curtains.

"Ew." Presley whines again. "You realize you guys could be waking up next to models instead of the tired, old mom, right?"

I slide my palm down her back and cup her ass. "I'd choose to wake up next to this MILF any day of the week. Besides, you think models don't drool in their sleep? They have bedhead just like everyone else."

Her head pops up and she hits me with a glare. "I don't want to know how you know that."

"No, no you don't."

Her eyes narrow into slits. "I will castrate you in your sleep."

"You two are doing way too much talking for the morning." Chance rolls over and sandwiches her between us, burying his face in her neck. "No castration talk before noon."

"No castration talk at all." I roll my morning wood against Presley. "You should be thanking Big Mac for last night instead of threatening him."

Presley coughs out a laugh. "Of course you named your dick Big Mac."

I grin with pride. "It's perfect, isn't it?"

"What's perfect is this bed," Chance murmurs. "Way better than the bed in our dorm room."

Presley hums as she rests her head back against Chances shoulder. "God, my body is so sore from the both of you. It's been so long since I've been fucked like that."

"Want me to fill up the bath for you?" Chance asks. "I'll cook us breakfast while you're soaking."

I smirk. "And I'll make you come while he's cooking."

She smiles. "A girl could get used to waking up like this."

I steal a chaste kiss before she can shove me back. "You're going to wake up like this every morning, pretty girl."

She pouts. "I wish."

My hands freeze along their exploration of her body. "You don't have to wish." I glance at Chance, who's watching me with a steady gaze. "We're here. We're together."

Presley leans up on her elbow, fully alert and awake now. "Well, not when the kids are here."

My chin jerks back. "Why not?"

"Because they can't know that we're sleeping together."

"Maybe not at first, but after some time, sure. That's what couples do."

"But we're not a couple." Presley scoots herself up and sits against the headboard. "We're...I don't know what we are. We got a little carried away last night."

Carried away?

Unease seeps into my gut as I sit up to face her. "Last night wasn't us getting carried away, or the result of too much alcohol. We're not strangers who had a one-night-stand. We're more than that."

Presley reaches out and clasps my hand. "I know that. I didn't mean to make it sound cheap. But we can't just throw ourselves into a relationship as if we're picking back up where we left off four years ago. Things are different now."

"Avery and Alyssa already love us. I don't see what the problem is here."

She wrings her hands in her lap. "I know they do, but…it's more than that. It's—"

"You're worried about what people will think of you," Chance finishes.

Presley's chin drops as she stares at the comforter.

She doesn't deny it.

What?

Presley was never one to shy away from her desires. She was outgoing and secure in who she was; it was one of the things that attracted me to her in the beginning. Chance was the one who had a tough time with societal views on our relationship, and that was understandable with the way he was raised.

But never Presley.

I tip her chin and bring her eyes back to mine. "You don't want people to know that we're together?"

"I work in an elementary school where parents make comments about my tattoos. Imagine what they'd say if they found out I was in a relationship with two men. And even if that wasn't a problem, I don't want Avery and Alyssa to be affected by my decisions. You've seen how cruel kids can be. I don't want to make their lives any harder than it already has been."

My heart sinks. "So, what then? We're together in private, and pretend like we're single to the rest of the world? Stay in hiding and let all the uptight, close-minded people win? Because that's not what I'm about. That's not what I stand for."

"I have to put the kids first, Stephen." Presley's eyebrows pinch together. "And we're not in college anymore. I'm a grown adult with adult responsibilities. I don't have the kind of lifestyle you guys do. You travel, you're in the spotlight, and you have more money than you know what to do with. You have people who handle your schedule, and drivers who take you wherever you need to go. I don't have that kind of life."

"But you can. You know we'd take care of you *and* the kids. They're important to you, so of course they're important to us. I'm not trying to take you out of your life, or change it in any way. I just want to be with you, and help you with anything you need." I swallow around the lump in my throat. "I just want to love you."

Tears well in her eyes. "You make it sound so simple."

"Because to me, it is that simple." I suck in a breath, knowing I'm not only trying to convince Presley, but Chance. "As long as we're together, we can handle anything that comes our way. Fuck anyone who doesn't stand with us. There will always be people with their anti-gay campaigns; people who get off on tearing others down; people who spread hate instead of love. But that doesn't mean we have to mold our lives around their beliefs. Look at Jason, Celeste, and Kourtney. They came out and took a stand, and changed the world of hockey. We can show the world that love looks different for everyone, and be happy together—the five of us."

"I don't know if the kids and I are ready for all that." Tears well in Presley's eyes. "And even if I was, we know Chance isn't ready for it either."

"I am."

Both of our heads snap to Chance.

"I understand why you're worried, and I agree that it won't be easy on the kids," he continues. "And if you need time, I'm willing to give you however long you need. You want the kids to be a little older? Done. You want to wait until they go off to college? Fine. You want us to sleep in separate rooms? I'll build an addition off the side of this fucking house. But I need you to know—" he pauses to look directly at me, "I'm ready to come out."

Presley and I are quiet. I think we're frozen. Stunned.

I never thought I'd hear those words from his mouth.

Presley slips her hand into his. "Are you serious?"

His jaw works under his skin as his coal eyes flick between the both of us. "Being around Avery has made me realize that I don't want to feel ashamed of who I am anymore. I don't want him to feel that way, so I should be able to lead by example, and show him that he deserves to love himself and feel confident in who he is. And so do I."

Tears stream down Presley's face as she throws her arms around his neck. "I'm so proud of you."

Emotion strangles me, making it nearly impossible to speak as I blink back my own tears.

Chance arches a brow. "I never thought I'd see the day when Stephen McKinley is speechless."

I chuckle, and tug him closer to me. "There's nothing I could say that would top the words that just came out of your mouth."

Chance holds each of us in his arms, and I let out a long breath of relief. If this is what he wants, then we'll both show Presley how possible our relationship is.

"What do you say, pretty girl?" I pull back and cup her face in my hands. "Are you willing to give this a try? You can set the pace. You make the rules. Just tell us that you want this, and we'll take care of you and the kids for the rest of our lives."

Another tear rolls down her cheek as she nods. "Of course I want this. I just don't know how it's going to look, or how to navigate it."

"We navigate it together," Chance whispers. "You're not doing this alone anymore."

Presley's shoulders shake as she sobs, and we hold her, letting her fall apart after years of holding it together for the kids.

And the three of us kiss, with morning breath and crust in our eyes, and I wouldn't want it any other way.

This is the best day of my life.

It's finally my turn.

Our turn.

Forever finally starts now.

"THE ONLY PERSON WHO SMILES THIS MUCH ON A MONDAY morning is a person who got dicked down over the weekend."

I smirk as I arrange the books on a display stand I've been working on. "I'm still not telling you about it."

When I went to pick the kids up from Dominique's house on Saturday morning, I refused to tell her anything that happened. Serves her right for sneaking around and plotting with the boys.

Dominique whines as she slumps into the chair behind my desk. "Come on. You can't punish me forever. The reason you get to smile like that is because I told the boys to dick you down in the first place!"

"Okay, you're not wrong there." I hold up my index finger. "But you didn't run it by me first, and you do not get to go behind my back and talk to the boys about said dicking."

"Fine, I promise I'll never do it again. Just please tell me what happened, I'm begging you."

Glancing up at the clock on the wall above us, I shake my head. "I'll call you tonight after the kids are asleep."

She lets out a frustrated groan. "Fine. I suppose I can survive all day."

I step back from the new book display. "Done. What do you think?"

Dominique's eyebrows shoot up. "Wow, I didn't even know we carried books like these in our library. This is amazing."

"That's the point." I cross my arms over my chest. "Kids should know that they have access to books like these."

The title of my display says, "All Families Look Different." I picked out specific books that illustrate families with two moms or two dads; families that are from different countries or speak different languages; families with disabilities; and families that look like Avery and Alyssa's, without a parent raising them, or with adoptive parents.

"I want the children in our school to know that being different is a good thing." I lower myself into the chair beside Dominique. "Maybe if we promote more of that at the elementary level, kids won't be so mean when they get to be Avery's age."

Dominique rubs my arm. "How has it been at school for him since the team paid them a visit?"

"Things seem to have calmed down. Avery said the bullies haven't bothered with him or anyone else."

"I hope it lasts."

"You and me both."

The bell rings, and Dominique scurries to her classroom while I head outside for my morning bus duty.

Wearing a shit-eating grin because I got dicked down this weekend.

"Ms. King, do you have a moment?"

I drop my car keys back into my purse and set it down on my desk. "Of course. Is everything okay?"

My boss, Principal Ware, gestures to the display I put up this morning. "Molly mentioned something about your new book display."

I clench my jaw and fight against rolling my eyes. Molly is the PTO president, and the stereotypical "I act like I'm a kind, Jesus-loving Catholic, but I'm really just a judgmental bitch who quotes the Bible when it suits me" kind of parent. She talks about everyone behind their backs, and then smiles in their faces. I know this because I've been on the receiving end of her two-faced comments regarding my tattoos.

Imagine if Regina George became a mom—before she got hit by the bus.

"Oh?" I feign ignorance. "I'm so glad she liked it."

I don't miss the smile my boss tries to hide. "We both know how Molly can be, so I'll cut to the chase: She doesn't think some of your book choices are appropriate for the kids."

My eyes flick to the book, *My Two Moms*. "Really? Which ones in particular?"

Principal Ware clears his throat. "The one with two moms, and the other with two dads."

My eyebrows shoot up as I try to maintain my composure. "And why does she feel those are inappropriate? Gay marriage is legal, and even celebrated in the state of New Jersey."

"Her issue is with the age of the students in our building. She thinks they're too young to be exposed to this kind of topic."

I cross my arms over my chest. "And what do *you* think?"

Because I don't answer to Molly.

He heaves a sigh. "I think it's a controversial topic."

Great. A non-answer.

"So, are you telling me this because you're asking me to take down the display, or...?"

"I'm not asking you to take it down, no. I'm letting you know so that you're aware." He grimaces. "I know Molly can be unpleasant to deal with."

I let out a humorless laugh. "Thanks for the heads-up, Principal Ware. And for the record, there are students in this school with two mothers, and there might be others who are realizing at this young age that they're gay, so I think it's important to show our support."

"I agree."

"I'd also like to point out that our school carries these kinds of books—I didn't bring them in from my own personal library."

He chuckles. "You're not on trial, Ms. King. I simply wanted to inform you before you heard something in the rumor mill."

I nod, and stuff down my simmering anger. "Thank you, sir. I appreciate it."

On the ride to pick up Avery and Alyssa from school, I call Dominique.

"What a little tattletale! I can't believe she went to the principal," Dominique's voice blares through my Bluetooth speaker.

"Seriously, like don't you have something more important to do?" I grip the steering wheel so hard, my knuckles turn white. "She's killing my vibe. I was in such a good mood today; I was feeling hopeful."

"Don't let Miserable Molly kill your vibe. She's not worth a second thought. She's just jealous because she's not getting any dick, and you've got two."

I tip my head back as I laugh. "God forbid that woman finds out."

"If she has anything to say about it, she can come talk to me. I'll sort her out *real* quick."

I smile at my best friend's loyalty.

"You said you feel *hopeful*. Care to share with the rest of the class?" she asks.

Warmth spreads throughout my chest as I roll to a stop at the red light in front of me. "Chance said he's ready to come out, and Stephen wants the three of us to be together—for real, like in a relationship."

"That's a big deal for Chance. I'm so happy to hear it."

"Me too. He's been through so much, and I'm really glad he's finally embracing who he truly is."

"And you know the kids love them. Shit, Alyssa looks at Stephen like he hung the moon, and Avery has really opened up with Chance around."

"I know. They've been so great with the kids." Tears sting the back of my eyes. "I want this so bad, Dom. It was so difficult to leave them, and now that they're back in my life, I want to run full-speed into them."

"That's the best feeling. You deserve this, Pres. You deserve to be happy. You've sacrificed so much for those kids, and they deserve to see you happy too."

"But then someone like Molly comes along." I roll my eyes. "And all my fears resurface."

Dominique sighs. "There's always going to be a Molly. The world is filled with ignorant, stupid people. But you can't worry about them. Surround yourself with people who love and support you, and enjoy your happiness."

"I know you're right." I chew my bottom lip. "And if it were just me, I wouldn't bat an eye. Molly can go fuck herself. But I have to think about the kids, and I want to make sure I'm doing right by them."

"You're showing them what acceptance and equality and human rights looks like."

"But I'm also putting them into the line of fire when it comes to people's ugly, hateful comments. I don't want Avery to start getting bullied all over again, or have kids start giving Alyssa a hard time."

She barks out a laugh. "You don't have to worry about our girl. She'll have no problem punching someone right in his mouth if he has anything to say."

146

I smile. "Yes, but I don't want to put her in that position to begin with."

"I hear you. But you can't shield them from everything. This is adversity, and it'll make them stronger."

"I hope you're right." I groan. "I wish my sister was alive so I could have her blessing with all of this."

"Maybe your sister is the one who sent these boys back into your life. Ever think of that?"

I sit in silence while I contemplate the possibility. *It's a nice notion.*

"The Lord works in mysterious ways. Just go ask Molly, and she'll tell you all about it."

I laugh loud and hard. "I love you, Dom."

"Good, because you're stuck with me."

"Fuck, yes!"

I fly around the back of the net and crash into Alexander, slapping his helmet. "Atta boy, Krum!"

Another goal brings the score to 2-1. Florida isn't making it easy for us; the game has been tense, and we were tied for the first two periods.

This final period is ours though, not only because I love winning, but because my people are here—Chance, Presley, Avery, and Alyssa—and they're all wearing my jersey.

My eyes dart to the glass as I skate back to our side of the rink. Alyssa waves frantically, holding up a giant foam finger, while Avery dodges it so he doesn't get hit in the face. My throat tightens at the sight of them, and a sense of belonging sinks deep into my bones. I've always dreamed of having a family of my own; of having people I love cheering me on at my games; of getting to take care of them, and share my love with them.

Chance says something to Presley, whispering it in her ear, and she tosses her head back as she laughs. Her hair is tied up in a messy bun, and she looks so fucking adorable in my oversized jersey. My heart swells. I never thought I'd see her again, yet here she is, filling the hole she once left in my heart.

Chance gazes down at her with an unbridled smile on his usually stoic face, and it takes my breath away. All I've ever wanted for him was to be happy; to know his worth; to feel loved. Losing Presley made me lose him too, and it was so damn hard seeing him on the ice and not being able to have him the way we used to be.

It feels like a dream, having them both back in my life again.

Chance's dark eyes meet mine as I purposely skate past their seats, and he shoots me a wink. He looks absolutely fuckable in a black backwards hat and my name across his back—something I know wasn't easy for him to wear.

Desire lights my skin on fire as Presley bites her bottom lip, a hidden promise for later reflecting in her gaze.

Fuck, I need to focus.

Can't win this game with a boner.

I snap back into position, and Florida sends the puck down the ice. I intercept it and pass it to Alexander for a breakaway. The crowd roars as he skates past their defense, and I fly up on his right. He passes it back to me and I take the shot.

The buzzer goes off, and that familiar rush of victory takes over me.

My head immediately snaps to my loves in the stands. Avery lifts Alyssa and spins her around, while Chance and Presley are on their feet, arms overhead, clapping and cheering.

For me.

My teammates slap me on the back as I make my way to the boards. I stop in front of Chance and Presley, and press my gloved hand against the glass. Presley reaches out and flattens her palm against the other side, gazing up at me with pride. To my surprise, Chance covers her hand with his to join us. It's a small gesture, but it's a momentous deal; he's showing me that he's serious about what he said—he's ready to be out, to be with me, with us.

Emotion strangles me as I reluctantly tear myself away from the glass and force myself to head into the locker room.

The locker room smells like sweat and victory, and the guys are all buzzing with excitement. I pull off my gear and shower at lightning speed.

"Let's go out and celebrate, Mac." Trenton nudges me with his elbow after we're dressed. "Where do you wanna go?"

I grin. "There's only one place I want to be right now, and it's not in a bar."

He coughs out an incredulous laugh. "Hell has frozen over. Mac doesn't want to party?"

"Nope." I wink. "Just a no-pants party of three for me tonight."

Jason laughs. "Yeah, same."

We high-five each other while the other guys hoot and slap us in the asses with their dirty towels.

"Be jealous, motherfuckers," I shout as I hold my arms out wide as I walk backward toward the door. "I'm about to have the hottest sex you'll never get to experience in your life."

The kids are asleep by the time I get to Presley's house.

She lets me peek in on them, and I chuckle when I spot Alyssa passed out in her bed, still clutching the foam finger.

"She was so pumped when you scored that last goal," Presley whispers as she closes the door to Alyssa's bedroom. "I doubt she'll have a voice left tomorrow."

I grin with pride. "And Avery? Did he enjoy the game?"

She nods. "I even caught him snapping a few pictures and videos—that's teenager for him having a good time."

I press her up against the wall in the hallway, breathing in her sweet scent. "What about you, pretty girl? Did you have a good time tonight?"

"You know I did." She lifts her arms around the back of my neck. "I still get turned on watching you play."

My dick twitches. "And I still get turned on seeing you in my jersey."

She brushes her nose against me. "Take it off me."

I scoop her into my arms and her legs wrap around my waist. I stride the rest of the way to her room, and lock the door behind us. Chance is waiting on the bed, sitting up against the headboard—still wearing my jersey.

I toss Presley onto the bed, drinking in the sight of them with my number sprawled across their bodies.

Palming my dick over my sweatpants, I groan. "Never thought I'd see the day Chance Kellerman would wear a Goldfinches jersey."

He arches a brow. "I only did it so it'd break your concentration on the game. Figured you'd end up losing, and give my team the upper hand when we play you next week."

I pull my hoodie over my head, and drop it to the floor along with my T-shirt and pants. "I'll let you lie to me if it makes you feel better. We both know the real reason you wore it."

He lifts his chin. "And why's that?"

I crawl onto the bed and kiss my way up Presley's bare thighs, keeping my eyes locked on Chance. "Because you want the world to know you're mine."

He watches me, and says nothing to deny it.

My dick hardens at the thought of everyone in that arena seeing my name on both of their backs—knowing that they support me, that they were there for me.

I slide my hands underneath Presley's jersey, and drag her thong down her legs. Then I nestle between her lush thighs, and skim a soft lick along her pussy.

"God damn, I've been thinking of this all day." I close my eyes and breathe her in, pressing open-mouthed sloppy kisses against her most sensitive spot.

Chance leans over and captures her mouth, swallowing her moan. "You're going to have to keep quiet, baby. Think you can do that for us?"

She shakes her head and lets out a breathy, "No."

I smile. "That's okay, pretty girl. Chance will help you."

I devour her pussy, relentlessly teasing and licking and sucking, not coming up for air until I've had my fill. Chance lies beside her and kisses her, lazily pumping his dick in slow strokes as he watches me work her over. When her thighs start to shake, Presley reaches down and grips two handfuls of my hair. Her back arches off the mattress, and Chance kisses her hard so she can't scream out.

Which is such a shame, because I love the sound of my name on her lips.

Chance and I kiss and caress every inch of her skin while she comes down from her high. Then she moves onto all fours, and tosses me a devious smirk over her shoulder.

I groan, and smooth my palm over her ass before giving it a firm smack. "You are the sexiest thing I've ever seen."

She arches a brow. "How are *you* going to keep quiet now, hmm?"

"I've been trying to figure out that mystery for years," Chance murmurs. I flip him off and he smirks as he shifts onto his knees in front of Presley. "Let's see who she can make come first."

I scoff. "I've got stamina for days, baby."

Presley shakes her head as she takes Chance's cock into her hand, backing her ass up to my hips at the same time—silencing us both. "Less talking, more fucking."

"Yes, ma'am." Chance's eyes roll back in his head as she sucks him all the way into her mouth. "*Fuck.*"

I rub myself against her ass, teasing myself before I reach over into her nightstand to look for condoms. There's a brand-new box inside, and I chuckle to myself. *My girl got prepared.* I tear off one from the pack, and roll it over my length.

Chance threads his fingers through Presley's hair and holds her head steady as he thrusts his hips forward. His muscles flex, his jaw slack as he gazes down at her, and my dick grows impossibly hard at the sight of him at her mercy.

I coat myself in her arousal, and press my crown against her entrance. I push slow inch by inch, until I'm buried as deep as I can go. Then I pull all the way out, and do it again. And again.

"I love filling you up like this, pretty girl—me inside your tight pussy while you swallow his cock."

Presley's back arches, and I can hear the sound of her breathy moans as her head stops bobbing in front of Chance.

"Our girl loves it too. She can barely suck me off while you're fucking her like that." Chance caresses her face with the back of his hand. "Don't worry, baby. I've got you."

His grip on her hair tightens as his hand forms a fist, and he begins fucking her mouth. I match his rhythm and plunge in and out of her, hard and fast.

She loves to be used, to let us take control. She trusts us, and she knows we're the only ones who can make her feel this way.

Chance leans over and grabs the back of my neck, hauling my mouth to his. We fuck Presley, and enjoy each other at the same time, each of us so in tune with the other.

"You ready to come yet?" I taunt Chance, nipping at his bottom lip.

He arches a brow. "Looking for an easy out?"

"Hardly." I slow my pace, and fuck Presley in slow, deep strokes as she lets out a muffled moan. "How many times do you think we can make our girl come?"

Chance reaches down and caresses her face. "We're going to take our time with you tonight, baby. You think you can handle us?"

She nods as she takes his cock deeper into her mouth, gagging as she does, and pushes her ass against me.

"Yeah, of course you can," Chance murmurs, his gaze fixed on her lips where she's wrapped around him. "Make her come, Stephen. I want to hear her try to moan my name while she's choking on my dick."

With one hand gripping her hip, I slip the other underneath her body and play with her clit while I drive into her, fast and hard the way I know she loves to be fucked right before she comes.

Chance talks her through it while she ascends. "Such a good girl taking the both of us like this, baby. You're going to soak his cock with that pretty little pussy while you take me down your throat. You love being filled up, don't you, hmm? Yeah, you fucking do."

My dick throbs as Chance continues, and I have to use all of my focus not to blow too soon.

Presley's moans get louder, so Chance thrusts his hips and gags her. Her pussy becomes impossibly wetter, the sound of my dick sliding in and out of her echoing throughout the room.

"She's close," I whisper. Her walls swell and clench me so tight. "Come for us, pretty girl."

"That's right, baby." Chance grips her face in both hands, holding her still while he thrusts in and out of her mouth. "Just like that. Let go."

Presley falls apart, her entire body shaking as her core spasms around me.

Chance's mouth drops open, and I know by that look on his face that he's close too. I haul his mouth to mine, and swallow his groans as he comes down Presley's throat. And once both of them are riding through the aftershocks, I finally allow myself to have my turn. My jaw clenches as I try to stifle my sounds.

Chance shifts on the bed and takes my face into his hands while I pump my release. "You look so beautiful when you come, Stephen."

I capture his lips, and surrender everything to him—to them.

They can have all of me, all of my heart.

It's always belonged to them, even after all this time.

And I'll fight like hell to keep them this time, no matter what.

"Would you stop fussing with your hair? You look great."

I drop my hands at my sides and take two giant steps back from the phone. "One last look. What do we think?"

"I think you look like a hot rock princess." Dominique fans herself with her hand. "Those fishnets with the combat boots look badass."

A smile creeps onto my face. "I haven't been to a concert in so long."

"I'm really glad you're allowing yourself to have some fun, Pres. Happiness looks good on you."

Warmth spreads through my chest. "Thanks. Okay, let me go. I'll call you tomorrow."

"You better."

We end the call, and I stare at my reflection in the mirror for one more lingering moment. I'm only twenty-six, but I feel a lot older. The last four years taking care of my niece and nephew have been a lot for me, and I haven't allowed myself to enjoy my twenties as much as everyone else usually does.

But tonight, in my tied-up Breaking Benjamin T-shirt and black leather mini-skirt, I feel like I'm getting a piece of myself back. The kids are at their friends' houses for a sleepover, and I'm going out on a date with my boyfriends.

I glance at the picture of my sister sitting on my dresser, and I press a kiss to my fingertips before touching it to the frame. "Love you, sis'."

The doorbell rings and pulls me from my thoughts. I snatch my clutch off the bed and head downstairs.

Stephen and Chance are both waiting on the porch when I swing open the door, each holding a bouquet of red roses.

Stephen wastes no time in lunging for me, and I squeal as he lifts and spins me. "You look fucking hot!"

I laugh as he sets me down and steadies me. "You look hot yourself."

His muscles pop in his fitted white T-shirt, brightening those crystal-blue eyes of his. I drink my fill of him, my gaze trailing down his biceps and along his forearms, smattered with freckles.

I gasp as I spot the black leather bracelet wrapped around his wrist. "Oh my God, is that...?"

"Of course it is." He holds it up proudly, gesturing to the three silver circles at the center. "I figured our first official date was the perfect time to break it out."

"You saved it after all this time?"

"You were always with me, even when you weren't."

My eyes shift to Chance, and linger on the matching bracelet on his wrist. "You too?"

He nods once. "Always."

I wrap my arms around his waist, breathing in his familiar scent. "You look sexy, my Grumpy Man."

The sleeves of his black dress shirt are rolled up, putting his vascular forearms on display. The top two buttons are undone, revealing his smooth olive skin. His messy dark hair falls over his obsidian eyes.

They look so different, my men. Opposites in every way, yet their contrasting traits complement each other so well. They are the perfect balance.

And I get to have them both.

"I'll be right back." I spin around and dart back upstairs, making a beeline for my bedroom. I rummage through my jewelry box, and pull out the necklace Stephen gave me years ago, and run back downstairs.

"Put it on for me, please?" I hand it to Stephen and turn around in front of him.

He leans down and presses his soft lips to the side of my neck, and goosebumps trail along my skin. He clasps the necklace, and I smile wide as my fingertips come up to touch the silver circles.

The three of us are back together.

Maybe this really could be forever.

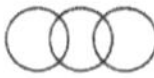

Chance smirks as he gazes down at me. "Did you think we'd be sitting in the nosebleed section?"

I laugh. "No, I suppose not with the two of you."

I expected good seats, but I didn't anticipate the VIP balcony area to the left of the stage. If I leaned down, I could reach out and touch Benjamin Burnley whenever he jumps onto the speaker below us.

Stephen leans in as he shouts over the music. "These seats are much more private. Plus, I didn't feel like getting into a fight in the mosh pit."

I scoff, feigning offense. "I don't know what you're talking about. I don't get into fights."

He tosses his head back and laughs. "No, you just cause them."

Chance nods as his smirk turns into a smile. "I thought we were going to die that night. That chick's boyfriend was the biggest dude I've ever seen—and I play hockey."

Stephen pats my shoulder. "Before you shove a girl onto the ground, make sure her boyfriend isn't Sasquatch."

I shrug. "She got what she deserved. Flick your hair in my face multiple times, and you're going to get shoved."

Chance shakes his head. "My little rebel."

The music changes and I cheer. *Angels Fall* is my favorite song. I hold my arms over my head as I belt out the first verse, closing my eyes and swaying to the melody.

Chance slides behind me, wrapping his hands around my waist, and his fingers skim along my exposed skin. I lean back against him, pressing against his hard body as he sings along.

Stephen moves closer to us, and I crane my neck to watch as he leans in and kisses Chance. My heart swells whenever I see them together, knowing how far they've come to get to this point—especially for a second time.

I try to move, to turn around in Chance's arms, but his grip tightens on my waist and he holds me in place. Stephen slips his fingers underneath my skirt, and my eyes dart around to check if anyone's able to see us.

"Relax," Chance's deep voice is at my ear, and I shiver.

"In front of everyone like this?" I ask.

"Let's give them a show, pretty girl." Stephen nips at my other ear. "You can be as loud as you want in here."

His fingers hook into the holes of my fishnets, and he yanks. I gasp as he tears open the crotch, and finds his way underneath my thong.

"Think you can make our girl come before the song ends?" Chance shouts.

Stephen chuckles. "You know I can."

His fingers swirl over my clit and I let out a loud moan, but the drums and bass swallow my sounds.

Chance slips his hand under my shirt and cups my breast. "Look at all those people down there, completely unaware that Stephen is rubbing that pretty pussy of yours. I wonder if the guitarist can see you from the stage."

My core clenches as adrenaline courses through me, mixing with desire. "You okay with that, letting them see what's yours?"

"Let them look." He pushes up my shirt and tugs down one of the cups of my bra, completely exposing my breast. "Let them see what they're missing." He pinches my nipple at the same time Stephen slips his long finger inside me. "This perfect body of yours belongs to us. You haven't given it to anyone else while we've been away, have you?"

I shake my head as sweat forms on my forehead. "No. Nobody."

Stephen pumps his finger in and out of me before adding a second. I cry out, and he uses the opportunity to slip his tongue inside my mouth. He kisses me, slow and sensual, the same way he's working my pussy.

"You knew nobody could take care of this body the way we did," Chance continues. "You were saving yourself for us, and you didn't even know it."

"I did though," Stephen says as he rips his mouth away from mine. "I knew you would come back to us eventually."

My chest heaves as the pleasure mounts, and I rock my hips against Stephen's fingers. "Y-you did?"

"I did." He taps on my necklace. "A circle is forever. There was never going to be an ending for us. We might have gone our separate ways for a while, but we were always going to come back around."

Chance trails his hand down my stomach and toys with my clit while Stephen's finger fucks me faster.

The faint sound of the bridge of the song playing in the background tells me that we only have another minute to go.

"You didn't want anyone else but us, did you, baby?" Chance whispers.

"No." My heart races as I reach up behind me and grab the back of Chance's neck with one hand, and cup Stephen's face with the other. "I belong to the both of you. Always."

Stephen kisses me hard while Chance sucks on my neck.

And as the crowd chants along to the final lyrics of the song, I come—loud and unrestrained. My body shakes, and Chance holds me up while Stephen milks every second of my orgasm.

"That's our good little rebel." Chance's deep voice is like liquid sex in my ear. "Coming for us in front of everyone like the slut you are. I knew she was in there, all this time just begging to come out and play."

Stephen slips his fingers out of me, and pushes them inside Chance's mouth. "Tell me that's not the best thing you've ever tasted."

Chance hums as his eyes close, and I get turned on all over again watching his lips wrap around Stephen's thick fingers.

"I got us backstage passes," Stephen says with a sly grin. "Think we can find a storage closet somewhere back there?"

Chance grabs us each by the hand, and yanks us toward the stairs.

God, I've missed this.

Junior Year

"Would you stop eating my fries?" Presley slaps Stephen's hand as he tries to sneak another. "Try it again and you're coming back with less than five fingers next time."

Stephen waggles his eyebrows. "Pretty girl is so feisty when she's hungry."

Presley scoots closer to me in the booth. "Protect my honor, Chance."

I wrap my arm around her waist, relishing in the feel of her snuggled against me. "You can't listen to him when he says he doesn't want fries. Next time, we need to get two orders just for him."

Stephen feigns offense. "Don't body shame me. I'm a growing boy. Plus, sharing food is romantic." He sticks one end of a fry in his mouth, and leans over the table. "Come on."

Presley giggles as she bites off the other end, and Stephen lunges forward for a kiss.

The pizzeria is crowded, everyone fueling up before attending tonight's big football game. I'd rather spend the night holed up in my room, just the three of us, but Presley begged us to come out being that her best friend's boyfriend is playing. Since she comes to every one of our games, we figured it was only fair.

The three of us have been inseparable for the last few months, and I've been floating on a cloud. It's surreal having found not one but two incredible people to share these feelings with.

Stephen keeps the conversation going, as usual, eyes wide and hands flying around him as he talks. Presley smiles across the table at him, entertaining his story about God knows what. Being part of their worlds gives me a sense of home that I've never felt. I feel safe. Cared for. Like I matter to someone—*two* someones.

I don't know how I got so lucky. I don't know how any of this happened. But I'm going to hold on as tight as I can and never let them go.

"Oh, I almost forgot." Stephen reaches into his backpack and pulls out two small wrapped packages. He slides them across the table to us with a sly grin. "I got you guys something."

Presley tears at the wrapping paper, her excitement matching Stephen's.

A present? Why? "What is this?" I can't help but ask.

"It's a gift." Stephen nudges it toward me. "Open it and you'll see."

Presley opens a long rectangular box to reveal a silver necklace with three interlocking circles in the center.

Her eyes fill with tears as she blinks up to Stephen. "Three circles for the three of us."

Stephen nods as he takes the necklace from her and fastens it around her neck. "Connected forever."

Forever.

The word seems too unreal.

I unwrap my box, and open it to find the same three silver circles as Presley's, but they're in the middle of a black leather band instead of a dainty silver chain.

"I have one too." Stephen pushes up his sleeve to show us.

"It's beautiful," Presley murmurs, clasping Stephen's hand and leaning her head on my shoulder. "I love us."

A lump forms in my throat. "Thank you," is all I can push out without giving way to my emotions.

I've never had anything like this before, and I'm terrified to lose it.

I lost my mom, and I haven't been able to trust anything in life since.

Until now.

"Can we always be like this?" Presley asks.

I tilt my head to look at her. "Like what?"

"The three of us, together. No matter what."

Stephen takes a bite of pizza, nodding immediately. "Of course."

I laugh. "You say it so easily."

"What's so difficult about it? We can work through anything that comes our way. We're there for each other in good times and bad." He shrugs and takes another bite of pizza. "It's not hard to stay true to the people you love."

My heart stalls out, and Presley sits up ramrod straight. "You just said *love*."

Stephen's freckled cheeks redden, but he lifts his chin with his ever-present confidence. "Yeah, I did."

"You...love us?" she asks.

"I do." His eyes lock with hers before flicking to mine. "Pres, you are the woman of my dreams, and Chance—you're the man of mine."

I don't know anything about love. Never have, and assumed I never would. I didn't have the best example of it growing up. But now...with these two incredible people in my life, it's hard to believe that it doesn't exist.

"I love you too, Stephen." Presley leans over the table and presses a soft kiss to his lips. Then she turns to me. "And I love you, my grumpy man."

They love me.

Not for who I'm pretending to be, but for who I truly am.

"I love you, Pres." My voice sounds raw as I speak the three words I never thought I'd say to someone, to anyone.

I kiss Presley's forehead, and then take Stephen's hand into mine—on top of the table, for everyone to see. "I love you."

Stephen grins like it's the best thing he's ever heard.

The three of us are connected now.

Forever.

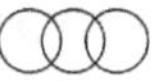

We're quiet after we get back to the dorm.

I didn't pay much attention to the football game. Couldn't even tell you who won. I was too focused on the three words shared between us during dinner.

Something feels different between us. Heavier. More serious.

Real.

I'm not good with my words, so I need to express my feelings through actions. I walk Presley backward until her shoulders hit Stephen's chest, sandwiching her between us.

I tip her chin and take her mouth, wasting no time in claiming her. Stephen lowers to his knees and pulls off her pants before coming back up and taking her shirt with him, until she stands between us completely naked.

She steps to the side, and runs her hands over her hips as she looks between us. "Stephen, kiss him."

My dick jumps at her request. I'm always the one in charge, the one who calls the shots when we're naked together.

Stephen obeys, not hesitating for a second before his lips are on mine. I open for him and our tongues tangle, stroking against the other while peeling each other's clothes off until our hands can roam freely over every inch of hard muscles and smooth skin. I match the intensity rolling off of him, and lose myself completely in his kiss.

I glance at Presley and find her fingers playing between her legs while she watches. Her eyes lock with mine. "Get on your knees, Chance."

I arch a brow as I lower myself at Stephen's feet. "Feeling bold tonight, are we?"

She smirks as she lifts her leg and sets her foot on the mattress beside her, and spreads open her pussy with her fingers. "You're going to see what a good boy you can be for me."

The sight of her wet, glistening pussy has me ready to oblige her, and she knows it.

"I'm at your service, rebel." I grasp Stephen's cock in my palm, and suck on the tip. "This what you want?"

She lets out a small moan. "Yes."

She can have the control. She can have it all. I'll do anything this woman wants.

My eyes flick up to Stephen as I take him fully into my mouth, groaning around his length. My tongue trails over his veins, relishing in the feel of his thickness stretching my jaw.

His fingers brush back my hair from my forehead, and then curl into the thick of it at the top of my head. "*Such* a good fucking boy."

I work him with my mouth while Presley rubs her clit, praising us the entire time.

Then Stephen's hips start to rock on their own, his movements fast and erratic. He's close.

"Enough," Presley says, and I let Stephen's dick fall from my mouth with a pop. She glances up at him. "On your knees next to him."

Stephen sinks down onto the carpet beside me. We wait in silence for our next order.

"Crawl to me—both of you. Come and have a taste of what's yours."

Each of us falls forward onto our hands, and we stalk over to our girl. We feast on her until her legs tremble, and we lap up her arousal when she comes.

Presley yanks us up by our hair, her pupils dilated and chest heaving with ragged breaths. She looks drunk on desire, and we've only just begun.

I cup her face and drag her lips to mine. "What's next, baby? Tell us what's on your mind."

"Fuck him," she whispers. "I want you to fuck Stephen while he fucks me."

My eyes fly to Stephen, nerves and excitement swirling together.

It's the one line we haven't crossed yet, the last wall of mine left to come down.

He nods as his beautiful, crystal eyes hold mine. "I'm ready if you are."

He said he'd wait for me.

He said he loves me.

He's been patient, and I know it's time.

"I'm ready." I grip the back of his neck and crash my mouth against his, as my other arm snakes around Presley's waist, pulling her into our kiss.

We're a mess of tongues and lips and breath and hands, each of us taking what we need from the others.

And what I need right now is control.

My teeth scrape Presley's bottom lip as I pull away. "Get on the bed and spread those pretty thighs for us."

She lies down on her back while I gather the condoms and lube in the bedside table. Stephen gets on top of her, and for a moment I watch them together. The way he caresses her face is the same way he caresses mine. The way he looks into her eyes with such sincerity, it's the same loving look he gives me. The way he kisses her is the same way he kisses me, with devotion and the promise of forever.

If Presley is the glue that brings us together, Stephen is the rock that remains solid and sure to keep us here.

I climb onto the bed behind him, and pepper kisses along his broad back while he rubs his cock over Presley's slick pussy. "You ready for us, rebel?" I ask.

She bites her bottom lip as she nods.

I bring my lips to Stephen's ear, pressing my dick against him. "And you, baby? You ready for me?"

He turns his head and reaches for me, bringing my lips to his. "I've been ready for a long time. I'm glad you finally got on the same page."

I chuckle. "I can't wait to fuck that sass right out of you."

I roll the condom on for him, and then he pushes himself inside Presley. My dick throbs at the sounds she makes while she's getting fucked, and my hand shakes as roll on the condom and pour the lubricant over myself.

Tonight, it's about more than sex. More than a primal, physical desire.

Tonight, it's about love. A deep connection tethering the three of us for the rest of our lives.

Forever.

Is that even a possibility?

My mind can't fathom such a surreal thought. But I know I'm all in, for however long this will last.

Pressing my crown against Stephen's opening, time stands still. I work myself inside him, watching as he takes me. He lets out short, shallow breaths, bracing himself as he's stretched open.

"Relax, baby," I whisper. "Let me inside."

Presley cradles his face and kisses him softly while I watch the way my cock disappears inside of him, slow inch by slow inch. I push against the resistance and then pull back out, only to push back in, deeper and deeper until his ass is filled with everything I've got.

My body shudders once I'm all the way in. "Fuck, baby. This feels too good."

He's squeezing me, his hole constricting so tight around me.

Stephen's eyes are squeezed shut, and he rests his forehead against Presley's. "This is incredible, filled with you while I'm filling her."

I smooth my left hand over his hip while using my other hand to caress Presley's leg, hiking it up around Stephen's waist so I can feel her while I fuck him. "You two better hold onto each other."

Stephen drags himself out of Presley, and when he plunges back inside, I rock into him. I match his pace, letting his body tell me what he needs. Our bodies are slick with sweat, our breaths panting and ragged. Each of us chases our own ecstasy while bringing the other to theirs. Our eyes are closed, lost in the moment, lost in each other, letting our sense of touch guide us where we need to be.

Soon, Presley breaks apart, Stephen comes with her, and that's when I lose my restraint. I fuck him hard, watching the look of pure euphoria on Presley's face as she climaxes and listening to the sound of Stephen's guttural groans.

When it's finally my turn, I'm overcome with so much emotion, stinging the backs of my eyes. I drain myself inside of Stephen, and then the three of us collapse into a heap on the bed, a tangle of legs and arms.

And it's in the sated silence with them that I know...

I am wholly and irrevocably changed forever.

Which means I am wholly and irrevocably fucked.

Only I can't seem to worry about it right now.

I RECEIVE A TEXT FROM MY BOSS ON THE WAY TO WORK MONDAY morning.

PRINCIPAL WARE

Good morning. Please meet me in my office
when you get in.

That's never good.

My stomach is in knots for the remainder of my short ride as I rack my brain what this could be in reference to. When I pull into the parking lot and spot the small crowd blocking the main entrance at the front of the building, my stomach twists even tighter. Several of them are holding up white posters, but I can't make out what they say.

What the hell?

I call Dominique before getting out of the car. "Hey, are you in the building yet?"

"No, I'm running a little behind this morning. Why, what's up?"

"I got a text from Ware asking me to meet him in his office, and when I got here, there's a bunch of people out front in the loop. It almost looks like some kind of protest or something."

"What the fuck could they be protesting about?" she asks.

"No clue. I'm going to see what I can find out and I'll let you know."

I walk in through the side entrance in the staff parking lot, and set my things down in the library before making my wait to speak with Principal Ware.

"Good morning, Presley." The secretary picks up her phone and dials the principal's office. "She's here."

Mr. Ware swings open his office door and ushers me inside. "Good morning."

Once I step inside, I spot two people sitting at the oval desk in the middle of the office—Mrs. Cleary, the head of Human Resources, and Dennis Rodriguez, our union president.

My stomach drops to the floor. The only reason a teacher would be called into a meeting with these people is if she's in trouble.

I wring my hands. "Uh, what's going on?"

Mrs. Cleary smiles and gestures to the seat across from her. "Have a seat, Ms. King."

I glance at Dennis as I lower myself into the chair beside him. I'm glad he's here; the only interactions I've had with him have been at union meetings, but he seems great at what he does, which is protecting our rights.

Principal Ware sits at the head of the table. "I'm sorry to spring this on you, but I wanted to speak with you before the school day starts. I've called this meeting in light of the accusations against you."

My chin jerks back. "Accusations? About what?"

"Over the weekend, you were spotted with two professional hockey players attending a concert in New York City."

I nod. "Yes, I was there."

Oh, fuck. Please tell me nobody saw the three of us fooling around on the balcony.

"Pictures of the three of you holding hands and kissing were posted online. It looks as though you are in a relationship with them." He pauses. "Is this true?"

I lift my chin. "It is."

"Well, Molly has been spreading the news all over social media, and there are a bunch of parents who have expressed their...feelings about it."

This bitch. "Is that what's going on out front?"

He grimaces as he nods. "Unfortunately, Molly has rallied some of the other moms, and they've staged a protest. Even called the local news station."

"A protest for what though, me being in a relationship? I don't see how it's any of her business who I date."

Dennis reaches across the table and pats my hand. "It's not."

"What does she want?" I ask. "Is she trying to get me fired?"

The three of them nod. "It seems so," Mr. Ware says.

"She can't do that." I glance around the table. "Oh my God, are you firing me? Is that what this is? I mean, isn't that discrimination?"

Mrs. Cleary holds up her palm. "You are protected from discrimination on your sexual orientation, gender identity, and relationship status in the state of New Jersey. You are not getting fired."

A breath of relief whooshes out of me.

Dennis nods. "The only thing that would cause your job to be terminated is if there is a legitimate reason tied to your professional conduct or performance. And who you choose to date in your personal life has nothing to do with what you do during work hours."

"And you have been nothing but a wonderful employee here at our school," Mr. Ware adds.

"Okay, so what happens now?"

"I've already alerted the police department to come remove these people from the premises. If Molly wants to exercise her freedom of speech, she can do so away from school property. We need to ensure the safety of the children upon arrival. You are to not engage with Molly or any of the other mothers out there; don't give them the reaction they're looking for. I would also like to remind you that you are not allowed to discuss anything school-related on social media."

"Of course."

"We're hoping she tires herself out," Mrs. Cleary says. "We are also preparing a statement to make it clear to Molly, and anyone else in our district that we stand in support with the LGBTQ community."

"This district does not stand for hate and bigotry—otherwise, I wouldn't be here." Dennis grins, confirming his place in the LGBTQ community.

Pride soars in my chest. "Thank you for that."

"Let's focus on the kids, and try to forget the mess that's outside. As far as they're concerned, today is a normal Monday," Mr. Ware says.

"And if the kids bring up anything they've heard from their parents over the weekend, what should I tell them?"

Anyone who works with children knows how inquisitive they are. I wouldn't be surprised if they're being brainwashed into thinking I'm a bad person because of this.

"Excellent question," Mr. Ware says. "Tell them to discuss any questions they have with their parents at home. If you receive any e-mails from parents, forward them to me."

"Got it."

Dominique is waiting for me in the library when I get out of the meeting. "What the actual fuck is going on? I saw those signs, Pres. They're disgusting."

I dig my phone out of my purse, and search up Stephen McKinley's name into a Google search. "Apparently, there are pictures of me and the boys from this weekend on the internet, and Molly got her hands on them. She's trying to get me fired."

Dominique scoffs. "As if she has the power to do that." She leans over my shoulder while I click on the top article. "Shit, girl. You've made it onto ESPN. You're famous now."

I let out a humorless laugh. "Hardly. This article is more about the boys than it is me."

The headline is ridiculous: *Rivals on the Ice, Partners in Life? The Unexpected Romance Between Two Pro Hockey Stars.*

"I wonder if this is going to cause any issues for them," I murmur, thinking aloud. I text the article to the thread between the three of us, hoping they've seen it and their agents are already working on damage control.

"So, what did Ware say?" Dominique asks. "Where does he stand on all this?"

"He said to ignore it, and not make any statements. They're hoping it blows over." I shrug. "There are laws protecting me from discrimination like this."

"You should sue her ass." She crosses her arms over her chest. "Fuck staying quiet. She can't get away with acting like this."

I grimace. "I don't want to cause any problems for the school."

"She's the one causing problems! You're just sticking up for yourself."

I exhale a long breath. "Let's just get through today. Hopefully, once Molly sees that she doesn't have a leg to stand on, she'll tuck her tail and go back to her own life."

Dominique shoots me a dubious. "I highly doubt that."

So do I, but I have to hope that this will all be over soon.

"WILL YOU TURN THAT OFF?" AVERY YELLS.

Alyssa whips around to glare at him over the back of the couch. "Shut up! I want to hear what they're saying."

Avery stomps over to her and rips the remote out of her hands, switching off the television. "You don't need to listen to that garbage, and neither does Aunt Presley."

I twist the burner on the stove to shut it off, and walk into the living room. "Your brother is right, 'Lyss. We don't need to concern ourselves with drama."

Her eyebrows pinch together. "But they're talking bad about you, and Stephen and Chance. They can't do that."

"The media spreads lies all the time, babe." I lower myself onto the couch beside her, and take her hand in mine. "It sucks, but that doesn't mean we have to feed into it. I don't want you watching stuff like that."

"I hate them," she grumbles, looking away.

"Hey." I tip her chin, turning her gaze back to mine. "We don't have room in our hearts for hate. We're not going to let them bring us down to their level. We are strong, and we rise above it. You got me?"

She nods.

I feel awful that the kids have to experience something like this. I wasn't prepared for the reporters camped outside our house when we got home from school today, and I wasn't prepared for my face to be plastered all over the news—but I can handle myself. It's Avery and Alyssa that I need to focus on.

The doorbell rings, and I jump up to let Stephen and Chance inside.

"Get your ass inside." Stephen shoves Chance through the doorway. "I don't need to bail you out of jail for beating up a reporter."

Chance flips them off, and their camera flashes go crazy before I close the door. "Fucking vultures."

I smooth my palms along his chest. "Calm down, Grumpy Man. Everything is fine. We're all safe inside."

His jaw clenches. "They shouldn't be out there. I'm getting you security."

Alyssa bounces into the foyer. "Like bodyguards? That's so freaking cool!"

Stephen scoops her up and flings her over his shoulder. "You don't need a bodyguard. You're a badass girl who can defend herself."

"Language." I rub my forehead. "Do you think they'll go to their schools?"

"They're not allowed on school premises, so they'll have to stay at a distance." Stephen sets Alyssa on her feet, and gives Avery a fist bump as we walk into the living room. "But I'm already handling it, so you have nothing to worry about."

My eyebrows jump. "Handling it how?"

"We're professional hockey players, pretty girl. We have management teams for shit like this." He grimaces at another curse word leaving his lips. "Sorry."

We each take a spot on the couch, Avery at my side with his nervous, wide eyes. I squeeze his knee for reassurance. "So, what is your team planning to do?"

Stephen sits back against the couch and spreads his arms wide along the back of it, totally relaxed as if this isn't a big deal. I suppose he's used to being in the spotlight like this. "My lawyer has delivered cease and desist letters to Molly and her posse of homophobes. If they want to picket, they'll have to do it somewhere else. I've hired a security team to guard your school for the next month, and I've hired them for Avery and Alyssa's schools as well. I'm having my own personal security team stay outside your house round-the-clock; unfortunately, there are no laws about paparazzi harassing you here, but my men will keep you all safe. This story will blow over, and it'll die down. The same thing happened to Jason, Kourtney, and Celeste when the three of them announced that they were together. Once another hot story comes out, everyone's attention will move onto that."

I glance over at Chance. "You okay?"

He was just outed to the world against his will, and though he said he was ready, that doesn't mean he's ready for being thrown into this media frenzy.

He nods once. "Let them say whatever they want about me. It's you three I'm worried about."

"We'll be okay with all this security," I say, even though I'm not confident in that statement myself. I flick my gaze to Avery and Alyssa. "Do you guys feel weird with this situation right now? Do you have any questions, or want to talk about any of it?"

Alyssa shrugs, smacking her gum as she chews. "This is so cool. We're gonna be famous."

Avery scoffs, not one for all of this attention. "We're not famous. They're doing this because there are angry, mean people in the world who hate the LGBTQ community. This is disgusting behavior."

Alyssa looks over at me, the smile falling from her face. "Oh."

This is all my fault. This is exactly what I was worried about. The kids are being thrust into this drama, and they don't deserve an ounce of it. Not only is it affecting my job, but it's affecting the two most important people in my life. I have to put them first.

I have to end this now, before it gets worse.

"Hey." Stephen pushes to his feet and moves into the center of the room. "Everyone, look at me right now."

We turn our attention to him, Chance being the last one to swing his reluctant gaze.

"I don't want to see these long faces. Especially not on you." He points at me. "I know what you're thinking in that head of yours, and you can just forget it."

I swallow down the lump of guilt in my throat.

"We are a family, and families stick together. Family is forever." Stephen swings his arm toward the door. "Those people out there? They're just doing their job, trying to make a buck off of our story. But they're not in control of us. We are. So, why don't we give them something good to write about? Instead of them snapping pictures of us looking upset and scared, why not show the world what a beautiful, happy, diverse family looks like? We can spin this any way we want. It's our choice to stay miserable, or to rise above this and fight back. The world is always going to be filled with hate— but we don't have to focus on them."

"Yeah!" Alyssa shoots up and pumps her fist in the air. "Those assholes can go fuck themselves!"

I gasp, Avery shouts, and Chance pinches the bridge of his nose.

Stephen grimaces as his shoulders jerk up to his ears. "I love your enthusiasm, 'Lyssa girl, but maybe not with the cursing so your aunt doesn't kill me."

She clamps her hand over her mouth. "Sorry."

I let out a small chuckle, and make eye-contact with Avery. "What do you say, kid? Want to take this situation by the balls?"

He grins. "Hell yes."

Chance smirks. "That's my boy."

Pride and love swirl in my chest.

Family.

I've felt a little broken since my sister passed, but having this support system now fills an empty loneliness that's been in my heart. She would love these guys so much.

Almost as much as I do.

"Did you know they made white hot chocolate? Chance bought me one the other night, and it's life-changing."

Trenton glances at my hot cup. "No, but I'm sure Giuliana does."

I scoff. "I don't know why everyone's under the impression that hot chocolate is for kids."

"Because adults need caffeine, not a cup of sugar."

"You don't know what you're missing, Warden. This is fucking delicious."

Jason nudges my knee with his. "You ready for this, Mac?"

I straighten my tie and flash him a wide grin. "You know it."

I've been waiting a long time to tell the world about the two loves of my life. The team scheduled a press conference so we can make a statement regarding the stories circulating about me, Chance, and Presley. Chance is planning on doing the same in Philly later today. I wish I could be there; I know this isn't easy for him. At least he has the support of his team.

This is more than just PR. This is standing up and letting everyone know: Racism and prejudice no longer have a place in the NHL. Inequality has gone on for far too long. Our teams are going to make sure everyone knows that moving forward, sports will be a safe space for *everyone*.

Jason pats my shoulder. "We're with you, whatever you need."

I arch a brow. "Feels like it was yesterday when I was giving you the same speech."

He chuckles. "Time flies when you're fucking two people at the same time."

"It sure fucking does, my friend."

Trenton laughs. "Our boy is all grown up. Look at you, in a relationship. Did you think you'd ever be here when you woke up naked in a stranger's house?"

I slap my forehead with my palm, and drag my hand down my face. "Don't remind me of that nightmare, okay?"

Coach knocks on the door before sticking his head inside. "They're ready for us."

Alexander wraps his arm around my shoulders as we walk toward the door. "I'm proud of you, Mac. And I'm so happy that you're finally happy."

Me too.

It's about damn time.

"You were incredible today."

I smile as my head falls back against the seat, and I kill the engine. "Thanks, pretty girl. You watched it?"

"Of course I did. I watched Chance's press conference too."

My heart clenches at the reminder. "So did I."

"I'm jealous I can't be there with you two tonight."

"How's my girl doing? Has she stopped throwing up?"

She heaves a sigh. "I think she's finally on empty. Hopefully she sleeps through the night without any issues."

"I wish you would've let me stay and help."

"You have a big game coming up. There's no way in hell I'd let you catch this thing."

"I'm invincible. Germs can't bring me down."

She chuckles, and the sound of her laugh soothes me. "It's concerning that you actually believe that."

"Well, get some rest, baby. I need you healthy for when I get back."

"Oh, yeah? And why's that?"

"Because you'll need all your strength for how good I'm going to fuck you."

She hums. "Maybe I'll make a video of me touching myself tonight to show you both what you're missing."

My dick jumps. "Fuck, yes. Definitely do that."

"Goodnight, handsome. Give Chance a kiss for me."

"I will." I pause. "I love you, pretty girl."

"I love you too, Stephen."

My heart soars as I end the call.

I love the two of them. I never stopped, even when we weren't a part of each other's lives. And now it's like we're picking right back up where we left off, as if no time has passed at all.

Chance's SUV pulls up to his apartment building, and I step out of the car.

His eyebrows draw together as he spots me. "What's wrong?"

I let out a low chuckle. "Everything's fine, relax."

"You came all the way to Philly because everything's fine?"

"I came all the way to Philly to see you." I clasp his hand, threading our fingers together, and I tug him toward his building. "Come on. Let's go inside."

He eyes my duffle bag. "You staying over?"

"Wanted to catch you before your flight leaves tomorrow."

"It's an early one."

I shoot him a wink. "I won't keep you up too late."

The hint of a smirk pulls at the corner of his mouth as he leads us inside. He knows damn well that I have every intention of keeping him up until sunrise.

We're quiet on the elevator ride upstairs, anticipation building in the silence between us. Normally, I'd be talking his ear off about anything and everything, just to annoy him.

But tonight is different.

My eyes bounce around Chance's apartment as I step inside. It's exactly what I expected—minimal decorations; minimal color; lots of black and gray. It doesn't feel warm and inviting. It doesn't really feel lived-in at all.

"Stop judging me," he says as he drops his keys into a dish on the entryway table.

I hold up my palms on either side of my head. "Not judging."

He puts his hands on his hips, his defenses rising. "Tell me why you're here."

Damn, he looks good. He's in a suit from his press conference, a charcoal color with a crisp black button-up underneath. His usual messy hair is styled neatly, putting his big brown eyes on full display. Chance is strikingly beautiful. Tall, dark, and handsome with an edge. And he's finally mine.

I toss my duffle onto the floor and step into his space. "I saw your press conference."

He arches a brow. "And...?"

My fingers slowly work the buttons on his shirt, popping them open one by one. "And I'm so proud of you."

His eyes tighten as he holds himself still, not one for praise.

I continue, unbuckling his belt next. "It was such a turn-on hearing you talk about our relationship in front of everyone like that." I slip his jacket off his shoulders, letting it fall to the floor. "You let the world know that you are mine, and that I belong to you—that the three of us are forever entwined."

His lips part with his shallow breaths.

I remove his shirt next, leaving him in a tight black tank top. "Fuck, you look good, baby." I dip my head and press soft kisses to his neck. "I know it wasn't easy for you to do what you did today, and I just wanted to show you how good it made me feel."

Chance reaches out and cups my face in his strong hands. "Is that what you think, that it wasn't easy for me?"

My eyes bounce between his. "I know you don't like talking about your feelings, especially in front of the press. You just came out and told the world you're bisexual. This is a huge deal."

He shakes his head as he leans in and nips at my bottom lip. "It's been a long time coming, Stephen. I was ready. I don't want to hide this anymore."

Pride surges through me as arousal seeps into my core. I always told him I'd wait for him—wait for him to come out, wait for him to admit his feelings to the world, wait for him to feel secure in who he truly is.

My tongue swipes along his lips. "You finally ready for me, baby?"

"You've waited long enough."

My patience snaps, and I yank his pants down to his ankles, dropping down to my knees in front of him. Chance tears off his tank top while I slide his boxers down his legs, leaving him towering naked above me.

His hand comes around to the back of my head, guiding my mouth to his hard cock. I suck him all the way in, forgoing any teasing, and let him hit the back of my throat. Tonight is about him, and I want him to take whatever he wants from me.

"You love gagging on this cock, don't you, baby?" He thrusts his hips forward, and I give it a second before I pull back to gasp for air. "You've always been such a good boy for me. You love being on your knees, letting me fuck this perfect mouth and fill it with cum."

My eyes roll in the back of my head as precum leaks from my dick, and I moan around him. I'm swollen and hard, already so turned on by Chance's dirty talk.

"You gonna let me fuck that tight little ass tonight, hmm?" His deep voice smooths over me like silk. "I'm gonna use you and make such a mess of you, baby."

I wrap my hand around my cock and squeeze it, needing relief.

Chance clicks his tongue on the roof of his mouth. "Uh-uh, baby. Hands behind your back. You don't get to touch unless I say you do."

I clasp my hands behind my back, loving the way he orders me around. I know how much he loves being in control, and I can feel his dick practically pulsing in my mouth because of how turned-on he is.

He fucks my mouth in harsh strokes, and it's not long before he gazes down at me with those wild eyes of his. "I'm gonna come, baby. Fuck, I'm gonna come."

I keep my eyes locked on his, and I suck him all the way to the back of my throat as he spills his load. I hum and close my eyes as I swallow him down, licking the remnants of him off my lips.

Chance wastes no time hauling me up and dragging me down the hall. We peel my clothes off, and crash into the walls as we kiss, until we fall into a heap on the bed. The comforter puffs up around us, cocooning us in like it's shielding us from the rest of the world.

"Hold on." I pull back, and push off the mattress.

"Where are you going?" Chance calls after me as I bolt into the hallway.

I slip my phone out of my pants pocket and bring it back into the bedroom. I prop it up against the lamp on his nightstand, and open the camera, setting it up for a video.

"We're going to make a video for our girl."

Chance smirks as I turn around and crawl back to him on the mattress. God, he's fucking beautiful. Completely naked with his smooth, olive skin on display, and his hair a mess from my fingers. My heart feels so full, so completely whole knowing that I have both of the loves of my life back.

I slow things down, and take Chance's face into my hands, pressing a tender kiss to his lips. I pull back an inch to look into his eyes. "I love you, Chance. I always have."

His Adam's apple bobs in his throat as he gazes at me. "I love you too."

We spend the night making love to each other—in between absolute filthy fucking—and we fall asleep in each other's arms.

A sense of accomplishment lulls me to sleep. I'm finally where I want to be in life. The perfect girlfriend; the perfect boyfriend; incredible kids to help raise; and my dream career.

Everything is so perfect.

Principal Sturges' name lights up my phone on my lunch break, and my stomach instantly twists.

It's been a while since he's had to reach out to me. The bullies have left Avery alone, as far as I know. Maybe this call is for a good thing, for once.

"Hi, Mr. Sturges. Everything okay?"

"Hi, Ms. King. Sorry to disturb you at work, but Avery got into a fight at lunch today. I'd like for you to come in and pick him up."

My heart sinks. "Is he okay? What happened?"

"He's okay." He pauses, and his voice lowers. "He, uh, started the fight."

My eyebrows hit my hairline. "He *what*?"

"I'll explain everything when you get here."

I let out a long sigh. "Let me talk to my boss, and see if I can leave early."

"I understand. Take your time."

I click on Avery's name and type out a text to him:

ME

What's this I hear about you starting a fight?

AVERY

I punched Austin in his stupid face.

ME

Why would you do that? I thought everything had calmed down with those boys.

AVERY

He called you a whore.

AVERY

I had to stick up for you.

I cover my mouth with my hand and squeeze my eyes shut as I read the disgusting five-letter word my nephew had to hear because of me.

God damnit.

This is getting worse.

The last thing I wanted was for the kids to suffer because of my choices.

ME:

I'm sorry I put you in that position. You should've just ignored him.

AVERY

He had it coming.

I let out a small chuckle. That little shithead really did have it coming.

ME

Did he hit you back?

AVERY

Nope. I knocked him on the floor with one punch.

AVERY

Can't wait to tell Chance.

ME

I hate to say this but I'm proud of you, kid.

ME

I just wish you didn't have to feel the need to defend me. It's supposed to be the other way around.

AVERY

We're family. We defend each other.

ME

I love you.

Love you too, Aunt Pres.

I pick up the phone in the library and dial my boss' extension.

"Hey, Presley. What's up?"

"Avery got into a fight at school. Any way I can leave a little early today?"

"Oh, no. Is he okay?"

I rub my temple with my fingers. "Yeah, he's okay."

"Hmm, let me see your schedule." I hear the faint sound of his computer mouse clicking in the background. "I can switch your free period at one-thirty, and you can leave at two-thirty. Does that work?"

"Absolutely. Thank you so much. I really appreciate it."

"Of course."

I hang up, and prepare for my next class. Being a school librarian isn't my dream job, but it allows me to have the same schedule as the kids. When I was presented with the opportunity, I jumped at the chance. This school paid for me to get my master's degree in order to take this position, and I was able to take online classes. It wasn't easy while simultaneously juggling two children full-time, and dealing with the loss of my sister—all while grieving my own broken heart after leaving the two loves of my life in college. Looking back, I don't know how I made it through that sad, stressful time. But these kids mean everything to me, and I was determined to make it work.

I might not love this job, but I need it. And the fact that Molly is trying to come for it is personal. She's trying to take food out of my niece and nephew's mouths, and I won't stand for it. Ideas have been bouncing around my mind all week. I want to do more than create a book display in this library. I want to create something that will help bridge the gap between children and the LGBTQ community. I want to teach kids about kindness, and diversity, and acceptance.

With the support of my school, my friends, and my men, I'm going to make sure Molly knows that there's no place in this town for her hatred and discrimination. The same goes for Avery's bullies.

It seems everyone needs to be taught a lesson, and punching people in the face isn't going to cut it.

◯◯◯

DOMINIQUE SNAPS HER FINGERS IN FRONT OF MY FACE. "HEY, you with me?"

"Sorry. I've been in my own head a lot lately."

"Thinking about what? Not wasting your time on Miserable Molly, I hope."

I chuckle. "No, not at all. I've actually been thinking about starting some kind of group for children where they can experience people in the LGBTQ community—kind of like how Drag Queens were reading books to kids in Manhattan—just to have them be in an inclusive and accepting safe space together."

Dominique's eyes widen. "I love that. Let's do it."

My smile widens. Whenever I want to do something, Dominique always says *let's*, as if it's an automatic given that she's going to do whatever it is with me. I'm never alone, and she's always by my side.

"I love you, Dom." I cover her hand with mine. "Thank you for being my friend."

"Pfft. You know I'm only in this for the pro hockey fame."

I toss my head back and laugh. "You bitch. I was trying to have a nice moment, and you ruined it."

"Sorry, wait—I'll do better. Try it again."

I toss a piece of bread at her. "Too late. The moment has passed."

"Damnit."

The sound of pounding feet has our heads jerking up to the ceiling.

"Why does it always have to sound like this when the kids play together?" Dominique scrunches her nose. "I swear, one of them is going to come through the ceiling one day."

"They better fucking not." I take a sip of wine. "I'll kill them if I have to spackle one more hole in the wall. Did I tell you that Alyssa put a hole in the fence outside the other day?"

Her eyebrows shoot up to her hairline. "The vinyl fence?"

"The vinyl fence that costs two-hundred-dollars per slat to fix? Yep. That one."

"How the hell did she manage that?"

"She shot the field hockey ball right into it." I let out a humorless laugh. "I didn't realize how strong that little shit is."

"She really is a beast." Dominique grins. "I love her."

Affection warms my chest. "Me too."

"Avery seems different lately. I love that he has positive male role models to look up to."

I nod. "His confidence has really grown since Chance took him under his wing. He's smiling more too. He's growing up right in front of my eyes."

"Any luck on getting Sturges to show you the surveillance footage of Avery knocking out that shithead Austin?"

I laugh. "He said it's against school policy."

She scoffs. "Did you slip him a twenty like I told you?"

"I'm not bribing the kid's principal, Dom."

"You have not one but two hockey players in your back pocket. You should be using that to your advantage more often."

I shake my head. "You're crazy."

My phone vibrates on the table, Chance's name lighting up the screen. I grab it and dart to the stairs. "Avery, he's calling!"

Avery bounds down the stairs and rips the phone out of my hand. "Hi, Chance. How was your game tonight?"

I strain to listen as he takes my phone into the kitchen, wanting to give him space but also dying to hear Chance's reaction. I love the way he is around Avery. It's a softer side of him I don't get to see often.

Dominique clutches her chest. "He's so excited to talk to him."

Emotion clogs my throat. "I know. I love it. I just wish the kids at school weren't such assholes. I know it's not common for a woman to be in a relationship with two men, but they don't have to be so cruel. I hate that I'm bringing this added stress to Avery's life. He has enough issues with them; he didn't need this on top of it."

"Look, kids are going to be assholes no matter what. But it's making him a stronger person. A little adversity is okay."

I shoot her a dubious look. "He has a dead mother, he doesn't know who his father is, and he likes art instead of sports. I think he had enough adversity before I added polyamory to his plate."

Dominique squeezes my shoulder. "You're showing him what a healthy, loving relationship looks like. Don't focus on the negativity. Look at all the good that's happening here."

"I know you're right, but it's hard to not feel like I'm messing up these kids' lives."

"All good parents feel that way, Pres. You're doing an amazing job. Trust me."

I lean my head on her shoulder as we listen to Avery finish his conversation with Chance.

Then he comes into the dining room and hands me the phone. "Chance wants to talk to you."

I ruffle his hair as I take the phone and smile down at Chance's handsome face. "Hey."

"Hey yourself." He's sitting against the headboard in the bed of his hotel room. "You okay?"

I nod. "I wish he didn't have to resort to violence, but I'm proud of him for standing up for himself."

His lush lips twist into a smirk. "That's my boy."

Affection wraps around my heart. "He really looks up to you. I appreciate your help so much."

"He's a great kid. He had an amazing mom, and an incredible aunt to make him that way. I just taught him how to throw a punch."

Tears well behind my lids. "You've done more than that, Grumpy Man."

That's Chance. Always selling himself short.

"How is everything there? Molly and the paparazzi...?"

This past week has been a whirlwind. Molly took her bullshit elsewhere after we shut her down, mainly keeping to social media to try to slander my name wherever she can. She has a small following, but more people have spoken out in support than not, and I'm shocked to see who has my back here.

The paparazzi are annoying as fuck, but the frenzy has died down a bit. Life is as normal as it can be when dating two professional hockey players.

"It's fine. Seems to be calming down." I look into his concerned eyes. "I can't wait for you to come home."

He bites his bottom lip. "I can't wait to fu—"

"Dominique is here!" I cut him off before he can finish his sentence.

"Oh, come on" Dominique whines. "It was just about to get good."

Chance chuckles. "Hi, Dom."

"Hi, handsome. Don't worry about your girl. Everything is fine here."

"Thanks for keeping her company for me." He shoots me a wink. "See you tomorrow, rebel."

Desire has my thighs clenching together. "Goodnight, Grumpy Man."

Tomorrow can't come fast enough.

"WHY DID YOU THINK TEQUILA SHOTS WERE A GOOD IDEA FOR this meeting today?"

Celeste blinks as she glances around at the four of us. "Is there ever a bad time for tequila?"

I laugh as I take the bottle from her and set it on the dining room table. "Thank you. I love tequila."

"Just not at ten in the morning," Cassidy finishes.

Celeste shrugs as she lowers herself into the seat beside me. "Alcohol helps my creative juices flow."

Kourtney pats her wife's shoulder and smiles at me. "So, what have you come up with so far?"

I let out a shaky breath as I stare down at the papers scattered across the table. "I need to narrow down the purpose of this organization. I feel like my thoughts are all over the place."

Kourtney nods. "Something concrete. A specific and direct plan."

"Exactly."

After Stephen told me all about Kourtney's website and how she started her business from scratch, I knew I wanted to have her on board for this. She was able to take her vision and bring it to fruition. And I need all the help I can get.

I clear my throat as I attempt to articulate my thoughts. "I want this to be about education: Educating children, and their families as well. I want it to be a safe space for them to ask questions, to clear up any misconceptions. I want to teach them why this matters."

Cassidy nods. "We also need to focus on the other side of that coin, and make sure it's a safe space for the queer people who are volunteering their time for this. It should be a give and take, something that benefits both parties."

"I agree." I suck in a deep breath. "But I don't want it to be so formal, like a class."

Celeste grins. "I don't know. *Queer People 101* has a nice ring to it."

We all chuckle. Aarya leans forward, her dark hair falling around her shoulders. "Do you want this to be something you take into schools? Or something that people go to outside of school hours?"

"I think we should start with something outside of school. We might have a better turnout if people *want* to be there, instead of forcing it down their kids' throats."

"Let's start with something once a month," Aarya says. "You can do it at the gallery I work at, so you don't have to worry about finding a space."

My eyebrows shoot up. "Really? That'd be okay with your boss?"

She flips her hair over her shoulder. "I'm the events coordinator, so he'll be on board with whatever I bring to the table."

"Each month could be a different theme." Kourtney's brown eyes light up as she speaks. "One month, a kid-friendly paint-and-sip at the gallery; another month could be playing kickball at the local park; another month could be a cooking class at my parents' catering kitchen."

My heart picks up speed as jot down everyone's ideas. "Wow, this is great. There will be something for everyone."

"You need to come up with a name," Celeste says. "Then I can help get the word out, and start marketing it around town; local media outlets too. I have a bunch of contacts from my PR days."

"And I can help you set up a website," Kourtney chimes in.

My eyes fill with tears as I glance around the table. "I really appreciate your help. I know we're not really friends yet, but—"

Cassidy holds up her hand to stop me. "We absolutely are friends, and this is what friends do. They help each other."

Kourtney reaches out and covers my hand with hers. "Mac told us a little bit about what happened with your sister, and how you raised these kids on your own. You don't have to be alone anymore, Presley. The boys are a team, and so are we. We all have each other's backs no matter what."

My vision blurs as I dab at the corner of my eye, and smile. "Thank you."

My sister was always my best friend, and after she passed, I found it difficult to connect with people. Nobody knew me the way Allie did, and I didn't have the time or desire to go out and socialize. Dominique was the only one who made the effort to form a friendship with me once I moved here—she didn't exactly take no for an answer, and I'm grateful for that.

It feels good to have a core friend group now; it feels like I'm getting back yet another piece of myself.

I'm finally setting down the weight of grief and looking forward to the new life I'm building.

Is that a power tool?

I drop the grocery bags on the counter in the kitchen, and bolt up the stairs. "Why do I hear the sound of a drill?"

"It's fine," Avery calls.

Nothing about this sounds fine.

The kids' rooms are empty, but the bathroom door is slightly ajar. I tap my knuckles against the frame and stick my head through the opening.

Avery is sitting on a giant hockey player's shoulders, drilling in a new light fixture above the sink.

"Uh, hi. What the heck are you two doing?"

Avery hands Stephen the drill, and climbs off of him. "We're just fixing a couple of things around the house."

I arch a brow at Stephen, who is uncharacteristically silent. "And why are we doing that?"

Stephen hikes a shoulder, trying to make himself busy so that he doesn't have to look me in the eye. "I noticed there were a few things on your to-do list."

"Oh, you just happened to notice it?" I widen my eyes as I look at Avery, who won't look at me either. "Wonder how that happened."

Thick as thieves, these two.

Stephen's eyes finally meet mine as he reaches out and brushes my hair behind my ear. "I'm teaching Avery some important skills."

Avery gestures to his handiwork. "I just put that whole thing up by myself!"

My chest warms with so much love. "It looks great. I'm so proud of you."

Avery beams. "Stephen's going to teach me how to clean the gutters, and then we're going to repaint my bedroom."

I hold up my hands. "Whoa, hold on. You're redoing your bedroom?"

He nods, chewing the inside of his cheek. "If that's okay with you."

I glance between him and Stephen, and nod. "Sure. What color are you thinking?"

"Not sure yet. Could we go to the store and look at some swatches?"

Stephen nudges him with his elbow. "Tell her your other idea."

"I'd like to paint a mural on one of the walls."

My eyebrows shoot up. "I think that's a great idea. I'd love to see what you come up with."

"Really?" His cheeks push up into his eyes with his wide smile. "I've been sketching some ideas."

Having Stephen and Chance around the house has been so good for the kids. I haven't seen Avery this full of life. I need to keep putting him in situations that boost his confidence, and give him a sense of control.

"It's your room," I say. "You should have a say over what it looks like."

He lunges forward and slams into me, squeezing me hard with a hug. "Thank you, Aunt Presley."

My eyes flick up to Stephen as I hold my precious nephew in my arms. *Thank you*, I mouth.

He shoots me a wink.

God, this man is so getting laid later.

My cheeks push up even further as I sneak a picture of Chance. "Oh, nothing."

His head whips around as he shoots me a glare, but Alyssa tugs on his hand. "Stop moving. You're going to make me smudge your nails."

"Sorry," he whispers. "It's your aunt's fault."

She giggles. "I'm actually surprised at how good of a job you did with my nails."

"Yeah, if hockey doesn't work out for you, you can open a nail salon." Stephen's shoulders shake with his silent laughter as he pokes fun at Chance.

Chance lifts his middle finger in the air, showing off his black nail polish.

"Who knew you were so good at painting nails," I muse.

Chance arches a brow. "I have lots of skills you haven't seen yet."

I bite my bottom lip, and goosebumps fly across my skin. "Can't wait to see these skills."

Stephen grins from his spot on the couch beside Avery. "Your skills are nothing like little man over here. I don't know how you can make strokes with a pencil and turn it into a masterpiece like this."

Avery's face reddens as he continues sketching. "And I don't know how you don't bust your ass on the ice when you play."

Alyssa grins, handing Chance a yellow crayon. "Ooo, Avery cursed."

He glances up at me. "Sorry."

I roll my eyes. "*Ass* is the least of my worries with this one in the house." I jerk my thumb toward Stephen.

Stephen holds a hand to his chest, feigning innocence. "I don't know what you're insinuating, Ms. King."

My heart feels like it's overflowing with joy as I watch these men with my niece and nephew. I used to love wild nights out, dancing and drinking, and then having loud, wild sex after. Now, I'm completely content with lying on the couch with my family while they color.

Plus, I still get to have wild sex.

"How's the nonprofit research coming along?" Chance asks.

I scribble another idea down onto my notepad. "Good. Tell me what you think of these names: *NextGen Unity; Safe Space Allies; Inclusive Hearts.*"

"*Inclusive Hearts,*" he says without looking up from his nails.

"I vote for that one too," Avery says.

I nod. "That one's my favorite of the few I've come up with."

When the girls were over earlier, we made a checklist of the things I needed to do to form a nonprofit organization. Once I come up with a name, I can get started on all the legal forms. It seems daunting, but I'm excited to do this.

Not everyone thinks like Miserable Molly, and I want to create something beautiful to make a difference in our community.

"Avery, I was thinking maybe you could design a logo for me."

His head jerks up. "Really?"

"Yep. Something that symbolizes *Inclusive Hearts*."

His eyes light up as he turns the page in his sketchbook. "I'm on it."

I chuckle. "It doesn't have to be right now. I know you're excited to sketch out your ideas for the mural."

"I want a new room," Alyssa says. "Can Avery paint something on my wall too?"

Stephen laughs. "We're going to have to get you an assistant to keep your art bookings organized. You're about to become a very busy man."

Seeing the proud look on Avery's brings hot tears to my eyes. After everything he's been through, he's finally getting to spread his wings and become the talented, smart, sweet man I've always known him to be—only this time, he believes it.

I love this diverse little family we're turning out to be.

Junior Year

THE SUN STREAMS THROUGH THE WINDOW, CASTING SOFT, HAZY beams of light across the room.

My lips automatically curl into a smile at the feel of Stephen's against mine, his soft, sated breaths tickling my neck.

He's so beautiful when he shuts the hell up every once in a while.

I've never felt so good with anyone like this, let alone two people. It's like a dream that I fear I'm going to wake up from at any moment, like this is all too good to be true. I'm not used to love like this. I've been trying hard to open my heart and accept it, but it's been an uphill battle against myself. Luckily, Presley and Stephen have been patient with me.

I reach out for our girl, but my palm is met with cool sheets beside me. I lift my head, glancing around the room. Stephen's clothes are strewn about with mine where we left them last night. But Presley's clothes aren't tangled with ours.

What day is today? I dig the heel of my hand into my eye, forcing myself to wake up and remember if Presley had an early class this morning.

Stephen stirs beside me, groaning. "Go back to sleep. I can literally hear you thinking."

"Did Presley say she was going somewhere this morning?"

His head pops up as he squints his eyes. "Nope. Where is she?"

I reach for my phone on my nightstand.

No new texts or missed calls.

Unease seeps into my gut. She's never slipped out in the middle of the night like this.

"She probably just went out to get coffee or bring back breakfast." Stephen's head flops back down on the pillow. "Call her and tell her I want a shot of espresso in mine."

I click on her name and press my phone to my ear. "It went straight to voicemail."

"Maybe her phone is dead."

I swing my legs out of bed, and tear apart the room looking for any small trace of her.

I dial her number again, and again, it doesn't ring.

Something's wrong.

Stephen moves to sit up against the headboard. "Why are you freaking out? I'm sure she'll be back soon. She probably didn't want to wake us."

"But where did she have to go this early? And why didn't she leave a note? And why isn't her phone ringing?"

He stands from the bed and takes my shoulders in his hands. "Hey, look at me. Breathe. We fell asleep together, and there's no sign of anyone breaking in here and kidnapping her. She left on her own free will, and she's going to have a good explanation as to why she left. Come back to bed, and let's give her some time to do whatever she's doing."

I shake my head. "I'm going to take a walk to her dorm. Maybe she's there grabbing some things."

Stephen sighs, and face-plants on the mattress. "Have fun."

"Call me if she shows up."

"Got it."

I throw on my sweats and stuff my feet into my sneakers. "I mean it. Call me immediately."

He lifts his thumb in the air without looking up.

How is he not worried?

This is it.

This is the rug being pulled out from underneath me.

Nothing this good ever lasts.

"Presley, I need you to call me back as soon as you get this message. Do you understand? Call. Me. Fucking. Back." I toss my phone onto the bed with a growl. "What the fuck?"

Stephen tugs at his curls, pacing our dorm. "I don't understand. Why would she drop her classes and not tell us?"

My chest heaves, and I'm still reeling over the news. "I don't fucking know. Everything was fine last night."

Wasn't it?

The three of us ate pizza, and then we came back to the room to watch a movie—most of which we didn't end up watching because we were ripping each other's clothes off. It was a normal night for us. I've gone over it, again and again, overanalyzing each and every second, every look, every touch, every word she said.

"Did she seem weird to you at all?" I ask. "At dinner, or after?"

"Not one bit." Stephen's wide blue eyes meet mine. "I mean, I didn't think so."

"So, why on fucking earth would she wake up, decide to drop out of college, and vanish into thin air? Something doesn't add up."

"Are you saying she planned this?"

I hold out my arms wide. "You don't just drop out on a whim, and leave the two people you supposedly love. That's probably why she's not answering, because she knows she fucked up and she doesn't have the balls to face us."

Stephen's head jerks back. "That's not her. She wouldn't do that. And what would she have to gain from it?"

"We've only known her for a year. Who's to say that was even really her?"

He shakes his head, adamant that I'm wrong. "No way. Something's wrong. She wouldn't leave like this unless something big happened."

I roll my eyes. "You're so naïve. You think everything is all rainbows and puppies all the damn time." I pause. "Come to think of it, you're probably the reason she left. You pushed too much, too soon. You told her you loved her, and she got spooked."

Stephen coughs out an incredulous laugh. "Are you kidding me? You're saying this is *my* fault? Maybe it was you. You're the grumpy asshole with the negative mindset. You said you loved her too, if I recall correctly, and look at you now—not even one day and you're already throwing her under the bus and not giving her the benefit of the doubt."

"Because what kind of person just fucking leaves and doesn't tell people where she's going? It's fucking bullshit. If she really loved us, she wouldn't be ghosting us right now. Wake the fuck up."

Stephen steps toward me and jabs his finger in my chest. "You keep us in the shadows like we're some dirty little secret. You can't even kiss me in public. You don't want anyone to know about us, and it puts a strain on our relationship. Presley wanted to be seen, Chance. She's carefree and fun. But you sucked all the fun out of it."

Bitter anger flares in my chest, and my eyes narrow as I grit my teeth. "Tell me how you really feel."

"You wanna point the finger at me, I'll point it right back. Take accountability for your shit and get your head out of your ass."

I glance at the clock, and shove past him. "Fuck this."

"You're seriously going to play tonight? Presley's missing, and you're just going to act like it's any other night?"

I whip around and get in his face. "The scout is coming. I can't not be there. Presley doesn't give a shit about us."

"So, that's it then?" He lets out a humorless laugh. "You're just giving up on her?"

"I'm going to pick up the pieces and move on with my fucking life. She sure as shit just did."

"And what about me, about us?"

I should cool down before we have this conversation. I need to get out of here, and blow off some steam. Come back to this with a clear head.

But what's the point? Presley was the reason we got together in the first place. Stephen said it himself—I suck the joy out of everything. I'll only bring him down. He deserves better. He deserves more. He deserves someone who will love him in public, and bask in the sun.

That's not me.

So, instead of fighting for him, I put the final nail in the coffin.

"There is no us, and there never will be." I hold up my wrist and unclasp the bracelet he bought me, dropping it onto the mattress. "This was fun while it lasted, but it's over now."

Stephen says nothing in response. His eyes well with tears as he watches me move around the room, grabbing my clothes and stuffing them into my bag. I can't bring myself to look at him. If I do, I'll break. I just need to get out of here and get on the ice.

The silence is thick, filled with the emptiness of Presley's absence. And in that silence, the bitter truth settles deep in my bones.

She's gone.

There's nothing like having home advantage.

The roar of the crowd, the sea of yellow-and-black jerseys, the kids holding up signs with your name on it—there's no feeling like it.

And winning always tastes a little sweeter when we're playing against Philly.

I thought it'd be different playing against Chance now that we're together; maybe we'd go easier on the other, or not fight as much. But it seems to have had the opposite effect. We're all over each other, blocking shots, creating openings for our teammates, and playing better than we ever have. We're explosive together on the ice. Then again, we've always been explosive off the ice as well. It's almost like hockey is our foreplay.

"You look a little winded," Chance shouts, his stick knocking into mine as he bumps me with his shoulder. "Tired already?"

"You'd like that, wouldn't you? Want me to make it easier for you?"

"Not a fucking chance." He darts in front of me and steals the puck, skating off in the opposite direction.

He passes it to one of his teammates, but Alexander is there to intercept. He skates back down the ice and takes a shot between two of Philly's defenseman.

The buzzer sounds, and I raise my arms overhead. "Fuck, yeah!"

The scoreboard changes: 1-0. The crowd is electric around us, cheering us on and booing the shit out of Philadelphia.

In the second period, our hits get harder, and Chance and I both spend some time in the penalty box. He grins at me with his bloody mouth, his dark eyes shining with the promise of what's to come when we get home later.

But there's aggressive plays, and then there's illegal hits—and that's where Chance's teammate, Ivanov, pushes the line. He plays like he doesn't give a fuck whether he gets ejected from the game, or fined for his attitude. And tonight, he's pissed that his team can't seem to score.

I'm flying down the ice with the puck toward the Sharks' goalie with Ivanov practically up my ass. His stick juts out under my skates and trips me up. He's not even trying to get the puck—he wants me to fall.

Where the hell is the ref?

Alexander glides alongside him and shoves him out of the way, allowing me the space to surge ahead. I make an attempt on the goalie, but Chance is there to stop it. He takes it all the way to Trenton, but my goalie stops it like he always does, and passes it to Alex.

And then Alexander shoots across the rink like lightning.

The crowd is deafening. Adrenaline pumps through my veins as I try to get ahead of him to set up the play. Chance is right behind him though, and Alex can't make a safe pass without losing the puck. He takes it around the back of the net, but Chance runs him into the boards trying to steal it.

Alexander is one talented motherfucker though, and he manages to get out from under Chance's pressure. With his head down, he focuses on getting into position to make another winning goal. With Chance right behind him, it's a risky move, but I have faith in my captain.

As a winger, it's my job to work with the center—which would be Alex—in order to make a play happen. I'm supposed to be a step ahead of everyone else, seeing opportunities and creating openings to score.

Somehow, I don't see this coming.

Ivanov whizzes past me, making a direct line toward Alex and Chance. He doesn't slow down as he approaches them, and Alexander is too busy trying to escape Chance and score to notice.

What the fuck is Ivanov doing?

My voice catches in my throat as I freeze, realizing what's happening only milliseconds before it happens.

"Stop!" I shout.

But it's too little too late.

Ivanov slams into Alexander head-on. It's a hard hit, and the crowd gasps as the air leaves my lungs. Alex is sandwiched between Ivanov and Chance, and it's so forceful that the three of them propel backward.

Alexander's helmet flies off just before he lands on his back, and his head bounces off the ice.

Fuck.

I drop my stick and my gloves, and toss my helmet as I make my way toward them. I reach Ivanov first, and I lift him off the ice by his jersey and rip off his helmet so I can pummel his stupid, smug face.

That was an illegal hit, and nobody touches my captain and gets away with it.

Both teams erupt in a fight, and I'm in such a blind rage that I don't realize what's happening around me until Jason pulls me off of Ivanov and shouts, "Alex is hurt."

I drop Ivanov and my eyes dart to Alexander. He's lying on his back, eyes closed, his arms and legs sprawled out and unmoving.

My pulse pounds in my ears.

Get up.

Open your eyes.

I crouch down beside him. "Hey, big guy. You good?"

He doesn't move.

I nudge him gently. "I know Giuliana had you up late last night, but you can't nap in the middle of the game." I let out a nervous laugh. "Come on, Alex. Time to get up."

Come on, Alex.

Open your eyes.

I glance up at our teammates, and each of them are wearing the same worried expression.

The medical team comes out onto the ice, and Jason pulls me away to give them space.

It feels as if time stops while we wait for them to finish checking Alex. I watch helplessly as they secure a neck brace on him, and then haul him onto a stretcher. A pool of red stays behind where his head just was. I stand frozen as they carry him off the ice.

His eyes still haven't opened.

Jason tugs on my jersey. "Come on. He's going to be okay. Let's finish this game so we can get to the hospital."

Hospital.

They're taking him to the hospital because he hasn't opened his eyes.

Bile rises in my throat as my thoughts immediately land on sweet Giuliana's face. What is she going to think when she hears her father is in the hospital?

My head jerks up to find Aarya in her seat behind Trenton's goal. Standing with her hands pressed against the glass, she looks beyond terrified —which is something I'm not used to seeing on her.

Ignoring the referee's whistle blows, I skate toward the wives in the stands.

I hold up my palm and press it to the glass. "He's going to be okay."

A tear slips down Aarya's cheek. It's a lie. She knows it, and I know it. We don't know if Alexander is going to be okay.

All I know is that an incident like this didn't need to happen. It wasn't necessary. Sure, players get hurt on the ice all the time, but two players *purposely* slamming into him like that? That was calculated, and violent.

I swing my gaze to Chance.

The man I love just played a part in hurting my best friend.

On purpose.

My skates move before I even realize what's happening. Trenton yanks me back by my jersey, but I shake him off.

Fuck this.

Chance knows I'm coming for him. He even doesn't try to defend himself. I launch myself at him, and slam my fists into his face over and over again.

Someone tries to pull me back, and I can hear voices shouting at me, but I can't make out what they're saying.

All I can see is Alexander's lifeless body on the ice.

Finally, Chance pushes me off of him, and throws a punch at my jaw. "It was an accident, Stephen."

"The fuck it was!" I swing again but the referee gets to me before my fist can connect.

"Let's go. Into the box."

On my way into the penalty box, I steal a glance at Ivanov. Wearing a devilish grin, he shoots me a wink.

And I fucking snap.

I throw punches as fast as my arms will allow me to, making sure I get in as many hits as I can before the ref stops me.

"Enough!" he yells in my ear. "You're out of the game. Go cool off."

I shove past Ivanov, and leave my team on the ice, down a captain and now down a winger.

But I can't seem to care.

I need to get to the hospital.

Internal bleeding. Head trauma. Brain surgery. Coma.

I couldn't understand half of the shit the doctor said, but I did make out those terms. My best friend is in a coma, all thanks to my boyfriend and his teammate.

"We're heading home." Jason pats me on the back. "You coming?"

I shake my head, staring at the tile floor. "I'm going to stay with Aarya. See if they'll let me back to see him after her."

Celeste squeezes my hand. "Let us know if anything changes. We'll be back in the morning."

After the team clears out of the waiting room, I take out my phone and click on Presley's name.

She answers after the first ring. "Hi. How is he?"

"He's breathing on his own, but he's still in a coma."

"Fuck." She pauses. "Dominique said she can stay with the kids. I'm coming to see you."

"No, don't do that."

"Why not? I don't want you sitting there by yourself."

"The team is still here," I lie. "Stay home. I'll update you if I hear anything new."

"I'm so sorry, Stephen." She lets out a heavy sigh. "Chance is sorry too."

Anger spikes in my veins. "Is he there with you?"

"No, but I spoke to him. He's really upset. He didn't mean to—"

"Didn't mean to? Are you fucking kidding me? Of course he meant to. He and that piece of shit Ivanov wanted to hurt Alex. They always play dirty, and this time they took it too far."

"Stephen," she whispers. "You have to know he didn't want this."

I shake my head and squeeze my eyes shut, at a complete loss for words. I saw the play; I saw the way they teamed up to hit Alexander from both sides. Presley might be able to believe that Chance didn't do it on purpose, but I know better. It's what he does, what he's capable of. He has anger issues. Always has.

And now my best friend has to pay the price.

Two days.

It's been two days since the game. Two days since Alexander has been in a coma. Two days since I've spoken to Stephen.

Two days since my heart has splintered in half.

Ivanov crossed a line that night. I had it handled; I was covering Alexander, putting pressure on the play. We were both scrambling for possession of the puck, heads down, and I caught a glimpse of him coming one second too late. I shouted for him to stop, tried to alert Alexander, but it all happened so fast.

This was the last thing I ever expected.

I've tried to call Stephen for the past two days, but he refuses to answer. I don't want Presley feeling like she's in the middle of this, so I told her to stay with him and be strong for him while he's waiting for his best friend to come back to him.

If he comes back.

Memories of my mother have been at the forefront of my mind. If it weren't for me, she wouldn't have run out in front of the car to protect me from my father. If it weren't for me, maybe Alexander wouldn't be in a coma right now.

It's like everything I touch turns to shit.

Like I'm destined for nothing but horror and sadness.

I've known it all along. I only deluded myself these last few months, letting myself believe that I could have things as beautiful and pure as love and happiness.

I was so fucking wrong.

Stephen's car pulls up to Presley's house, and rolls into the driveway. I get out of my car and make my way up the path to meet him before he goes into the house.

He does a double-take over his shoulder, and glares at me with tired, sunken-in eyes. "Get the fuck out of here, Chance."

"Can we just talk?"

"I have nothing to say to you." He turns and walks toward the porch stairs. "Do not follow me. You're not welcome here."

"Stephen, please." Presley's voice has both of our heads snapping up to the front door. "Talk to him. We can sit together and talk it out."

"There is nothing to talk about, Pres." Stephen's jaw clenches. I've never seen him so angry before. So closed off. "Alex is in a coma because of *him*. There's nothing he can say to make this better."

"Chance!" Avery pushes past Presley and bounds down the stairs, jumping into my arms. "You're here."

"Hey, bud." I wrap my arms around him and hold him tight.

"I missed you," he says, his voice muffled against my chest.

Unexpected tears sting my eyes. "Me too."

Alyssa runs out the door next. "Chance, are you staying?"

I hug her to my side, emotion clogging my throat. I don't know what to say, don't know if I belong here anymore.

"Chance is going home," Stephen says. He crosses his arms over his chest, drawing a clear line in the sand between us.

The kids look to Presley.

I don't want to do this in front of them, and I know Presley doesn't either. I need to walk away, as much as it kills me.

I ruffle Alyssa's hair, and squeeze Avery's shoulder. "It's okay, guys. I'll catch you later."

"No, don't go." Avery grips my wrist as he turns to his aunt. "Please, Aunt Presley. Let him stay."

Her shoulders droop as she glances at Stephen, unsure of what to do. "Let's go inside so we can talk."

I shake my head. "It's okay. I have to get ready for a game tomorrow," I lie. "Just wanted to stop by and say hi."

"Can I come with you?" Avery asks. "I'll come to your game, and I'll be quiet on the bus. I promise. Please, I just want to stay with you."

My heart wrenches in my chest. "You have school tomorrow, kid. But I'll FaceTime you from the hotel. How does that sound?"

His eyebrows push together as he drops his head.

I tip his chin. "Take care of your aunt, okay?"

He nods, but he won't meet my eyes. Presley tries to reach for him as he walks past her, but he shakes her off and storms into the house.

Alyssa slinks back inside, void of her usual spunkiness.

Fuck, I shouldn't have come here.

Presley comes down the stairs and she pulls me close to her. I breathe her in as she lifts onto her toes as she puts her arms around the back of my neck.

"Don't give up on him," she whispers. "Don't give up on us."

But it's already too late.

I pull back and turn to Stephen. My hand twitches, dying to reach out and touch him. But he won't even look at me.

"So, that's it, huh?" I arch a brow, hot tears filling my eyes. "All that talk about us being together forever, no matter what...it was conditional."

His eyebrows hit his hairline. "*You* did this. This isn't my fault. You ruined everything like you always do."

His words hit me like bullets. "I didn't mean to! It was an accident."

"Bullshit." He charges down the stairs and shoves me back. "You and Ivanov play rough, and you knew exactly what you were doing that night."

I step forward so we're chest to chest. "It's not bullshit. I didn't mean for this to happen. You just need someone to blame to make yourself feel better."

"This is what you do. You let all your pent-up anger from your past eat away at you, and you lash out at everyone else. Your rage cost my best friend his life." He throws a punch, and I don't put my hands up to block it. "He's in the hospital right now, while his family cries at his bedside, not knowing if he'll ever come back to them."

Presley tugs on his arm. "Stephen..."

"It's okay, Pres." I arch a taunting brow at him. "Let him get it out."

He needs someone to take out his pain on. I'll bear it all for him.

The anger radiates off his body, his eyes like cold sapphire stones. I've never seen him like this before, and it terrifies me that my actions have brought him to this point.

Stephen's fist connects with my jaw again. "Come on, fight back, you prick." Another punch. "You love violence so much; you know you want to hit me back. This is what fuels you."

"It's not. Not anymore."

Not like it used to. I've come a long way from the man my father poisoned.

Or maybe this is who I truly am, and have been all along.

Maybe I'll never be able to escape it.

I lift my hand and he flinches, but he doesn't pull away as I press my palm against his cheek. "I'm sorry, Stephen. I'm so sorry."

It's all I can offer, though it's not enough.

For a fraction of a second, his eyes soften. My heart clenches in my chest, and I hold my breath, waiting for whatever's about to come out of his mouth next.

Please forgive me, baby.

I didn't mean to do this.

Can't you see that?

Don't you see me?

Without a word, his arm cocks back and he punches me again. "For someone who tries so hard to not be like your father, you're sure following right in his footsteps."

Betrayal pierces my heart like an arrow. His words wound me more than his fists ever could.

I wipe my lip with the back of my hand, and blood smears across my skin.

Presley's shoulders shake as she cries.

This is all because of me.

All I do is cause problems and pain.

I let my eyes roam over the two loves of my life one last time before I turn and walk back to my car.

Leaving my bloody heart at their feet.

FIRST RIVAL GAME AFTER GRADUATING COLLEGE

I CAN FEEL HIM BEFORE I SPOT HIM WARMING UP ACROSS THE rink.

It's like my body picks up a frequency only he emits. The hairs on the back of my neck stand up; my skin buzzes; my heart thumps a furious rhythm against my chest.

I watch Stephen as he glides around, laughing with his teammates, and engaging with the crowd. The charismatic showman.

He looks happy. He should. He deserves to be.

Then he spots me, and his smile falls. I told myself I'd be fine tonight. I told myself I'd be able to act like I don't miss the two of them every second that I'm awake, and dream of them every time I close my eyes. I told myself it's just one game. I can survive one game.

But everything rushes at me in the instant we lock eyes; the memories, the tender moments, the laughs.

I blame Presley for breaking us. How could we be *us* without her? How could we go back to two when three was what set us on fire? But I can't deny that I pushed Stephen away and made sure whatever we had left was destroyed. Not only did I lose the only two people I've ever loved, but I lost a man who had my back no matter what. I lost my best friend.

And it's my fault. It always is.

Echoes of our last conversation on graduation night haunt me as I'm hit with Stephen's cold stare.

"We can stay together," Stephen pleads. "We can figure out where Presley went, and find out what happened. We don't have to end this."

I let out a humorless laugh. "She left us, Stephen. She made a choice. And I'm not going to let you settle for me when we both know you were happiest with her here."

"Being with you isn't settling." He steps closer to me and takes my hand, unclenching my fist and pressing my palm to his face. "I love you. I don't want to lose you."

Emotion strangles me, lodging itself in my throat like a boulder.

"I love you," he repeats. "We can figure this out together."

I want to believe him. I want to give in. But I know better. Presley left, and though I'll never understand why, I know some part of it has to be because of me. I was bringing them down. And I won't let that happen to Stephen. He deserves so much more than what I can offer him. He doesn't realize it now, but he will.

I pull back from his touch, and his hand drops at his side. "There is no we without her. She's gone, so it's over."

"You don't even want to try?"

"What's the point? You're only fooling yourself if you think this'll work."

His eyes narrow. "Why are you saying this? I know you don't mean it. I know you love me."

A searing knife slices into my chest. I want to tell him he's right; I do love him. But it'll only hurt worse in the end, so I might as well cut it off now.

"This isn't real." The lie burns like acid on my tongue. "And now the fantasy is over, so we can get back to reality. I'm here to play hockey, and leave everything in my life behind."

Hurt flashes in his eyes as they fill with tears. "Even me?"

I swallow the bile climbing up my throat. "Especially you."

I force myself to look away, and push away the painful memory.

I don't have time to feel all of these emotions right now. I have to prove my worth on this team, and that's where my focus needs to be. Hockey is the only thing I have in this life, and I can't fuck it up.

As soon as the puck drops, my skates dig into the ice, propelling me forward. Adrenaline floods my veins. My team comes away with the puck, and I instantly spot an opening on the right side. But as I approach it, there he is right beside me.

I speed up, preparing to accept the pass from my teammate, but Stephen's stick juts out and he steals it away before skating off in the opposite direction.

Fuck.

I fly down the ice after him, tunnel vision taking over in this silent war between us. The anger, the pain, the resentment, the heartache, the guilt—it all surges inside me like a tidal wave, and I'm helpless to stay afloat. I shove him into the boards, and take the puck back down to my side of the rink. The crowd roars around us, but it sounds like a whisper compared to the sound of my pulse in my ears. Before Stephen can get to me, I pass the puck off to my teammate, but the goalie stops his shot at the net.

We're at a stalemate for the first period, but we start the second like we've been shot out of a cannon.

Stephen and I play our hearts out while simultaneously gunning for each other. He's right behind me, and no matter how hard I try, I can't seem to shake him. Every move I make, every shot I attempt, every pass—he's right there with me like my fucking shadow, taunting me with the memory of what we once were.

Anger flares in the pit of my stomach, and when Stephen gets possession of the puck, I smash into him. Hard.

This ends now.

He stumbles but regains balance. I drop my gloves and my stick, and the last thing I see is that smug fucking smirk on his face before I slam my fist into it.

Stephen's fist connects with my jaw in return, but I don't feel any pain. It feels too good, taking out my aggression on him. This kind of contact is better than no contact at all; this is the only way I can get my hands on him.

We trade blows, until I grab onto his jersey and slam him back against the boards.

Stephen grins, blood dripping from his nose. "This make you feel better, baby? You always did like it rough."

"Fuck you." My arm cocks back to punch him again, but the referee pulls me off him before I can have my fill.

Though I don't know that I'll ever have my fill of this man.

It's never going to be enough, because it'll never be what it once was.

And at the end of the night, my team loses the game.
0-1.
It's fitting.
A big fat zero. An empty nothing.
Just like me.

"ANOTHER CONTAINER."

Alyssa looks up at me as she kneels beside the Tupperware on the porch. "When is he going to come back?"

I blow out a long breath between my lips. "I don't know, kid."

Every night this week, Chance has left dinner on the porch—cooked and ready, with enough left for the kids to take for lunch the next day. I talk to him on FaceTime before bed, and call to see Stephen as well. But neither of them has been here in days. After their fight out on the lawn the other night, I told Stephen that it isn't fair to anyone to have him here without Chance, and vice versa. My house needs to be a neutral zone, for me and for the kids.

I don't want *one* of them. It's both, or nothing.

I'm holding out for both, but I don't know how this will all turn out—especially if Alexander doesn't wake up. This animosity between the boys was there before I came into the picture, and with Stephen's best friend in a coma, it's back stronger than ever.

I've never seen Stephen like this before. I'm worried that he won't be able to move past this, regardless of Alexander's outcome. His friends are his family, and I know better than anyone how difficult it is losing someone close to you. I'm trying to stay positive for him, but deep down I'm anxious.

Avery takes the food from Alyssa and walks into the house without a word. The kids have been talking to Stephen and Chance on the phone daily, but our house just isn't the same without them here, together. I hate that it's taking a toll on the kids.

"Okay, kids. Back in the car."

Alyssa stops in her tracks. "What? Where are we going?"

"We're taking a road trip."

Avery perks up. "To Philadelphia?"

"To Philadelphia."

He grins and bolts back out the door, still carrying the container of food in his hands.

"Wait!" Alyssa runs up the stairs. "I have to get something." A minute later, she returns clutching two bottles of nail polish, one in each hand. "I want to paint his nails for his game tomorrow!"

I give her a sad smile. "Not sure he'll be in the mood for that, babe."

"Duh. That's why I'm gonna cheer him up."

I laugh. *Yeah, she totally will.*

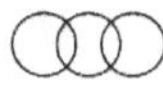

Nerves dance in my stomach as we walk toward Chance's door.

I called ahead and told him we were coming, yet I'm still anxious about how he'll respond to us being in his space. I know he isolates when he's upset, plus he has a game tomorrow—the first one since Alexander's accident—and I don't want to cause him more stress than he's already under.

But all my worries dissipate when he swings open the door and hugs the kids tightly to his chest.

Alyssa invites herself in, and makes herself at home. "We brought dinner. Well, technically, you brought dinner, but then we brought it back to you. You know what I mean. Oh, wow—your TV is huge!"

Avery follows her into the apartment, shaking his head.

I grimace. "Sorry. She's...Alyssa."

Chance offers me a sad smile. "Don't apologize."

I slip my arms around his waist, and breathe in his clean scent. "How are you holding up?"

His shoulders slump as he wraps his arms around me. "Better now that you're here."

"Are you able to skip tomorrow's game? Do hockey players get sick days?"

He hikes a shoulder. "I think it'll make things worse if I don't show up."

I blow out a long breath through my lips. "I just wish Alex would wake up. I hate being in limbo like this."

He nods, clenching his jaw. "Come on, let me give you guys a tour."

The tour doesn't last long, and my heart sinks when I take in the bare walls and lifeless rooms. It screams solitude, and I know the last four years couldn't have been easy on him.

"What's in this room?" Alyssa swings open the last door at the end of the hallway.

"Wait, that's not—"

Her eyes widen when she steps in the doorway. "Whoa."

Chance reaches up and rubs the back of his neck. "It's not finished yet."

Avery and I peer into the room, and a gasp leaves my throat. "Chance..."

He leans against the doorframe and watches me as I step further into the room.

One side has wall-to-wall shelves, filled with books. The other wall is accented with giant windows overlooking the city, with various types of comfortable chairs set up underneath that look perfect to curl up on while you're reading. An easel stands in the far corner of the room beside a table with paint brushes and stacked canvases.

Avery glances over his shoulder, his eyes darting between us. "Is this for us? For me and Alyssa?"

Chance nods. "It was going to be a surprise."

Alyssa clamps her hand over her mouth. "Sorry."

He chuckles. "It's okay. I wanted you guys to have something to do when you come over. I wanted to make it feel more...inviting."

I slip my hand into his and give it a squeeze. "You wanted to make it feel like a home."

"Thank you." Avery smiles, and nudges Alyssa.

"Oh, yes. Thank you!"

My stomach growls. Loud.

Chance's eyebrows shoot up. "Uh-oh. Her stomach is growling. That only gives us five minutes."

Avery holds up his wrist, pretending to glance at a watch. "Hurry! We have to get the beast fed!"

My mouth drops open. "I am not a beast."

Alyssa pushes past everyone and runs frantically out of the room. "Get to the kitchen! Now!"

"I'll get the plates," Avery shouts as he and Chance scramble to get out of the room, leaving me behind.

I lift my arms and let them fall, slapping my palms against my thighs. "What the hell?"

"I love your nails."

Chance smirks as he gazes down at his newly painted navy-and-silver nails. "I can't tell her no."

"Welcome to my life." I lean my head against his shoulder, stretching my legs out on the couch. "It was really sweet of you to build that room for them."

"I just want them to feel welcome here. I don't know if I'll be able to spend time at their house anymore."

Guilt pricks at my gut. "I hate this so much."

"Me too." His voice lowers. "I'm scared."

I lift my head to look at him. "Of what, baby?"

"Scared if Alexander doesn't wake up; or if he does, that he won't have a memory." He swallows. "I'm scared that Stephen won't be able to forgive me. Scared that I've ruined everything."

"It's not your fault, Chance." I shift and straddle his lap, putting myself right in front of his face. "I know you have it in your head that you are the reason for your mother's death, but your father was the one behind the wheel that night. He was the one who was drunk. He was the one responsible. You were trying to help your mother. You were just a kid." I clutch his face between my hands. "You cannot hold onto this any longer, do you hear me? You have to stop blaming yourself, and let it go. It's not serving you."

A lone tear rolls down his cheek, and his bottom lip trembles.

"Let it go," I whisper. Leaning in, I press a kiss to his cheek, swiping away his tears. "You don't deserve this eternity of pain you're forcing yourself to live in."

His shoulders shake with his silent sobs.

I slide my arms and legs around his body, and squeeze him with all my might—with all of my love, as if it can heal him all the way to his soul.

"Life happens to us all, good and bad. The only things you can take responsibility for are the choices you make. You choose to drive drunk? Yes, that's your fault. You decide to throw a punch, or cheat on your husband, or gamble all of your money—these are all choices you'd have to face the consequences of. But other things are accidents. They just happen, and I don't know why, but I'd like to think we're faced with them to make us stronger."

He rests his forehead on my shoulder. "I don't think Stephen sees it that way."

"He has to navigate this for himself right now. You know, he's never experienced trauma before. Me and you? We've lost people. We've suffered through grief. His life has been pretty much perfect up until this point, and he doesn't know what to do with all of this pain. We have to be strong for him, and be patient while he figures this out."

I lean back and tip his head to look into my eyes. "I have faith that he will come back to us. He just needs some time."

He huffs out a humorless laugh. "We've already been apart for four years. What's some more time, huh?"

I smile and press a soft kiss to his lips. "Don't give up on us, Grumpy Man. We're going to make it out of this together."

"You know, Stephen told me we'd find you again. He told me that we'd be together one day, and I didn't believe him."

"I'm sorry that I put you both through that." I let out a sad sigh. "I'm sorry I put myself through that. It would've been so much easier to have you there, helping me through it. Then again, maybe it's like what I said—maybe I needed to go through with it on my own. Who knows."

"My mother always used to say that we don't know what the reason for all of this is until we meet our maker in the sky." A soft smile touches his lips as he remembers her. "I have a few choice words for this maker."

I giggle. "You don't talk too much about her. When was the last time you went to visit her grave?"

He shakes his head. "I haven't. Not since her burial."

My eyes widen. "I'd like to come with you someday, if you'll let me."

Chance brushes a strand of hair out of my eyes. "Okay."

Well, that was easy. "Thought you'd put up more of a fight."

"I'm done fighting. I just want to love you."

I smile against his lips as he leans in. "That sounds great."

"Daddy, look. I drew you another picture. This one's funny. I made you into a unicorn, and gave you rainbow wings. Unicorns have magic, and maybe if you had some magic, you'd wake up."

God, this is the worst kind of torture. Day in and day out, watching Alexander's daughter talk to him while he lies there, lifeless.

Giuliana pats him gingerly on his head, careful as to not upset the bandage wrapped around it. "I wonder if he's dreaming. What do you think, Uncle Mac?"

I clear my throat and try to speak around the lump lodged in it. "I think people can dream when they're in a coma. I think they can hear us talking to them too."

"Maybe he'll have a dream about a magical unicorn now." She giggles, her thick brown curls bouncing around her cheeks. "That'd be funny."

It's been six days. The longer he stays in a coma, the worse his prognosis gets. I've done what the nurses told me not to do, and Googled every possible outcome. Memory loss; brain damage; death. This is like a sick nightmare that I'm stuck in, and I need someone to shake me awake.

"Can we get hot chocolate?" Giuliana looks at me with those big, round, puppy dog eyes, the same exact ones her father has, and she knows I can't say no—to her or hot chocolate.

"Of course. We'll have to leave the hospital to get the good stuff though. You okay with that?"

"Sure." She places her tiny hand on her father's chest. "Daddy, we're going to get some hot chocolate. Do you want some too? We'll be right back, so don't worry. We won't be gone too long."

Tears sting the backs of my eyes as I lift her into my arms, and carry her out of the room. Aarya is asleep on the cot in the corner, so I shoot her a text to let her know where we are in case she wakes up.

"Can we invite Presley and Chance?" Giuliana asks. "I want to play with Alyssa and Avery."

"Uh, I'm not sure, kid." I contemplate the right words to say. Sure, she's only four, so I could easily lie. But she's intelligent and intuitive, so it feels wrong to lie to her.

"Are they busy?"

The elevator door dings and we step inside. "Well, the truth is, I'm not speaking to Chance right now. But I can ask Presley if you can have a play date with the kids one day soon."

Her eyebrows furrow. "Why aren't you talking to Chance? Did you get into a fight?"

I blow out a sigh as I carry her into the lobby of the hospital. Fuck it. I'm going for honesty. "You know how your dad got hurt during a hockey game?"

She nods.

"Chance was one of the players on the other team who hurt him."

She stares at me, and I can see the wheels in her head spinning. "He hurt him on purpose?"

I don't know how to answer this question. It feels wrong to say yes, and it feels wrong to say no. I've been going over it in my head like I'm riding a merry-go-round made of knives, trying to understand why Chance had any part in this.

"It's hard to say what really happened. I don't...I don't know if Chance tried to hurt Daddy on purpose, but he wasn't playing safely, and in the end, Daddy got hurt."

"Daddy always says hockey is a dangerous sport." Her eyes widen. "Did you know they're allowed to punch each other, and nobody stops them?"

I chuckle. "Yes. It's crazy, right?"

She nods. "I think it was an accident. Nobody would want to hurt Daddy on purpose. He's so kind, and he's a great hockey player. Plus, Chance loves you. So, he wouldn't want to hurt your friend."

I hug her tightly to my body before setting her down on the sidewalk outside. "You're probably right."

My heart says she is, but my mind can't get over the fact that Chance and Ivanov are known for being overly aggressive. We know accidents happen on the ice all the time, and we've each had our own share of scares. In this season alone, I've watched both Trenton and Jason end up getting hauled off the ice.

But nothing of this magnitude.

I wish it were me. I wish I could switch places with Alexander. I feel guilty that I wasn't able to protect him, to stop Ivanov from getting to him. I was too wrapped up in Chance, too focused on the wrong things. My head wasn't completely in the game, and I fucked up.

"My teacher said that sometimes people do things that they don't mean to do." She looks up at me as we walk hand-in-hand down the block, her curls bouncing around her shoulders. "There's this boy in my class, Marcus, and he hits the other kids."

I arch a brow. "Has he ever hit you?"

"No, but he hit my friends. Miss Kelly asked him why he hit them, and he said he didn't know. Then she had to explain it to us, and she said that sometimes people do things without thinking." Her eyes narrow. "Isn't your brain always thinking?"

"It is, but some people are impulsive. That means their brain reacts before their mind can catch up to it. That's probably why Marcus hits, because he gets angry and his brain makes his body react before his brain can think rationally."

She's quiet as she thinks on it for a moment. "So, maybe Chance's brain didn't tell him to stop before he hurt Daddy. Maybe he was being *im-plus-ive*."

I toss my head back and laugh. "Impulsive."

"Yeah, that."

I suck in a lungful of air, and feel a little bit lighter when I exhale. "I love you, kid. You know that, right?"

"Duh." She smiles as she looks up at me. "I love you too, Uncle Mac."

I slip my phone out of my pocket. "Let's call Presley and see if she wants to meet us at the arcade."

Giuliana gasps. "Really? That's gonna be so much fun!"

We could all use a little bit of fun right now.

"I took the kids to see Chance yesterday."

My heart constricts. "I bet they were happy to see him."

Presley nods. "He's really beating himself up about this. I'm worried about him."

I grunt. "He's not the one in a coma."

She peels at the label on her water bottle. "He's always felt responsible for his mother's death, and now this. There's only so much weight someone can withstand before they crack."

Bile rises in my throat, my stomach churning with guilt. I said some awful things to him that night he showed up at Presley's house. I compared him to his father, which was as low a shot as I could've taken at him.

I didn't mean it. He's not his father. But I was just so furious—I still am —at the way everything went down on the ice.

"This isn't me," I admit. "Anger and resentment and all this turmoil. I feel sick." My eyes wander to Avery and Alyssa, helping Giuliana shoot basketballs several feet away in the desolate arcade. "And I hate that you're all in the middle of it."

"Hey." Presley cups my cheek and turns my face to meet her eyes. "You're going through a lot right now. Alex is like a brother to you, and you're scared. It's understandable. You don't have to always be the funny man, you know. We're here for you. You have our unwavering love and support. And you will get through this, regardless of the outcome."

My phone buzzes with a notification. My shoulders jump, and I fumble to get my phone out of my pocket, hoping it's a message from Aarya saying that Alex has woken up.

AllyCat418 wants to chat.

My heart sinks. "I keep meaning to cancel my membership on this site."

"What site?" Presley leans over and glances at my screen. "Is that Kourtney's website?"

I nod. "I haven't been on it since the night I saw you on the KissCam."

She grins. "Let me see."

I hand her my phone, and she explores the site. "This is incredible. There's something for everyone on here."

"Kourtney did an amazing job with this."

She clicks on my inbox. "That's funny. This username is *ScoringChance*, and that's Chance's birthday; February seventeenth."

My eyebrows pinch together. "Wait, what?"

She hands me back my phone, and I scroll through the private message exchange between me and the anonymous stranger from a couple of months ago.

"Scoring chance is a hockey term, isn't it?" Presley asks.

I stare at the username in disbelief. "It is."

"You don't think it could be Chance, do you?"

"I wouldn't be able to tell from this thread, but..." I close my eyes, trying to rack my brain to remember what was in the background of his video when we chatted. "We had a video chat once, but it was too dark to make out anything."

My heart accelerates.

Presley points to one of his messages. "He said he isn't out yet."

I shake my head. "There's no way. That would be too much of a coincidence. Come on, what are the odds we match up on a dating app one week before we run into you at our game."

"The same odds that I'd show up at both of your games, and end up on the KissCam." She bites her bottom lip as she rereads our conversation. "I've always said we were written in the stars, Stephen. I think there's a real possibility that this is him."

Longing and anticipation twist my heart in a vice.

"Only one way to find out." Presley nudges me with her elbow. "Message this guy. See if he'll show you a picture of his face."

"I know you believe in all that zodiac mumbo-jumbo, but it's not real. It's not him, Pres."

It can't be.

"There's no harm in asking." She bounces on her heels. "Come on. I'm dying to know."

"Aunt Presley!" Alyssa comes waddling over with Giuliana on her back. "We're hungry. Can we get some pizza?"

"Sure." Presley side-eyes me, and lowers her voice as she whispers, "Chicken shit."

"This isn't lying. I call it *strategic persuasion.*" I arch a brow at my niece. "And it's for a good reason, not for sneaking candy into your room."

She crosses her arms over her chest. "That was one time."

"Won't they be worried though?" Avery asks. "Stephen is already worried enough about Alex. Won't this make him scared?"

I heave a long sigh. "I thought about that, but you're not going to be hurt—you're just going missing for a couple of hours."

"What if they want to come check his room for clues?" Alyssa asks.

Avery rolls his eyes. "What clues would they be looking for?"

I smooth my hand over her soft hair. "I really shouldn't let you watch all those crime shows."

"Too late now." She shrugs. "Okay, so, you're going to call them and tell them that you can't find Avery. Then what?"

"They'll want to split up and look all over town for him. Then after an hour or so, I'll call them and tell them that I found him, and to come over. This will get them both here at the same time, and they'll have to talk it out." I grimace. "And hopefully, they're not both mad at me."

"For the record, I think this is a terrible idea," Avery says.

Alyssa bounces in her chair. "This is so fun! It's like we're spies on an undercover mission."

"All spy missions are undercover."

"Whatever." Alyssa slides my phone closer to me across the table. "Call them now."

I fill my lungs with a brave breath, and scroll through my contacts. "Your phone is off, right, Ave?"

He nods. "It's off."

"Good. They need to think your phone died."

I click on Stephen's name, and hold the phone to my ear.

Here goes nothing.

"Hey, pretty girl. How was work?"

"Hey, is Avery with you by any chance?"

"What? No. Why would he be with me?"

"I can't find him, and I was hoping you knew where he was. He wasn't at school when I went to pick him up, and the principal said he never came to school today."

"Oh, shit. Maybe he cut with his friends. Have you tried their parents?"

"Yes." I pause and close my eyes, mustering all my strength to not give myself away with my terrible acting. "I'm worried. This isn't like him."

"It's okay, baby. I'll help you find him." It's quiet before he asks, "Have you called Chance?"

"He's my next call."

"Okay, you call him and I'll take a ride around the neighborhood." I hear the sound of his keys clanging in the background. "Don't worry, pretty girl. We'll find him."

Guilt pricks my conscience, and I have to remind myself that I'm doing this for good reason. "Thank you. I love you."

"I love you too, baby."

I end the call and click on Chance's name next. Nerves bubble in my stomach. Chance is the intuitive one of the two, and I'm really hoping he doesn't call my bluff.

"Hi, rebel." His deep voice rolls over me like warm butter. "How's my girl today?"

"Please tell me you have Avery with you right now."

"I'm home alone. Why, what's wrong?"

"He cut school today, and now I don't know where he is."

"Fuck," he hisses. "Let's check the gallery, and I can take a ride down to the arcade. Maybe he ditched with his friends for a day of fun."

"I don't know, that just doesn't sound like him. Plus, his friends' parents said he isn't with them."

"It'll take me a couple hours to get to you, but I'm on my way. Do you have Alyssa?"

"Yes."

"Okay, I want the two of you to stay home in case he comes back."

"Are you sure? Shouldn't I be out looking for him?"

"Someone needs to be home for him, baby. You stay there by the phone. Tell Stephen to check the gallery, and any other places he likes to go in town. I'll check the arcade, and we'll be in touch if anything comes up."

Alyssa clamps her hand over her mouth to keep herself quiet, and Avery smirks as he listens to the conversation.

"Okay, thank you, Chance."

"Of course. Everything's going to be okay, baby. Try not to worry too much. He's a good kid. He won't be doing anything bad."

"You're right. I love you."

"I love you more. Talk soon."

I let my head fall against the table with a thud when I end the call.

Alyssa giggles. "Now what?"

"You guys want pizza for dinner tonight?"

"Yes!" they both shout.

"That's it?" Avery asks. "Now we just wait?"

I nod once. "Now, we wait."

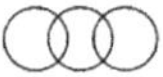

"Where is he?"

I yank Stephen by his arm and close the front door behind him. "He locked himself in his room, and he won't talk to me. I don't know what happened."

He presses a kiss to my forehead, and turns for the stairs. "I'll try to get him to open up."

I shoot a warning glare at Alyssa, who's practically buzzing around me like a neurotic bird. "Keep it together," I whisper.

"I'm trying!" she whisper-yells back. "*You* keep it together."

God, I am so bad at this. But my plan seems to be working. All I need is for Chance to get here so this can come to a head.

While Stephen is upstairs trying to coax Avery to open his bedroom door, Chance pulls up to the house.

Show time.

My heart is in my throat as he barrels through the door. "He's here? Is he okay?"

I nod. "He's upstairs, but—"

Chance takes off up the stairs, and I run after him. He stops short when he gets to the top step, and his hand tightens around the banister.

Stephen's head whips around, and his jaw clenches. "He won't open the door."

"So, we'll break it down." Chance rolls up his sleeves. "Avery, we're coming in one way or another. You can open this door right now, or I will take it off the damn hinges."

The door flies open, and Avery's wide eyes meet mine. "Tell him, Aunt Presley!"

Stephen and Chance flick their gazes to me, and I swallow the dry lump in my throat.

"Surprise!" Alyssa shouts.

Oh, God.

Stephen tilts his head. "Huh?"

Chance pinches the bridge of his nose. "You've got to be kidding me."

"What?" Stephen glances between the two of us. "What's going on?"

"We tricked you!" Alyssa squeezes past me and stands in the middle of my two men. "We hate that you're fighting, and we knew we couldn't get you to talk to each other, so we came up with a plan to get you both here at the same time."

Stephen arches a brow at me. "You lied to us?"

I give him a sheepish smile. "I call it *strategic persuasion.*"

Chance grunts. "That's messed up. You used the kid against us."

Avery holds up his index finger. "I gave my consent. Come on, hasn't this gone on long enough? You guys need to talk it out."

Chance glares at me. "I've been wanting to talk. It's not me you had to persuade. It's him. And tricking him isn't the way to do that."

He turns and heads back downstairs, and my heart drops to the floor. "Stephen, please. Stop him. Talk to him."

But his phone goes off in his pocket, and he pulls it out to glance at the screen. "Fuck, it's Aarya."

The door opens and closes downstairs as Chance walks out.

Shit.

"I'll try to stop him." Avery bolts down the stairs with Alyssa right behind him.

Stephen's eyes widen as he listens to Aarya. "Oh, my God."

I grab his arm. "What? What is it?"

He drops his arm, and lets his phone fall to the floor. "He's awake."

MY FEET FALTER WHEN I GET TO ALEXANDER'S ROOM.

Aarya said he hasn't been able to speak yet, but he recognized her, so that's good news.

I have to lighten the mood. Make him laugh. It's been so heavy this last week without him, and it can't be easy waking up to find out all that's gone on in his absence. Knowing him, he's sick to his stomach about Giuliana going through this.

I take a moment to breathe in deep, and then I head into the room.

Aarya clutches his hand, and Giuliana sits on his lap, talking a mile a minute. She smiles wide when she spots me. "Uncle Mac, look! Daddy's awake!"

My eyes meet his, and my heart seizes in my chest. "It's about fucking time, man. If you needed some time to rest, you could've just taken a vacation like a normal person."

A slow smile spreads across his face, and he lifts his free hand to flip me off behind Giuliana's back.

Tears burn my eyes and blur my vision.

He's back.

He's okay.

Aarya rises from the bed and takes Giuliana with her. "Come on, kid. Let's go get an Irish hot chocolate for your Uncle Mac. I think he could use one."

"What does Irish mean?"

Alexander arches a brow at his wife, and she shoots him a wink. "I'll explain it on the way."

She kicks her feet as she beams. "Bye, Daddy. See you soon."

He presses his hand to his mouth, and blows her a kiss. She catches it, and her sweet laughter floats into the hallway.

Hot tears spill out of my eyes as soon as she's out the door. "Thank fuck. I was not going to be able to hold it together much longer."

Alexander opens his arms as wide as the wires will allow him, and I take long strides toward the bed so I can hug him.

"I'm so happy you're okay," I whisper, holding him tightly. "I never want to go through anything like that ever again."

His body shakes as he hugs me with as much force as he can muster. "Thank you," he whispers.

Aarya said the nurse told her that his throat will be sore for a little while from the feeding tube, and not talking all week.

I pull back and wipe my eyes with the backs of my hands. "Damn, I'm fucking glad you remember who I am. It would've been exhausting to force you to be my friend all over again."

His shoulders shake with silent laughter as he shakes his head. He sputters, so I hand him the cup of water sitting on the tray beside his bed.

"Aarya is a trooper. She was here every day, and kept Giuliana in good spirits." I squeeze his hand. "I hope you know how much that woman loves you."

His eyes water again and he nods. "I know."

I slide over a chair, and kick back my feet onto the bed. "Want me to catch you up on anything you've missed, or do you just want to enjoy the quiet for a little longer?"

His head tilts, and he pushes out the words, "How's Chance?"

My jaw clenches. "Don't worry about that right now, man. You're awake and you're just getting your bearings."

He holds up his palm, as if to stop me. "This wasn't his fault."

I shake my head. "You might not remember too clearly, but I saw—"

"I heard him."

My chin jerks back. "What do you mean?"

"Right before I got hit..." He coughs, and lifts the cup to his lips for another sip. "He saw Ivanov right before I did, and he shouted for him to stop. I heard it."

Regret and shock churn in my stomach, twisting my insides until I'm sick. "Are you sure?"

He nods once, keeping his brown eyes on mine.

I close my eyes. "Fuck."

Shouldn't I have known this though? Shouldn't I have given Chance the time to explain himself? Instead, when everything fell apart, I pointed the finger at him and turned my back on him.

Alex purses his lips. "What did you do?"

I let out a long exhale, scrubbing my palm over my face. "Nothing you need to worry about right now. Save your voice, and rest up so you can get the hell out of here."

For now, I'm going to enjoy the time with my best friend—time I wasn't sure I'd ever get again.

Chance's leg bounces as he stares down at his hands in his lap.

Presley sits between us on the couch. Luckily, Dominique was able to take the kids for the night so we can talk. I'm not sure how this talk is going to go, and I didn't want the kids eavesdropping.

I'm not usually at a loss for words, but it's been about two full, painful minutes, and neither of us has said a word to get this thing rolling.

"I guess I'll start," Presley says. "It's good to hear that Alexander is awake and alert. No memory loss or anything like that."

I nod. "He was in good spirits today when I saw him."

Presley smiles. "I bet Giuliana was happy."

"She was talking up a storm, filling him in on every little detail that he missed." I chuckle, but then my smile fades. "He, uh, he mentioned that he remembered what happened in the game right before Ivanov hit him."

Chance's face is a statue. If it weren't for his bouncing leg, I'd think he was frozen.

Presley reaches out and squeezes my hand.

This is painful.

"Alex said you tried to stop Ivanov," I blurt out.

Still no reaction from Chance.

Presley's wide eyes shift from me to him, blinking, waiting for him to say something.

"I'm sorry I blamed you." I pause, swallowing down the ball of nerves lodged in my throat, hoping Chance will say something. Anything. At least acknowledge that I'm speaking.

"Can you please look at me while I'm apologizing to you?"

Chance flicks his stormy eyes to mine.

"I'm sorry. I was so angry, and scared, but I shouldn't have blamed you for what happened. I never should have said the awful things I said to you."

Chance's jaw flexes under his skin, and the seconds tick by without a word from him.

Presley keeps my hand in hers as she leans over and reaches for Chance with her right hand. "Is there anything you want to say, baby?"

Finally, he breaks his silence. "I understand you being angry and scared. I was feeling the same way. I understand you thinking what Ivanov did was reckless and dangerous. I agree. I understand you needing time to cool off after the game. I needed space as well." Chance lifts Presley's hand and presses a kiss to her knuckles before letting it go. "But what I will never understand is why you thought I'd try to hurt Alexander on purpose."

My heart drops into my stomach. "I know. You're absolutely right—"

"No." Chance's voice booms. "You *don't* know. You didn't even hear me out, or let me explain. You shut me out, and instantly pointed the finger at me without a second thought. It's like you don't know me at all." He rises from the couch and stabs his chest with his finger. "Do you know how much that fucking hurts?"

Yes, baby. There we go. Let it all out.

"I'm so sorry for hurting you." I push off the couch to meet him in the middle of the room. "I didn't mean what I said about your father. That was a disgustingly low blow, and I swear I didn't mean it."

He clenches his fists at his sides, his entire body rigid. "You can't just take back the words after you hurl them at people, Stephen. The damage is already done."

"I know that." I step forward and grip his face in my hands. "I know I've hurt you, and I just need you to know how sorry I am. I know it doesn't take away the pain I've caused, and I know it doesn't wipe away what I said. But I'm going to work at earning your forgiveness and trust every single day if you give me the chance."

Tears well in his eyes as he stands strong, unmoving. He's not pulling away from me, so that counts for something.

"You hurt me." His voice cracks as a tear spills down his cheek. "You tossed me aside like I didn't matter."

"Just like you did to me!" I stab my chest with my finger. "When Presley left us, you pushed me away and told me our love wasn't enough."

"Oh, so this is all because you want to get back at me? Come on, what else have you been holding onto for all these years? Let's lay it all out on the table."

Anger swirls in my chest. "I've been the only one holding on to the three of us for these last four years, so don't try talking to me about who pushed who away."

Chance shakes his head. "You know what scares me the most? If Alexander never would've woken up, you wouldn't be standing here right now. You didn't have faith in me to know that I would never do something like that."

My heart splinters at his words. I could continue fighting with him, tell him that he didn't have faith in us either at one point in time. But we've come so far since then. We've been given our second chance, and I could either be stubborn and keep wedging this distance between us, or I can let the past go and figure out how to move forward. Together.

"Please, let me make this up to you. I want to prove to you that nothing like this will ever happen again."

"You didn't have my back." He shoves me back a step. "You didn't trust me."

I choke back a sob. "For years, we've been at each other's throats! We talked with our fists, and we took out our aggression on the ice. I just thought—"

"You thought I hurt your friend—and for what? What purpose would that serve?" Chance's voice gets louder. "Do you even hear yourself?"

Presley stands up and moves toward us. "Look, the bottom line is, Stephen made a mistake. Everyone fucks up in life. Look at me; I hurt you both in a way I'm still trying to figure out how to make up for. But you both forgave me. You knew that our love was strong enough to overcome any obstacle."

She's not wrong. We've each hurt the other while trying to find our way.

"Presley fucked up when she left us. You fucked up when you walked away from me and gave up on helping me find her. Now it's my turn to fuck up." I press my palms against my chest. "I'm allowed to fuck up every once in a while too, you know. I can't be held to this impossible standard where I never make a mistake. I'm not perfect, but I will always own up to my mistakes and take responsibility for my actions. And that has to count for something."

Tears overflow, the dam I've been trying to hold together all week while Alexander was in a coma finally breaking. "I'm so fucking sorry, Chance. I hate that I hurt you. I hate that you had to go through any of this because of me. I wish I could go back and do it over again, but I can't. All I can do is try to make it better moving forward. Please, baby, let me make it up to you."

The three of us are standing in front of each other with tear-streaked faces, laying it all on the table. All of our imperfections; all of our mistakes; the good the bad and the ugly. We've been through a lot together, and we've been able to make it this far.

I believe our love can carry us through anything.

But it's not me who needs convincing.

It's the beautiful, broken man standing in front of me.

I lace my fingers through each of their hands. "Please, baby. Say you'll forgive me. Let me love you the way you deserve to be loved."

Chance rolls his lips between his teeth and glances down at Presley. "Did you hear that, rebel? He said he's not perfect. Think we can get him to say it again so I can record it?"

An unexpected laugh bubbles out of her. "I don't think we'll get that lucky."

My jaw goes slack. "Was that a joke? Are you...joking? Does that mean you forgive me? Because if you're just being an asshole, then—"

Chance steps into my space and grips my shirt in his fists, pulling me nose-to-nose with him. "Don't you ever shut the fuck up?"

His lips crash into mine, and relief floods my senses. My shoulders relax, and my body melds against him as his arms wrap around my shoulders to hold me close while he kisses me.

My tongue surges inside his mouth, and he opens for me, just as eager as I am to take all of this pain away.

I reach for Presley, and she lifts onto her toes to join us, kissing each of us with such passion and reverence that I can feel it all the way down into the marrow of my bones. That's where these two have etched themselves, into the fibers of my being that make up my soul.

With them, I'm whole. I'm complete.

Presley pulls away panting, and tugs us by the hands. "Let's take this upstairs."

But Chance and I glance at one another. "I was kind of hoping we could go get the kids," Chance says.

I nod. "They're probably worried sick about us right now, and I've missed them like crazy."

Presley's eyebrows shoot up. "Let me get this straight: You're both turning down all of this,"—she gestures to her sexy as sin body—"for a couple of kids? Kids who *lied* to you, might I remind you."

Chance's head tilts back as he lets out a hearty laugh, and my chest warms at the sight of the smile on his handsome face. "You threw them right under the bus for some sex. That's shameful, rebel."

"So shameful." I lift her up and toss her over my shoulder, giving her plump ass a firm smack. "Come on, baby. Let's go get our kids."

I clench my jaw and roll my eyes. "Just ignore her, Dom. She's not worth our energy."

Dominique scoffs. "I beg to differ. She's definitely worth the energy it'd take for me to punch her in her stupid face."

I chuckle. "No violence today. I refuse to give Miserable Molly a reason to shut us down, or paint us in a bad light. This is happening, and she can't do a damn thing to stop us."

Today is the first event for *Inclusive Hearts*. I'm still going through the process of registering it as a nonprofit organization, but I figured there's no reason we can't start coming together now and spreading the word around the community.

It royally sucks that Molly and her minions showed up to try to tear us down, but we aren't going to pay her any mind. Her disgusting, discriminatory actions speak volumes about her—not us.

"This is a great turnout." Celeste struts over and bumps me with her hip. "The media will want an interview in a little while."

My pulse thumps faster. "Is there anything specific I should say? I need some of your PR expertise."

"They're definitely going to ask how you feel about Miserable Molly, but I'd try to keep it as positive as possible. She's not the focus of why you're doing what you're doing here."

I nod. "Got it."

Aarya purses her lips. "I hate that what she's doing is considered *peaceful* protesting. There's nothing peaceful about those assholes."

Cassidy pulls me to the side and wraps her arm around my shoulders. "I'll keep a close eye on Aarya and Dominique for you so you don't have to worry about our guard dogs attacking anyone."

I laugh. "Good plan."

They're both feisty females, and I wouldn't put it past Aarya to cut a bitch.

Kourtney walks over to us and holds up her phone for me to see. "Almost everyone who RSVP-ed has checked in. The app is running smoothly."

"Thank you so much for all of your help on that."

My heart is overflowing with all of the love and support I'm receiving from my friends and family on this project. As much as I enjoy my job at the school library, I haven't felt fulfilled; I haven't had a purpose. Creating *Inclusive Hearts* has breathed new life into me, and I couldn't be happier to contribute to such an important cause.

In addition to our friends, Stephen and Chance's teams both showed up with their loved ones. I told Alexander that he didn't have to come being that he's still recovering from his injury less than two weeks ago, but he insisted on bringing Giuliana. Aarya said he's going stir-crazy at home, especially since he hasn't been cleared to play yet, so at least this gets him out of the house.

"You need to check on your man." Celeste points to Stephen, who has appointed himself in charge of the hot chocolate station, but is drinking it instead. "I swear, that's the only reason he suggested a hot chocolate station —so he could have a vat of it to himself."

I laugh as I make my way over to him. "How many cups have you had, baby?"

His shoulders jump as he spins around. "What? Only one. Why, what have you heard?"

I arch a brow as I reach out and swipe my thumb over his top lip. "You have a chocolate milk mustache that says otherwise."

"I'm just tasting it to ensure quality. You don't want everyone to go home later and talk about how bad the hot chocolate was."

My head tilts back as I let out a loud laugh. "Yes, because *that's* what will have the town talking—not the group of queer people poisoning the minds of young children."

Stephen wraps his arms around me and presses a kiss to my forehead. "Ignore Molly and her signs. You're doing a beautiful thing with this organization, and I'm so proud of you, pretty girl."

Warmth seeps into my chest. "Thanks, baby. I love you."

"Not as much as I love you."

I pull back and point my index finger in his face. "Now leave the hot chocolate for the rest of the guests."

He feigns innocence, splaying his fingers on his chest. "I don't know what you're talking about."

My gaze roams around the baseball field at the local park. Kids of various ages and adults are squealing with laughter as they play kickball; everyone is interacting and having a great time.

And to think, this might not have happened without Miserable Molly. Her reaction to my polyamorous relationship sparked this fire inside of me to try to make a change in our community.

Throughout all of the bad, there is always something good that stems from it. You just have to look for it.

I scan the crowd for Cassidy, and make a beeline for her. "Hey, can you help me with something?"

"Of course." She salutes me. "What do you need?"

"I want to take some hot chocolate over to Molly and the other moms."

Her eyeballs nearly pop out of her head. "You...what? Why?"

I hike a shoulder. "It's cold out, and they could use a little warmth in their frigid-ass hearts."

She grimaces. "I don't think this is a good idea."

"I'm not going to start trouble." I make an X over my heart with my index finger. "Promise."

Her shoulders slump. "Fine. Let's use the cart."

Cassidy and I load up eight cups of hot chocolate onto the cart, and roll it across the street.

Molly steps out in front of the group, handing her sign off to one of her friends before facing me.

"Hi, ladies." I plaster on a smile. "I wanted to offer you some hot chocolate to keep you warm while you're out here."

Molly glares at me. "We don't want any of your hot chocolate. What we want is for you and your friends to get out of here, and stop trying to turn our children gay."

"I can promise you that nobody is trying to turn children gay. That's the main reason I put together this organization, to educate people who have misconceptions about the queer community."

"I don't have any misconceptions." She plants her hands on her hips. "These children are too young to understand what it means to be gay, and you're confusing them. I won't stand for it."

I ignore her comments because nothing I say will get through to her—certainly not here, with an audience.

Instead, I stick my hands in my coat pockets, mainly to keep myself from strangling her right here on the sidewalk. "Well, I just wanted to come over here to say thank you. You're the one who inspired me to start this organization. Your bigotry and hatred made me realize what's lacking in this community. I wouldn't be standing here with all of these people without you, so thank you."

Several of her friends murmur to each other, while Molly sputters.

I lift one of the cups and hold it out to her. "Are you sure you don't want some? My boyfriend made it, and he's a self-proclaimed hot chocolate connoisseur, so it'll probably be the best hot chocolate you've ever tasted."

She scoffs. "Your boyfriend? Which one? It's hard to keep things straight with the way you're spreading your legs to multiple men."

Cassidy steps forward, but my hand shoots out to grab her wrist and pull her back. "Oh, he's right there." I point my index finger at Stephen across the street. "The six-foot tall ginger who's wearing the fuck out of those gray sweatpants."

Molly's cheeks redden. She's clearly rattled that she isn't getting a rise out of me. "You're a whore, you know that? That's what all the moms at school are saying about you."

My heart rate spikes, but I hike a nonchalant shoulder to appear unfazed. "They don't say the nicest things about you either, Molls, though I'm sure you're already aware of those rumors." I haven't heard any rumors, but she doesn't know that, and now she'll be wondering what everyone's saying about her. "It's such a shame that women behave like that, isn't it? In this kind of political climate, we should be banding together and supporting one another instead of tearing each other down. They're playing right into the hands of the patriarchy."

"This is just the beginning. You won't get very far with what you're trying to do. I won't allow it." Molly balls her hands into fists and speaks through gritted teeth. "You're a poison in this town, Presley. I can't wait to put you down like the bitch you are."

God, how easy it would be to lay her out with one punch.

I swallow down the words itching to climb out of my throat. "I'm so sorry for the hate you're harboring in your heart. I truly hope you find happiness in your life."

She scoffs. "I am happy. You don't know anything about my life."

I gesture to the group before me with their insulting posters, and start walking backwards. "This isn't what happy looks like, Molls."

She continues yelling, but I spin around and link arms with Cassidy—mostly to drag her ass across the street with me so she doesn't hurt anyone.

"You have a lot of self-control," Cassidy says, shaking her head. "I don't know how you let her speak to you like that, and remained so calm. My blood is boiling for you."

"She's not worth it, Cass. Besides..." I direct her attention to the camera crew who no doubt recorded the whole scene. "The whole city is going to see her true colors, and know that we are nothing like that."

Scanning the field for Avery and Alyssa, I find them together as they teach Giuliana how to play kickball, and my heart squeezes at the sight of Chance laughing with Alexander as they watch the kids from the sidelines.

Today is one of the best days I've ever had, and I get to spend it with the most important people in my life. I feel so fortunate that the universe brought me back to Stephen and Chance.

I pity Molly. I truly do. How awful it must feel to be her? To wake up filled with hate every day. To always be so twisted up with anger. To need to tear others down because you can't find love from within yourself.

"Pres!" Celeste shouts my name from the far side of the field. "They're ready for you."

I suck in a deep breath and straighten my shoulders, tipping my face to the sky.

Wish you were here, Allie.

Hope you're watching.

"Who wants to go first?"

"Me." Presley shoots up out of her seat like an overexcited kid. "It's been so long since I've gotten a tattoo; I've been itching to get a new one."

Quinn, the tattoo artist, laughs and waves us into the room. "Come on, then."

We're led down the hall into one of the rooms. Colorful artwork hangs from the walls, some of them on sketch paper and others framed.

"Did you draw all of these?" I ask.

Quinn gestures for Chance and I to sit in the chairs against the wall. "Some of them are mine, but I like to collect original pieces from other tattoo artists when I travel for conventions."

Presley whips off her sweatshirt and lays face-down on the padded table while Quinn preps her station. Chance picks up one of the albums on the end table and flips through various tattoos while we wait.

"So, I have to know...why the three circles?" Quinn asks. "I love hearing about the meaning behind everyone's tattoo choices."

I push up the sleeve on my forearm, and show her the bracelet. "I got these for us when we were in college."

"Ah, that's cute. You guys best friends?"

Chance glances up from the book. "No, we're together."

"Cool."

Affection warms my heart. I'm so proud to see how far he's come, and how comfortable he is in his skin now.

We lean in as Quinn sets the stencil between Presley's shoulder blades. It's so strange to see such a clean slate of skin on her back when her chest, neck, and arms are covered in ink.

After Presley okays it, the buzz of the tattoo gun fills the room. I watch as she closes her eyes and lies peacefully on the table without flinching. It's like she enjoys the pain of the needle hitting her skin, as if it calms her. Every once in a while, she'll open her eyes and smile up at me and Chance. The tattoo was her idea, and I love that she wants such an important piece of us on her body forever.

After about fifteen minutes of tattooing and constant wiping, Presley sits up and glances at her reflection in the mirror.

She grins. "I love it. Thank you."

Quinn sanitizes her station before prepping it again, and I decide to go next. I'd like to consider myself a tough guy; I play professional ice hockey, after all. But none of the hits I've taken compare quite the same to the searing pain of the needle. I opted for the spot over my heart, and now I know why Presley winced when I chose it.

She holds my hand from the chair beside the table. "How are you doing, baby?"

My eyes remain squeezed shut as I clench her hand. "This fucking sucks."

Chance chuckles. "You big baby."

"If I could move, I'd flip you off."

Quinn smiles. "You know, men have the worst pain tolerance. Women handle tattoos so much better."

"See?" I shoot a glare at my boyfriend. "It's not my fault. It's science."

Presley pats my hand. "It's okay, baby. It'll be over soon."

Not soon enough.

Chance gets tattooed last, choosing the spot on the inside of his wrist for his, and by the end of the afternoon, all three of us are walking out to the parking lot with permanent ink linking us together forever.

Chance opens the passenger door for her, and she bounces onto the seat. Then he steps in front of me and swings open the back door before I can get to it.

"So chivalrous." I lean in and press a kiss to his lips before hopping in the back of his SUV.

While Chance takes us home, my phone beeps with a text from my family's group chat.

MOM

Stephen, invite Presley and Chance for dinner next week.

WILLA

No fair! I want to meet them too.

CHELSEA

Guess you shouldn't have moved four-hundred miles away.

WILLA

Fuck off, Chels. No one asked you.

DAD

Let me know what they like to drink so I can make sure the fridge is stocked.

MOM

I'm going to make grandma's pesto chicken recipe.

ME

Sounds good. We'll bring dessert.

KATHY

Ooo can you bring those macaroons you got from the bakery last time?

WILLA

Let's Zoom so we can all have dinner with you guys!

ERIN

I second this. I won't be able to see you guys until Christmas.

MOM

That's a great idea.

I glance up from my phone and meet Chance's eyes in the rear-view mirror. "Everyone's excited about meeting you next week."

Presley twists in her seat. "I can't wait. Are you sure it's okay if I bring the kids?"

"Please, my mother is dying for more grandkids."

She laughs. "Hope she's not expecting one from me anytime soon."

"Are you kidding? She's probably in the middle of crocheting our future child a blanket as we speak."

Chance smirks. "How many kids do you guys want to have?"

I shrug. "I'll have as many as you guys want. Definitely more than one though."

Chance nods. "He or she needs at least one sibling."

Presley chews on the inside of her cheek. "Why don't we start with two, and see how we feel after that? I don't think I could have six like your mother."

"The woman's a saint. I don't know how she did it with all of us growing up."

Chance grunts. "Especially with you."

I flip him off and he grins.

"Oh!" Presley smacks Chance in the thigh. "Give me your phone for a sec. I almost forgot."

Chance hands it to her, and I lean over her shoulder to see what she's doing.

She swiped past the different apps until she spots the *FreeMe* icon. "Aha! It's here. I knew it."

I roll my eyes, knowing exactly where she's going with this. "Doesn't mean anything. Lots of people have the app."

She holds up Chance's phone in front of his face, letting facial recognition log him into the app, and then she clicks on his messages.

Sure enough, my username is at the top.

Oh, shit.

She gasps. "I was right! It's him Oh, snap. In your face, McKinley. I'm right, and you're wrong."

I snatch the phone from her hand, and scroll through our messages to one another. "This was you? *ScoringChance217* was you?"

Chance rolls to a stop at a red light, and his eyebrows pull together. "What is this all about?"

"I'm the guy you jerked off with on video chat a few months ago."

Chance glances from the phone to me before turning to Presley. "How did you figure this out?"

She leans back against her seat. "I saw your username and knew it was your birthday, but Stephen didn't believe me."

I shake my head as I reread our exchange in the app. "I can't believe I didn't realize it the moment he messaged me."

"It was pretty obvious," Chance says.

Presley beams. "I told you, we're written in the stars. This just proves it. The universe was trying to get you two back together. Look how everything worked out."

Chance links his fingers with Presley's and presses a kiss to the back of her hand before placing it down on his thigh. He glances up at the mirror again, locking eyes with me. "You believe in fate now, Stephen?"

I smile. "I think I'm gonna have to."

"I have an idea."

"What's that, pretty girl?"

Presley gives us both a devious smirk. "I want you guys to go in different rooms, and I want you to video chat on *FreeMe* as if you don't know each other."

Chance skims his lips over her neck as he slides his arms around her from behind. "And what will you do?"

Her eyes fall closed. "Whatever you tell me to."

My dick twitches at the idea of role play, already straining against my pants to get started.

I love it when the kids are at their friends' houses.

I bend down and lift Presley into my arms, snatching her away from Chance, and bolt toward the stairs. "Chance can take the spare bedroom."

"What the fuck?" he calls after us.

Presley giggles in my arms. "You're such a little shit."

"I'm *your* little shit." I stalk into her bedroom, and toss her onto the middle of the bed. We scramble to strip off our clothes, until she's fully naked and I'm in my boxers.

I prop myself up against the headboard, and open the app. There's already a message from Chance waiting for me.

ScoringChance217: Hey. Been a while since we talked.

Me: You ghosted me after our last video call.

ScoringChance217: Sorry about that.

ScoringChance217: Can I make it up to you?

Me: Depends on how you plan to do that.

A picture comes through, and Chance's beautiful cock fills my screen when I click to enlarge it.

Me: It's going to take more than just a picture...

A notification for a video chat pops up, and I tap to accept.

The room he's in is dimly lit by the lamp on the nightstand. His camera is facing his lower body, his hand wrapped around his dick as he pumps himself in slow strokes.

Beside me, Presley slides her fingers over her clit, matching Chance's speed as she rubs herself.

"Are you alone?" Chance's deep voice sends a shiver down my spine.

"No. I'm here with my girlfriend." I move the phone to show him what she's doing to herself. "Is that going to be a problem for you?"

Chance groans. "Not at all. Why don't you taste her for me?"

I move to settle between her legs, and when I point the camera to give Chance a glimpse of her glistening pussy, she spreads open her lips with her fingers.

"Fuck," Chance hisses. "So perfect."

Presley takes the phone from me so I can have my hands free. I flatten my tongue and slide it over her in one slow sweep. "Mmm, she's sweet too."

The sounds of Presley's moans fill the room, and I can hear Chance breathing heavy in the background. "Just like that," he whispers. "Lick her nice and slow. Make her beg for it."

I keep a steady pace, and soon her hips rock to match my rhythm. "Your tongue feels incredible, Stephen."

"Look how much he enjoys it," Chance says. "I bet his dick is rock hard, leaking at the tip like it's weeping to be inside you."

I grind my dick into the mattress, trying to relieve the building ache. "You should come here and have a taste of her. I don't think she'd mind, would you, pretty girl?"

She arches her back and moans. "Please, Chance. Come here."

All of the pretending goes out the window. Within seconds, I can feel Chance's presence in the room.

His hands smooth over the backs of my legs, over the swell of my ass, and up along my spine until his fingers grip the back of my neck. He pulls me up, and I rise onto my knees as he slams his lips against mine. His tongue surges inside my mouth, swirling around to savor the taste of Presley.

He pulls back and points to the edge of the bed. "Come here, rebel. Hang your head off the side for me so I can feel those pretty lips wrap around my cock."

Presley shifts until she's lying horizontally across the bed with her head hanging over the edge of the mattress, legs spread wide so I can continue to have my way with her.

I lean down and caress her face. "Chance is going to fuck your mouth while I fuck your pussy. I know how much our girl loves to be filled up by her men at the same time."

"Please, hurry," she whispers.

"So needy." Chance clicks his tongue against the roof of his mouth. "You're such a greedy little slut for us. I can't wait for you to drain us of every drop."

I tear open a condom from the nightstand drawer, and roll it over my length before taking my spot between Presley's thighs. I grip her ankles and hike up her knees to her chest, spreading her open wide.

Chance taps his crown against her lips. "Open for me, baby."

At the same time Chance slides inside her mouth, I slide into her pussy. The both of us let out loud sighs of relief.

I'm mesmerized by the sight of Presley's throat swelling around his cock, and it takes all of my restraint to keep my hips from drilling her against the mattress so I can come hard and fast.

"I love watching the way you take us, rebel." Chance's eyes are wild, his pupils dilated and making his irises appear even darker than usual. "You were made for us, you know that? This body was made for the both of us to enjoy. You belong to us."

His chiseled abdomen flexes and ripples as he thrusts his hips. I absolutely love the dusting of dark hair leading from his navel to the base of his shaft, such a stark difference from the rest of his silky olive skin. He's leaner than I am, and I'm obsessed by the defined cuts and striations in his muscles. I want to lick each and every one.

"You good over there, baby?" Chance arches an eyebrow at me.

I grin. "Just thinking about all the things I'm going to do to you after."

He hums as he gazes down at Presley, brushing his knuckles against her cheek. "You love watching us together, don't you, baby? You get off on seeing me fuck your boyfriend."

Her pussy clenches, and I close my eyes in ecstasy. "Fuck, she gets so wet when you talk like that."

"That's because she's such a needy girl." He pushes himself all the way into her throat, and she gags before he pulls back. "She loves hearing me tell her filthy things because she knows how depraved it is, and that turns her on."

Between the slippery, wet sounds of her arousal coating me as I pump in and out of her, and the slurping sounds she's making around Chance's cock, I'm ready to blow.

"You ready, pretty girl? I know you're close. I can feel how swollen you're getting. You're squeezing my dick so tight."

That tips Presley over the edge, and her body starts to shake as she moans around Chance's cock. I'm right behind her, and grip her ankles with bruising force as I give her my release.

"Oh, fuck," I pant. "Your pussy feels so good. You're so wet. So perfect. I love you so much."

White-hot heat explodes behind my eyes, and I lose all sense as I fuck her through my orgasm.

I'm completely spent by the time I finish, and can barely keep myself up on my knees. But I come down just in time to watch as Chance pulls himself from Presley's mouth, and jerks himself off as his cum spills onto her chest.

I don't have time to wonder why he didn't let her swallow it down, because as soon as he's finished, he tips his chin at me. "There you go, baby. Clean her off like a good boy, and then get on all fours so I can fuck you after."

I drop down and run my tongue over Presley's tits, lapping up every last drop of Chance's warm cum.

Presley runs her fingers through my curls, humming her approval. "He is *such* a good boy. He listens so well. I wonder what else he'll do."

I rise up onto my knees, gripping onto Chance's newly tattooed wrist and holding it up between us. "This is forever. *We* are forever. You don't have to wonder what else I'll do, because when it comes to the two of you? The answer will always be *anything* and *everything*. Whatever you want, whatever you need, consider it done, because I am yours and you are mine for all of eternity."

Maybe we're written in the stars.

Maybe we're fated lovers.

Or maybe we're just plain fucking lucky.

Either way, I'm exactly where I want to be.

With my boyfriend, and our girlfriend.

"STEPHEN, HOW IS ALEX DOING? WHAT CAN YOU TELL US ABOUT his recovery?"

My heart beats a little faster with each question, waiting for the inevitable. The press conference is live, and I just know reporters are going to hammer Stephen with questions about me.

Stephen must know it too, because despite how good he looks in his gray suit and crisp white shirt—his blue tie making his eyes pop even more than they already do—he looks uncharacteristically nervous. His jaw is tight, and he's sitting up straight in his chair instead of leaning back in his usual relaxed stance. Gone is the happy-go-lucky man who always cracks jokes in the conference room. He's all business today.

"Alex is doing well. The doctors want him to take it slow, but he's itching to get back out on the ice." He lets out a nervous laugh. "You know how stubborn us athletes can be."

Another reporter asks, "How long until we see him play again?"

Jesus. It's only been a couple of weeks since he woke up. These people are like vultures.

"Let's leave that up to the doctors," Stephen says. "Alex is making progress, so that's all that matters."

A reporter near the front raises his finger for the next question. "People have concerns about the brutal hit that caused Alex's injury. What are your thoughts on Kellerman not being held responsible for his actions?"

My fingers tighten around the remote, and I hold my breath as I brace myself for Stephen's response.

Here we fucking go.

Stephen clears his throat. "The league has fined and suspended Ivanov for what he did. He has a history of excessive violent plays, so hopefully his team can get a handle on him before he hurts anyone else."

Great answer. He must've rehearsed this, anticipating questions about me.

But the reporter doesn't let it go. "My question wasn't about Ivanov." He pauses, and I don't miss the twitch in Stephen's left eye as the camera stays steady on him. "Many of us are wondering why your boyfriend didn't get the same punishment since he was involved in the play that put your captain in the hospital."

Fuck, this guy's a dick.

Stephen's voice is steady, despite the undercurrent of anger I pick up on. "My boyfriend didn't blatantly slam into Alexander head-on, and knock him onto the ice. He and Alex were both busy scrambling for the puck when Ivanov initiated contact. The correct player was reprimanded, and I don't think there needs to be any more speculation on the matter."

The reporter tries to speak again, but Stephen cuts him right off, leaning forward on his elbows. "I don't appreciate the way the media has been trying to pit us against each other. The focus should be on Alexander and his recovery, not on my relationship. And let me make this clear: Chance would never purposely cause harm to someone. He loves this game more than anyone else I know—and I know a lot of hockey players who bleed hockey. So, if you're not going to treat him with respect, then keep his name out of your mouth and off your pages."

My throat tightens with emotion, and I blink to clear my vision. Stephen didn't have to say a word. He could've changed the subject, or made some generic statement. Yet he not only defended me and made it clear to everyone that he doesn't blame me for Alexander's injury, but he made it clear to *me*. He proved what he said during his apology the other night, and made sure I know where he stands.

With me.

I lift my phone from the armrest of the couch, and type out a text.

"Do I look okay?"

"You look more than okay, pretty girl." Stephen shoots her a wink as we step onto the porch of his parents' house. "Don't be nervous. Everyone's going to love you."

Presley slips her hand into mine and gives it a squeeze. "They're going to love you too, baby."

"Should I call them Mr. and Mrs. McKinley, or should I use their first names?" Alyssa practically bounces beside us. "Or do I just call them grandma and grandpa?"

Avery rolls his eyes, and I chuckle. "You should always start with Mr. and Mrs. out of respect. If they want you to call them something else, they'll let you know."

She nods. "Be respectful. Got it."

Stephen swings open the door, and we are met with noise.

So. Much. Noise.

Dishes clanking, TV blaring, people yelling. The house is alive. Vibrant. Chaotic.

A giant Labrador slides across the wood floors as it bounds toward us, and I breathe a slight sigh of relief.

Thank God there's a dog. If all else fails, I can disappear into another room with it.

Presley's eyes narrow as she glances up at me. "Don't you dare leave me for that dog. We are in this together, bucko."

I hold up my palms on either side of my head. "I don't know what you're talking about."

"Uh-huh. I see that sketchy look in your eyes. I know what you're thinking."

I can't help but laugh. She knows me too well.

Alyssa squeals as the dog jumps up and licks her face.

"They're here!" A woman's voice screeches as she appears in one of the doorways. "Oh, my God. Chewbarka! Get down. No jumping."

Avery and I exchange glances. "Chewbarka?" he mouths.

Stephen undoubtedly named this poor dog. I'd bet my entire salary on it.

The short, blonde-haired woman shoves Stephen out of the way as he tries to hug her, and she throws her arms around Presley, engulfing her in a bear hug. "It's so nice to meet you, Presley. I'm Stephen's mother. You can call me Patty." She pulls back and widens her eyes. "Or just skip all the pleasantries and call me Mom."

Stephen barks out a laugh. "Dad, come and get your wife. She's being weird."

"Already?" A tall man with copper-colored curls just like Stephen's enters the room. "Patty, we talked about this."

Patty pays them no mind as she turns her attention to me. "Hi, my handsome boy. It's so nice to finally meet you."

I hold out my hand to shake hers, but she smashes into me like a linebacker and wraps her arms around my waist.

My nerves simmer, and I hug Stephen's mother with as much force as she's giving me. I haven't hugged my own mother since the day she died, and the memory of the way it felt has faded with time.

Patty steps back and holds my shoulders at arm's length. "I'm so happy you're here. We've been rooting for you."

I let out a nervous chuckle. "I'm happy to be here too."

She turns to the kids, and makes a fuss over them. She's elated to have Alyssa call her grandma, of course, and she gets a smile out of Avery—though I'm sure it's more because he's laughing at her antics.

Stephen's father shakes my hand after introducing himself to Presley. Patrick seems laid-back and calm, a stark contrast to his energetic wife. I can see so much of Stephen in his parents, and it's obvious where he gets his personable nature from. They're warm and inviting, leaving no room for my insecurities.

"Come, come. Take a seat anywhere at the table." Patty waves her arm around the dining room. "I hope you all brought your appetites."

I hang back, letting everyone else pick their seats. It's a habit, since I got punched in the face after taking my father's seat at the table when I was eight.

Patrick claps me on the shoulder, and gestures to an empty seat. "Come sit next to me. We can talk hockey."

Relief floods me. *I like this guy.*

I tug on Avery's sleeve and guide him to my left. Knowing how awkward he feels, I want to keep him close to me.

Two women enter the room, carrying bowls of mashed potatoes and mixed vegetables to the table. Stephen introduces them as his sisters, and soon everyone's sitting at the long table digging into a delicious meal.

I've never had a big family dinner like this. The closest I've gotten to it has been dinners with my team and their families over the last few years, but that didn't feel like *mine.*

Between Stephen, Presley, and the kids, I've found this sense of belonging. And something tells me Patty and Patrick are going to become part of that too, that they'll treat me and Presley like their own.

It doesn't scare me anymore. Not like it used to. It's been a journey for me, learning how to accept love...but I refuse to let my father and my past dictate my future. He doesn't get to ruin the relationships I have with the important people in my life. He doesn't deserve that satisfaction, and neither do I.

Like Stephen once said: My father isn't worth it, but I am.

As dinner winds down, each of us beyond stuffed from Patty's amazing cooking, she pushes her chair back from the table. "Alyssa and Avery, I have a little something for you guys."

Kathy and Chelsea groan, while Stephen scrubs a hand over his face. "I apologize for what's about to happen," he says.

Patty returns from the hall with two blankets in her arms. "I like to crochet in my spare time, and it's tradition that I make a blanket for each of my grandchildren." She holds up each of them respectively, beaming with pride. "I hope you like them."

Alyssa snatches it from her hands, excitement all over her face as she wraps the orange blanket around herself. "I love it! And it's my favorite color."

Patty smiles. "Stephen said that was your favorite. Good thing too, because I would've gone with pink."

Alyssa scrunches her nose. "Eww, no way."

Avery takes the blanket from Patty, black with gray stripes. "Thank you. This is very kind of you."

"You're so welcome, sweet boy."

Kathy leans back against her chair, wearing a mischievous smirk that I've seen one too many times on her brother. "Did you make one for Presley?"

Patty rolls her eyes. "Oh, don't start this now."

Chelsea chuckles. "She definitely did. I'd bet a hundred bucks that there's a blanket in that spare room of hers."

Stephen whips out his wallet, and tosses a hundred-dollar-bill onto the table. "There's no way she made one for us already."

Kathy bolts into another room. "Let me get my purse."

Patty crosses her arms over her chest. "You people are being ridiculous."

Presley rubs circles on her back. "It's okay. Don't listen to them. You're just full of love and excitement, and there's nothing wrong with that." She turns to glare at Stephen. "You're a lot like your mother, you know, so I don't think you have a leg to stand on here."

I snort-laugh, and Stephen shoots me a glare.

Patrick leans in and whispers, "He's totally like his mother."

I nod. "I made that observation the second I walked in the door."

Kathy returns with a stack of twenties, and tosses them onto the table in front of her. "I'm with Chelsea, and I'm adding in an extra fifty to bet that it's a yellow blanket."

Patty's eyes widen. "Did you go in there?"

"Aha!" Chelsea jumps up. "You did make a blanket. God, you're weird."

Stephen's head whips to his mother. "Are you kidding me? Already?"

"Sue me, okay? My baby boy is finally happy, and I'm excited." Patty dabs at the corners of her eyes. "Oh, I'm just so glad you're all here."

Presley flicks her eyes to me. "We're happy to be here, Patty. This is exactly where we're meant to be."

I grin as I turn to Stephen. "Some would say we're written in the stars."

The corner of his mouth curves up. "Yeah, I think we are."

THE END

Trenton & Cassidy's story: Heart Trick, Book 1
Jason, Kourtney, & Celeste's story: Odd Man Rush, Book 2
Alexander & Aarya's story: Puck Pact, Book 3

More books from Kristen HERE

THE END OF THE EAST COAST SERIES

I just want to take a minute to thank each and every one of you for loving this series! Your outpouring of love and support means the world to me.

For those of you who don't know, I never intended on writing a hockey series. I wasn't going to write a hockey romance at all. I didn't want to jump on the bandwagon when it first started; I'm not someone who enjoys "writing to market" because I don't plan out what I'm going to write. Inspiration strikes me, and I go with it. But then I got an idea for feuding neighbors and thought, "Why can't I just make it hockey?" Then, *Heart Trick* was born.

Halfway through writing Trenton and Cassidy's story, another idea formed about Jason, Kourtney, and Celeste. Readers always ask me to write a FF story, so I figured this was a great way to test the waters and see what I was capable of.

I never expected everyone to love *Odd Man Rush* as much as you do! Especially when other authors were trying to steer me away from writing a FFM story. But you know me—tell me I can't do something, and I'll tell you to watch me. I'm so proud of what this book has done, and the message it carries.

At that point, I had only planned on writing one more book in the series. I saved Krum Cake's book for last because he's my favorite, and I knew I wanted to surprise everyone with his single dad storyline. I had a feeling Puck Pact would be the series favorite, and I was right. We all want to crawl to Daddy Krum!

But then my messages were flooded with readers begging for McKinley's story. I love creating side characters so lovable that people want them to have their own books, but this was one I wasn't sure about. I didn't love McKinley. I didn't feel a connection to a specific storyline for him. I know some of you are probably disappointed that I didn't make his story with Erika, as I had toyed with the idea in the other books. Honestly, I respect the trans community too much to not put my all into doing that topic justice, and I didn't feel ready for it—as much as I wanted to.

I can't explain how or when Chance and Presley's characters came to me. But I can tell you that I had a thought that went something like, "What if one of the guys who caused Alex's coma was actually in a relationship with McKinley...?" (you know I'm a sick fuck like that) The idea took hold of me, and I became a woman obsessed. I hope you're not too mad at me for making Chance hurt our Daddy Krum, but I think I gave it a different perspective, and it pushed Stephen to have a little character growth as well.

Sorry for making you all relive Alexander's accident, and giving you another Giuliana-in-the-hospital scene. I just had to get one more ugly cry session in before the series ended.

So, yeah, that's how we got to where we are now. I'm amazed at how well this series is doing, and I can't wait to hear what you all think of Ice Rivals! I hope you all know how much I appreciate each and every one of you. You are the reason I get to do what makes my heart sing, and I couldn't be more grateful. As always, my DMs are open. I try to answer every single message you send me. I can't wait for you to see what other books are coming to you this year.

Here's to book number sweet sixteen.

xo Kristen

ALSO BY KRISTEN GRANATA

East Coast Hockey Series

Heart Trick

Odd Man Rush

Puck Pact

Ice Rivals

The Collision Series

Collision

Avoidance

The Other Brother

Against the Odds

Steamy Contemporary Standalones

Inevitable

Someone You Love

What's Left of Me

Bring Me Back

RomCom Standalones

Hating the Boss

Back to You

Novellas

Dear Santa

Trick or Truce